Harvest Homicide

A China Connection

Also by Steven M Wells

Ginger's Story: A Golden Retriever Reflects Upon Her Life With Humans

Killer Cuvée

Harvest Homicide

A China Connection

A Novel

Steven M Wells

Gwen. Enjoy!
Steve

Published by Overlake Media
Copyright ©2014 Steven M Wells
All Rights Reserved

ISBN-10 0615981062
ISBN-13 9780615981062

This is a work of fiction. Names, characters, places, and incidents are the products of
the author's imagination or are used fictitiously. Any resemblance to actual events,
locales, or persons, living or dead, is entirely coincidental.

www.thewinemakerseries.com

In memory of Lou Kinzel

Part One

Good name in man and woman, dear my lord,
Is the immediate jewel of their souls:
Who steals my purse steals trash; 'tis something, nothing;
'Twas mine, 'tis his, and has been slave to thousands:
But he that filches from me my good name
Robs me of that which not enriches him
And makes me poor indeed.

William Shakespeare
Othello—Act 3, Scene 3

Prologue

Most people drink their white wines too cold, Eric thought as he retrieved a bottle of Meursault from the refrigerator and set it on the kitchen table. He knew the wine would be the proper temperature by the time he sat down to eat. He set a wrapped turkey sandwich and a bag of chips he had picked up from a grocery store on a plate, and then he searched his office computer for music to accompany his mundane dinner. Locating the folder labeled O*pera*, he scrolled down until he found Bizet's *Carmen*. He pressed *play* and arrived back in the kitchen as the prelude came from speakers in the room's ceiling. Performed by the London Philharmonic Orchestra, the music was arranged with a number of instruments, including clarinet, bassoon, cornet, cellos, and strings. He opened the bottle of white Burgundy and poured a glass of the pale yellow liquid. He admired its brightness and inhaled hints of hazelnuts, honey, and wet stones, typical of that appellation's Chardonnay.

As Eric savored the glass of wine, he surveyed a stack of unopened mail spread across the dining room table. He still wasn't used to seeing his address in Walla Walla, Washington, printed on his letters. His life had changed dramatically since giving up a high-paying job at a large aerospace company in Seattle and moving to Walla Walla three years ago to make wine. It was now a rare evening that he found himself at home and not working in his winery. As he ate his dinner, moved by the ceremonious refrain from the "Toreador Song," he reflected on his love of winemaking. With seven vintages under his belt—three of them in Walla Walla—he knew he was still learning his craft.

Eric had learned his winemaking skills from the Viticulture and Enology program at a Seattle college. The program was the launch point for students of all ages to start or enhance a career in the state's burgeoning wine and restaurant industry. Washington State now boasted of over seven hundred operating wineries. Many graduates made a hobby out of winemaking, while others planned to someday launch a second career. Still others simply jumped in full time and started making wine straight away. Eric was in the last category, being fortunate enough to have sufficient resources.

He was happy with the quality of his wines. He believed each vintage to be progressively improving and he was gaining recognition in the region as a "Winemaker to Watch." His wines had been mentioned in many local magazines, featured on wine and travel-related radio shows, and had even made some of the Top 100 wine lists in Seattle.

With this year's vintage, he wanted to achieve the next level of acclaim, including a top score from the nationally recognized wine experts. Together with a local brand and marketing consultant, Eric developed a strategic plan centered on the next vintage of his Bordeaux blend, Eagle Cap, named after the wilderness area in the beautiful Wallowa Mountains in nearby Oregon. This vintage was currently aging in barrels in his winery, undergoing a process French winemakers call *élevage*, to be released in a little over a year's time. His strategic plan had two high-level goals by which he'd measure success: to be included in the leading wine consumer magazine and to receive at least two nationally recognized 90+ scores.

To be featured in the magazine, a winemaker needed to have a great story to tell in addition to making an exquisite wine. His publicist's job was to gain exposure for his label through interviews, local interest stories, and a positive relationship with the editors of the magazine. Eric believed that if he worked hard enough and his publicist delivered on his end, he would achieve success. Only then would he feel that he had moved from good to great.

As he listened to the opera's score and Plácido Domingo's verve, Eric found himself comparing winemaking and music. Both successfully synthesize many components into a combination of something much more. *Carmen*'s melody, harmony, atmosphere, and orchestration come together to produce a vivid sensory experience. Complex wines are similarly crafted by passionate winemakers from many parts. Eric blended Eagle Cap from four different grape varieties: Cabernet Sauvignon, Merlot, Cabernet Franc, and Petit Verdot. These varieties came from multiple vineyards. After fermentation, each lot of grapes was put into new French oak barrels from different forests and cooperages to impart even more unique characteristics to the wine, including aroma and "mouthfeel." Blending wines and composing music both required artistic creativity as well as technical excellence. Eric believed only experience would add to his skills, so he often sought the palates of others as he made his final blending decisions.

Eric ate the rest of his roast turkey on rye and washed it down with the last of his wine. Before he could dream of glory, he had to finish this year's wine crush, which was nearing completion. With his two golden retrievers for companionship, the efforts of his part-time assistant, and friends in the community to offer advice, he felt greatness was within his grasp.

1

October 15th

Seattle

Luc DuPont's office windows began to vibrate moments before he saw the locomotive come into view. He looked up from his computer screen and watched the Amtrak Cascades roll past his office window. Since opening Honorable Wine Merchants in the old warehouse building three years earlier, he had grown accustomed to the passenger trains rumbling by several times daily, completing or starting their scheduled runs between Vancouver, British Columbia and Eugene, Oregon.

He was working on the latest edition of a monthly newsletter he planned to send by email that evening to over three thousand fans and customers of his wines. He printed off a copy of the final text and put on his reading glasses. Like the occasional pain in his right knee from playing too much recreational basketball, the glasses reminded him that he was getting older. This thought always depressed him. With a pen in hand he began reviewing the copy.

> Dear Friends of the Vine,
> The wines I'm prepared to share with you this month come from Italy and the Capriva del Friuli in the DOC of Collio. This picturesque region is home to outstanding white wines from the region's best vineyards planted in clay and sandstone. Picture yourself in the shadow of the Alps as you experience the first taste of these full-bodied and rich wines. Imagine cool Adriatic winds keeping you comfortable during the warmer temperatures of a summer day. Now, thanks to my efforts, you can experience the beauty of Friuli in a glass.

The vineyards of this region yield only three and a half tons of grapes per acre, a much lower yield, yet of much higher quality, than other regions of Italy. By using the *metodo friulano*, or "Fruili method," these wines are made in a reductive style with minimal oxygen impact, keeping flavors fresh and acids high. I hiked through many vineyards in Collio and visited all the best wineries to bring you one of the most memorable 100 percent Pinot Grigios you will ever taste.

Imagine sitting in the courtyard of a palatial *castello* on top of a gentle *ronco*, a terraced hillside, surrounded by magnificent Italian gardens. You laugh and sing with the Friulian aristocracy, enjoying the fine company of descendants of Charlemagne, who owned the *castello* for 300 years. In fact, if you were there in 1773, you might have welcomed Giacomo Casanova, who stopped by to visit. Perhaps you shared stories of debauchery and romance over several bottles of luscious and aromatic wine, aged for many months in clay amphorae while covered in rich soils. This is the home of the wines I bring you today.

The Costello di Collio 2013 Pinot Grigio is made from grapes trellised in a Guyot style. Picked in the first ten days of September, they show an amazing balance of acid and ripeness. The grapes are soft pressed to preserve the integrity of the skins. The *must* is cold settled and allowed to age after fermentation on fine lees to build balance and add structured aromas and extracts. The wine is bright with a pale golden hue. The nose offers fruit notes of apple and damson plums and a floral note of hawthorn. As it breathes, aromas of pineapple, grapefruit, and pear blend with floral scents of acacia and broom. You will appreciate this wine's softness and structure, followed by a warm mouthfeel adding just the right amount of balance. Enjoy this fine wine with grilled fish and vegetable risottos.

After making a few corrections, Luc added his standard purchasing guidelines specifying to his customers that he had reserved an allotment of two cases each and they had one week to place an order. Furthermore, the offer was not transferable to anyone else. He chuckled to himself as he added this last part; he had learned that building an image of exclusivity was necessary to build loyalty in his customers and keep them willing to pay top prices.

Luc had always been a bit of an entrepreneur. Back when he was in college in Michigan, he had concocted his first scheme to make money from trading. Twice during fall quarter, he rented a truck and drove it to Colorado where he bought several hundred cases of Coors beer. This was when it was distributed only in eleven western states and consumed enthusiastically by loyal fans. He timed his trips to arrive back in Ann Arbor before a big football weekend, where he always sold out the entire truck within twenty-four hours, netting a profit four times his costs. This scheme allowed Luc to finish college with no debt. He majored in marketing, a degree he found useless unless he wanted to take a job at a big consumer products conglomerate like Procter and Gamble. Since he'd already gotten a taste of making large profits with minimal effort, he decided to head out on his own. This decision didn't sit well with his father, who was from a blue-collar family and had done well in home construction and remodeling.

Luc knew his father had all but given up on him anyway. Known simply as Big Joe around the industry, he expressed his displeasure when Luke decided to change his name after college to a more elitist spelling of *Luc*. Even then Luc had big plans for his life, and those plans didn't include working-class ethics or a sense of duty to his parents. In fact, he had nothing but disdain for his father's class.

Well, here he was, twenty years later, running his own wine club and distribution facility out of a warehouse south of downtown Seattle. He smiled at the thought. He really hadn't come that far from his college days, selling Coors out of the back of a truck. Now his product was more expensive, but his success still depended on his ability to find customers who were motivated as much by image as by quality and were willing to pay a premium price for perceived exclusivity. He had found wine to be the perfect product for his marketing and entrepreneurial skills.

Luc remembered his personal journey with a degree of nostalgia. He'd traveled around Europe for many years after college, enjoying the company of women and drinking a lot of wine. It was then that he first met his Italian-born wife and his life embarked on its current course. Seeing her across the dance floor in a disco in Sienna, he was immediately taken by her long chestnut hair and a figure that some might call voluptuous. She was then twenty-three, a few years younger than he. Initially attracted to her bright hazel eyes and a disarming laugh, it wasn't until he learned that her family owned vineyards and a winery in Tuscany, where they had been making wine for generations, that he resolved to marry her. He recognized then that his lifelong skill of looking for opportunities and seizing upon them was becoming his *forte*. He was honest about this recognition, seeing it not so much as skill but a willingness to be bold and grab what he wanted.

Refocusing his attention on the newsletter, he finished a few notes and got up from his desk. He walked out his office door to the desk of his administrative assistant, Gwen, and handed her the letter with instructions to format and email it by the end of the day. After he left Gwen's desk, he noticed two men sitting in what was an informally arranged waiting area with a sofa and coffee table. They were sipping bottled water.

"Who are they?" Luc asked.

"They asked to see you," Gwen said. "I told them that you were busy and couldn't be disturbed. They just said they'd wait, so I gave them bottles of water and asked them to sit."

"What are their names?"

"They wouldn't say, just that they wanted to wait and speak with you."

"All right, show them in. I'll find out what they want."

He returned to his office while Gwen ushered them in. Each man shook Luc's hand, bowed briefly, and presented business cards with both hands extended before sitting down.

"I'm Mr. Huang," said the man on the left.

"I'm Wei," said the other.

Luc thought Mr. Huang might be the more senior of the two, based on his age and conservative attire. He wore a dark suit and tie. The other man was dressed in tan slacks and a sport coat. Luc could tell by the fit of the jacket that the younger man had a large chest and strong arms, indicated by the tightness of the fabric around his biceps. He also thought it likely they were both Chinese from the printed characters on the reverse side of their business cards.

"How may I help you?" Luc asked.

"We saw this ad in a wine newspaper," Mr. Huang said. "W
interested in finding wine and want you to help us." He handed Lu
copy of an advertisement. Luc recognized it immediately as some ad
copy he had started running several months earlier in various Chinese
trade weeklies.

Wine shipped to you in bulk
container from Washington Winery.
You bottle and design label in China
to suit your customers

You travel to Washington in United States. I provide transportation,
a translator, and accommodations for our trip to many wineries in
Washington. The winery you choose will produce wine to suit your
taste. Sweet to dry; white to red; taste and aromas you desire. A variety
of available grapes let you create your own blends. We produce wine
that could be sold in United States for USD $100.00 a bottle and we
sell it to you below cost. Contact Honorable Wine Merchants today.

Luc had targeted the ad toward Asian markets and offered to
help foreign wine buyers find their way around wineries and wine in
Washington. Besides running his wine club and importing wine from
around the world, Luc also was trying to tap into what he knew was a
growing market of wine consumers in China. He saw it as yet another
opportunity to make some easy money from a hot trend.

"What type of wines are you looking for?"

"We are looking for wine that tastes like high-quality French
Bordeaux. We hear that there are very good Cabernet and Merlot
grapes being grown in Washington, and we would like to find some
wine we can export to China," Mr. Huang said.

"But why come to Washington? Why not go to France?"

The man named Wei pulled a document from his pocket, unfolded
it, and handed it to Luc. "Because of this article."

Luc flipped through the document and scanned its content, which
he quickly recognized. It was the stuff of folklore. A widely respected

ist, writing for a popular food and wine maga-
ine the issue of fake wine. She researched the
see if she could find a winemaker to help her
'82 Château Mouton Rothschild, a wine rated
nts. To help in her quest, she went to a noted
ate of Washington, who was well-known for his
auvignons, and highly regarded Bordeaux-style
blends. After many trials and errors, they ended up with a '95 blend
of his wine and poured it into an empty bottle from the real '82
Mouton, along with a new cork that would have to be removed sur-
reptitiously when opening the bottle. The next step was to try to fool
some well-regarded oenophile friends of the author into believing
that it was indeed the real thing. She assembled a dinner party at her
house in New York and asked each guest to bring along a bottle of
their favorite Bordeaux. By the end of the night, after tasting some
stunningly famous wines, they picked the fake as the best wine of
the night. When the author later confessed to her guests that they
had been duped, she faced a hostile reaction from one, who hadn't
spoken to her since.

Luc put the article down and turned to his guests. "Yes, there are
some great wines like that made in Washington. How much are you
looking for?"

"We want about fifty barrels."

Luc was surprised by the quantity. He quickly did the math in his
head. One barrel of wine would produce around twenty-five cases. Fifty
barrels was around 1,250 cases, or 15,000 bottles. If he could locate
wine for around $3,000 per barrel, it would represent a sale of about
$150,000. His usual commission was 10 percent which would represent
a minimum of fifteen thousand dollars in his pocket. "That's a lot of
wine. How much are you willing to pay?"

"We will go as high as $6,000 per barrel if the wine is of high qual-
ity," Mr. Huang replied.

Luc was startled. That was a lot of money to pay for wine still in
the barrel, especially considering it had to be transported and bottled.

However, he greatly appreciated the possibility of a large commission. He glanced over at Wei, who had remained silent and seemingly smug. After sizing up his guests for a minute, Luc replied, "I would be happy to try and help you."

"Most excellent," said Mr. Huang. "Wei is our wine expert. He will taste each of the wines you represent and inform me when he has found the right one. It should taste like it comes from the Médoc region and has been appropriately aged. We will make all arrangements for shipping by container ship once we agree on the wine and a price. When do you think we can get started?"

The comment about coming from the Médoc triggered a question in Luc's head. It suggested they knew wine pretty well and were probably looking for something expensive. He decided to focus instead on the possible commission he would earn. And since they appeared to be wealthy, he decided to inflate his normal commission of 10 percent. "We haven't discussed my fees. I normally charge 20 percent for my services, but considering the size of your order, I will cut my regular commission to 15 percent."

"That is acceptable," said Mr. Huang.

"Good. I'll call one of my associates and ask him to get started. I'm sure I'll find wine that will meet your requirements. You said Wei will be doing the tasting. How well does he know wine?"

"Wei spent many years in France during his youth while his family lived there. He also holds a Master of Wine designation and participates on many wine tasting panels in Hong Kong. He will appreciate good wine."

"Impressive. How may I contact you?"

"I will be returning to Shanghai. You may contact Wei at the local number he has written on his business card. How long do you think it will take to find us some candidate wines?"

"I think I can have a number of good samples for you to try in a week. I assume Wei will return to do the tasting?"

"Yes, I will," Wei replied. "I'll be staying in Seattle until I hear from you."

As both guests stood up, Luc quickly stood with them. He shook their hands and they left his office. After a few moments had passed, giving Gwen enough time to escort them to the front door, Luc walked out of his office and said to her, "Put a call in to Jeff Russell. Tell him I've got a job for him."

2

October 24th

Prosser

Ricardo Álvarez woke to the sounds of Spanish music coming from his clock radio. It was eleven o'clock in the evening, time to begin another long night in the vineyards. Each year around mid-October, his body ached and he swore he would never go through another harvest again. Yet every year, as the grapes started turning color and growing larger, he looked forward once again to helping nature yield its bounty.

He laid out his clothes on the bed next to his sleeping wife and then headed for the shower. After washing, shaving, and toweling off, he looked over and saw that she had awakened and now stood in the doorway of the steaming bathroom. She was holding a hot cup of coffee for him. Even after only a few hours of sleep, she looked angelic with long, thick, dark hair accenting her round face. A smile told him she understood that he was the one who had to go out and work that night. He knew she hated grape harvest, when he often worked through the night, but she also understood it was the nature of farming. For the most part, she kept any frustration she might feel to herself. Occasionally, her tongue might get the better of her and she'd give Ricardo a sharp rebuke in Spanish. But she supported him unconditionally. Just the way it should be, thought Ricardo. The first American-born child of Mexican immigrant parents and a legal citizen, he shared his parents' values and believed that men should work hard, honor their family, believe in God, and attend church. He was proud of his heritage.

After dressing in Wrangler jeans, a red and black cotton work shirt, and lace-up lugged-sole work boots, Ricardo took a quick glance in the mirror before walking out of the bedroom. Even though he was thirty-five years old, he felt he looked younger. His still wet black hair was swept back on his head, and he sported a small mustache, which he thought made him look handsome. The skin on his face was a bit leathered from hours in the sun, but its olive tint helped hide the wear on his face that he knew was there. One benefit of working at night was avoiding the hot summer sun.

He poured a second cup of coffee into his travel mug, kissed his wife good-bye, and headed outside. It was a pleasant evening, about fifty degrees, and a light fog was forming over the Pasco, Washington neighborhood where he lived. He got into his truck and glanced at the rosary beads hanging from his mirror. Another day full of grace, he prayed. He put the truck in gear, backed out of the driveway, and began the short trip toward Prosser. He planned to meet his boss, Walt Conner, at the vineyard, where they'd map out a work plan for the evening. Ricardo, or Ricky as everyone called him, managed a vineyard crew for Walt.

He knew he was lucky to be working for Walt, one of those rare Anglo bosses who practiced what he preached. Walt appreciated the importance of family and a strong work ethic and supported those values in his workers. Instead of hiring seasonal migrant workers just during harvest, he employed his workers year round. He always found work for them, whether it was harvest, pruning vines, repairing trellises, replacing damaged plants, or repairing equipment. He gave them medical insurance, regular vacations, and fed them like they were his family.

Ricky drove in the dark for the next thirty minutes, listening to a Spanish language radio station. He was bilingual and had learned Spanish as a child from his parents, who were now living back home in Mexico, north of Monterrey. His English language skills were formalized in school, but at home his parents had spoken Spanish to their children so they would retain their Mexican heritage. Now it was his turn to take care of them. He remembered that it was time to send them the monthly check he had promised, as well as make plans for his next trip to visit them in Mexico. He soon pulled his truck onto the soft soil of the parking area, near the vineyard they planned to pick that night. Walt had purchased the large vineyard several years earlier and signed a long-term contract with the largest wine producer in the state to provide grapes for some of their single varietal value-priced wines. As Ricky stepped out of his truck, he looked ahead and saw a couple of his crew talking to Walt while standing next to a portable table covered with donuts, coffee, and fruit. Just beyond them he spotted the Korvan grape harvester they'd be using that night. Ricky liked to call her *Compañera*, the Spanish word for "girlfriend."

"Good morning, boss," Ricky said.

"Good morning, Ricky," Walt replied. "Ready for a long night?"

"One more cup of coffee and I think I'll be ready for anything," Ricky laughed. "Tell me about the grapes we're picking tonight."

"We've got ten acres of Cabernet Sauvignon. The winery's enologist sampled the grapes yesterday, and she says they're ready. I tend to agree. She thinks the seed tannins are ripe and the brix and pH are in the right range. She doesn't want to lose any more acid during the stretch of warm weather we've been experiencing. The long-term forecast predicts rain in four days, and she doesn't want to risk getting the fruit wet."

"How's my sweet *Compañera* running today?" Ricky asked.

"She's ready to go," Walt replied. In a tone that sounded like a father giving advice to a son, he continued, "The mechanics gave her a once-over this afternoon and fueled her up before delivering her here this evening. I think she's ready for her date with you tonight."

"Excellent," Ricky said. "I know just the way to treat her. She's like the old mare I had as a boy. Give her some loving words and some tender touches, and she'd plod along all day."

"Which is why I always won all our races!" joked one of Ricky's crew standing nearby. They all laughed at that one. Ricky picked up one of the donuts from the table and playfully pretended to throw it at the jokester.

17

Ricky joined everyone at the table for some food and said a proper hello to the crew. After a few minutes of idle chatter, he looked over at Walt. "I think we're ready to go, boss."

Walt surveyed his crew. "I don't know what I'd do without you and your team, Ricky." They were hard-working, and unless one of them or a family member became seriously ill, they never missed a day. He had mixed feelings about using a mechanical harvester. A lot of vineyards used them, but the arguments about fruit quality remained a major source of debate. He agreed with the general opinion that hand-picked grapes were superior because the process was gentler and resulted in full clusters, a preferred option for making white wines. Still, his primary customer was more concerned with receiving large volumes of high-quality fruit in a timely fashion than with hand-picked full clusters of grapes.

According to Walt, a mechanical harvester performed well when it was used properly and the trellis system was well maintained, with the catch wires pulled taut through the vines. Walt liked using the machines on thick-skinned berries, such as Cabernet Sauvignon or Merlot. Another advantage of using machines was the ability to pick at night. Given how close the vineyards were to the winery, many grapes could be delivered within an hour of picking, arriving on the crush pad early in the morning. By processing grapes at the winery early in the day, they avoided having them sit out in the sun. Winemakers prefer cool grapes because they are less likely to go through spontaneous fermentation by wild yeasts. Cool grapes, especially white varieties, are less susceptible to browning and losing flavor if they get too warm prior to fermentation.

Most of all, Walt realized that widespread use of mechanical harvesters was just a matter of time. The numbers were compelling. It took a crew of ten to handpick three to four acres in a ten-hour shift. With an eight-person crew and a mechanical harvester, he could harvest up to ten acres in a shift. Plus, it was getting more difficult to find harvest crew. The work was hard, skill was required, and able-bodied workers were scarce. After the market crash of 2008, and without a reasonable immigration policy, many migrant workers returned home to Mexico and never came back. Walt wished the United States would come to a consensus, resolve some of the immigration issues, and implement a stronger guest-worker program. He knew that local folks wouldn't do the work; even second-generation Latino workers were reluctant. For now the best solution was to keep his crews working on premium vineyards in Walla Walla, so he could provide his best grapes for smaller, artisanal wineries, like the one his friend Eric Savage owned.

Walt addressed the crew. "We should be done by 7:00 a.m. We'll meet you for coffee about halfway through and then meet back here for breakfast when we're done. Remember, be careful. You guys are too important to risk getting hurt. I know you would rather be home in bed, but we only have a few more weeks to go until we can celebrate another successful harvest. Stay alert and no mistakes."

Ricky climbed up into the cab of the harvester. It was quite comfortable with heat and a sound system. Large windows provided 360-degree visibility all around the harvester. Bright, oversized headlights lit the ground in front of him as he started the machine. He planned to go down the first row near where they had parked, then turn around and head back up the adjacent row. He knew Walt had promoted him to driver because he was cautious and alert. He also had a good sense of how well *Compañera* was removing the grapes. Listening to the sound of the bow bars against the vines gave him all the information he needed to make the necessary adjustments to their frequency of movement. After driving only fifty yards, he usually had her dialed in for optimal performance.

Ricky pointed the harvester down the first vine row while a tractor pulled the fruit bins behind and to his right. Several workers walked along inspecting fruit, ready to haul full bins back to the parking area where they were loaded onto a truck. He made some slight adjustments to the frequency of the bow bars and could see fruit falling into the bins, clean of leaves, largely unbroken, and free of juice. That was how the winemakers wanted them. The rows in this vineyard were about a quarter-mile long, and one of the biggest mistakes a driver could make was to start driving down a row that had already been picked. In the dark it was an easy mistake to make. Because there wasn't a way to turn the machine around, once a driver committed to a row, he or she was forced to continue to the other end at five miles per hour, which wasted everyone's time. Walt was never happy when this happened, and Ricky had only made this mistake once.

After a couple of hours, they all took a break and had some coffee and donuts. Harvest wasn't the healthiest time of year for Ricky's diet, but all the hard work kept him trim, and he was too young to worry about cholesterol and triglycerides. After a quick twenty-minute break, they went back to work. Ricky glanced at his watch and noted it was 3:30 a.m. They were making good time and had probably picked over a third of the vineyard. At this rate they should be enjoying breakfast around 7:00 a.m., just as Walt had predicted.

"*Compañera,* you are a sweet girl," Ricky said aloud, even though no one could hear. "Keep it up—we're halfway home, and soon we can both go back to bed." He gave her a quick pat on the dashboard.

As he drove down the fourth row of vines after their short break, listening to the hum of the bow bars oscillating back and forth, Ricky felt sleep begin to overtake him. He took a sip of the now cold coffee sitting in a nearby cup holder and turned on the radio. He was enjoying some lively music when he noticed something odd on the ground ahead of him in the vine row. He stared as it got closer, trying to comprehend what he was seeing. It began to disappear below his field of view. Too late he realized what it was. At that moment he felt the steering wheel of the harvester pull to the left and the machine pass over what felt like a large object. Ricky quickly shut off the engine of the harvester and exited the cab via the ladder that led down to the ground.

The workers pulling bins alongside him had to stop their rig unexpectedly when they realized they were moving too far ahead. "*Qué pasa! ¿Por qué te detienes?*" They wondered why he had stopped.

Ricky's feet hit the ground and he scampered underneath the harvester. There, aided by the glow of the bright headlights of the machine, he saw the body of a young man lying on the ground between the front and rear tires, extending out lengthwise from either side of the leafy vines above him. He was dressed in a pair of slacks and a button-down dress shirt. Business casual, Ricky thought. He felt horrified to realize he'd driven over him. The tire marks across the man's back testified to it. He knew he had to call Walt right away.

Ricky climbed back into the cab to fetch his radio. Depressing the "transmit" button, he yelled, "Walt, this is Ricky, over." The few seconds he had to wait seemed painfully long.

"This is Walt. What's wrong?" Walt recognized the concern in Ricky's voice.

"Walt, there has been a terrible accident. I just drove over someone. Please come right away."

"I'm coming now. I should be there in five minutes." Walt was pretty sure of the location of the harvester based on the current time and his experience of knowing how far the crew would have traveled since the break. He jumped on his ATV, switched on the headlights, and roared off.

3

October 25th

Walla Walla

Eric's alarm rang at 6:30 a.m. that late October morning. After turning it off, he sat up slowly in bed. Toward the end of harvest, each day started and ended with his body feeling tired and sore. Sleep always came easily at night, but there was never enough of it. Such was the life of a winemaker. Most of the grapes he had under contract with various growers had been picked, pressed, and put in barrels. Only six tons of Cabernet Sauvignon hadn't yet finished fermenting. Once that was done, he could declare victory over another season. But the first task ahead of him that morning was punching down. His assistant, Melissa, would punch down that evening.

Eric's dogs, Max and Ginger, soon arrived at the side of his bed, eagerly anticipating their breakfast. After finishing a hot shower, Eric glanced at his body in the mirror. Though still in his forties, harvest always made him feel older. His muscles were still well-defined, but his six-foot-three frame drooped from exhaustion. While he could still wear thirty-four-inch jeans, as in his college days, his full brown head of hair showed some gray areas and wasn't quite as thick as it used to be. As he shaved, he studied the dark circles below his blue eyes. He sighed, not wanting to accept that he was growing older. He still felt young; he just couldn't cheat the calendar. After putting on his clothes and shoes, he went downstairs to make coffee.

As the coffee brewed, he fed his dogs and put a frozen breakfast burrito in the microwave for the drive out to the winery. Within thirty minutes of his alarm going off, he and the dogs were out the front door and piling into his much-used red Ford F-250 pickup truck parked under the carport. He carefully drank his coffee and ate his burrito as he drove south out of Walla Walla. Max and Ginger sat huddled up against the cab in the truck bed behind him, out of the forty-degree wind swirling past them.

He drove twenty minutes before turning onto the gravel parking lot of the winery and parking the truck. After buttoning up his coat, he stepped out of the cab and walked to the rear where he let Max and Ginger jump out of the back. They ran off together toward the building, sniffing around the ground, checking for any scent of visitors from the previous evening. Eric unlocked the door and hurried inside his office to get out of the cold.

The design of his winery was mostly utilitarian, but with some decorative touches. The main building had a symmetric peaked roof of about thirty degrees which ran along its length. An extension off to one side housed the office and tasting room. From above, the building resembled the letter L. The roof was covered in vertical, slate-gray metal panels, and the exterior walls were made from board and batten, stained in a natural finish. Industrial-style, bowl-shade lamps, hung from curved tubing on the sides of the building, created a soft glow of circular light on the ground below. Around the walkways of the building, old wine half-barrels contained straggling remnants of last season's plantings. The honeysuckle, impatiens, marigolds, and geraniums he'd planted in early spring had been thriving just a few weeks ago, but the near-freezing overnight temperatures had taken their toll.

Eric had designed the building himself exactly the way he wanted it. Sliding barn-style doors hung on either end of the main building. In the rear, near the crush pad, where he frequently moved equipment and fermentation bins in and out of the winery, a larger door allowed for easy movement. A similar though smaller door was located on the front of the building. That's where he brought in supplies and moved out cases of finished wine.

Once he'd unlocked his office door and turned off the alarm system, Eric went inside the production part of the winery and opened the sliding doors to provide ventilation. Because bins filled with fermenting wine produce so much carbon dioxide, he knew it was important to make sure the odorless and deadly gas that built up overnight was allowed to dissipate. When he entered the winery before ventilating the fermenting gases, the acidic carbon dioxide gas irritated his nose and made him feel dizzy as oxygen was displaced in his body. It was a serious matter. He always checked his carbon dioxide meters to ensure acceptable levels before working inside.

The Cabernet Sauvignon was fermenting in four open-top, steel fermentation bins. Six days ago, the grapes had been delivered to the winery by truck early in the morning. A group of volunteers worked with Melissa and Eric to sort, destem, and crush the grapes before placing about one and a half tons into each bin. To control spoilage bacteria during the crushing process, Eric added sulfur dioxide to the mixture of grape juice and skins, known as *must*, and let it soak for twenty-four hours before adding rehydrated yeast to begin fermentation.

As Eric arrived inside the winery that morning, a pungent smell indicated fermentation was going well and the yeast were producing lots of carbon dioxide. The smooth temperature curve of the *must*, which he plotted daily, was also a positive indicator. The gas bubbles rising to the surface of the fermentation bins brought grape skins up along with them, forming a cap. After about ten minutes of allowing fresh air into the winery, he prepared to punch down the cap on each fermentation bin, a process known as *pigeage*. Traditionally, this was done by stomping through the vats of grapes, but nowadays, winemakers use a tool that looks a little like a stainless steel canoe paddle, with a T-handle on one end, and a stainless steel disk on the other, for pushing down into the cap. He or Melissa punched down twice daily during the two weeks of fermentation. On some days he used a hose with a pump to circulate wine from inside the bin and then spray it gently over the cap of grape skins, a process known as *remontage*, which adds more oxygen to fermenting wine. Both procedures help balance the temperature of the *must*. Eric knew from experience that color and tannin extraction from the grapes depended on regulating temperatures and keeping the cap of grape skins moist.

As Eric moved over to begin punching down the next fermentation bin, he looked at his watch and noted the time was 7:30 a.m. Each bin took under ten minutes to punch down; with only three more to go, he'd be done by 8:00 a.m. Just as he was starting on the second bin, his cell phone in the front pocket of his jeans began to vibrate. Not wanting to risk dropping his phone into the bin, he decided to ignore the call until he finished his work. He wondered who'd be calling him this time of the morning.

Once he had finished the last bin, cleaned the punch-down tool, and returned it to the equipment rack, Eric put the bin covers on and walked back to his office. He pulled his phone out of his pocket and found a message from the sheriff's office. As he listened to it, he heard a familiar voice.

"Eric, this is Sheriff Scott Thompson. I need to drop by for a visit this morning. Sorry for the short notice, but something has come up. I need to ask you a few questions. I should be out there about eight thirty. If you won't be there, give me a call. Otherwise, I'll see you soon."

Eric hadn't seen the sheriff since before the beginning of harvest. Their reasons for seeing each other back then had to do with the mysterious murder of his ex-wife, Bridget, something he had been trying his best to forget. He and Scott had grown closer through the experience.

Yet there had been a time when Scott, like most people, suspected Eric had murdered his ex-wife. She'd been found dead in her flat in London where she'd moved after their divorce. The local police had determined the death had been caused by drinking a bottle of Eric's wine which had been laced with poison. To make matters worse, Eric had let it be known that he was upset with Bridget for divorcing him.

Within hours after Scott visited his house that fateful day to inform him of Bridget's death, Eric left for London in an impromptu search for the killer. During the ensuing adventure, Eric met an FBI agent who helped solve the crime. Now back in Walla Walla with his reputation cleared, he really didn't want to think about any of it. What could Scott want now, Eric wondered?

He went to his office to check email while he awaited Scott's arrival. He decided to make a pot of coffee and wait. He was leaning against his desk sipping from a cup when he saw the patrol car pull into the gravel parking lot of the winery. He went to meet Scott at the office door. After exchanging greetings, they returned to the office where Eric poured Scott a cup of coffee, and they both sat down.

"It's good to see you, Scott, but I'm guessing this isn't a social call. Normally, you'd come by after lunch and we'd have a glass of wine together. What's up?"

"Eric, I hate to come calling so early, and actually I'd prefer this to be a social call. I'd rather have a glass of your wine than this coffee, but I need to ask you some questions."

"Ask away."

"You know Jeff Russell, right?"

"Of course, he's Walt Conner's son-in-law." Walt was a legend in the valley and regarded as one of the best vineyard managers in the state. Eric felt fortunate to have annual contracts with Walt and believed he provided the best fruit for his wines. Over time, Eric had grown close to Walt and his affable wife Susan, who continually tried to fix Eric up on dates with eligible women. "Yes, I met him two days ago, here at the winery. He came to taste my wines. Melissa was here with me."

"Why did he want to taste your wines?"

"He said he had a customer who was looking to buy a quantity of bulk wine. What's going on, Scott?"

"One of Walt Conner's guys found him dead in a vineyard early this morning."

"What? Does Walt know? He must be devastated." Walt's daughter had gone through a painful divorce many years earlier and had a two-year-old daughter at the time. Eric knew Walt was relieved she had survived the divorce and now seemed happily married to her second husband, Jeff. Eric had met him at a few social events.

"I think you know Ricardo Álvarez, one of Walt's crew chiefs." When Eric nodded yes, Scott recounted the early-morning events in the vineyard. "Poor guy, he was convinced that he had killed him. After Walt arrived on the scene, he had to calm Ricardo down first before examining the body. Only then did he realize it was Jeff. He's now at home with his daughter and Susan. They are all very upset."

"What was Jeff doing in the vineyard?" Eric asked.

"We don't know. When we got there it was pretty clear he'd been dead for a while. He was dressed in business clothes and from the looks of the lacerations around his neck, he was likely strangled. We won't have the preliminary autopsy report until later this afternoon."

"So why are you talking to me, Scott?"

"We got an emergency search warrant so we could check his cell phone and noticed his appointment with you a couple of days ago. I thought you might be able to give us some help."

"Jeff works as a wine broker and said he was looking for a really good Bordeaux blend. Someone had told him he should talk to me and taste my wines. I tried to say no on the phone, but he was very persistent. So I scheduled the appointment with him, but I also made sure he understood that I had no plans to sell any of my wines in bulk. Luckily, demand is pretty good and I sell most of my cases directly. That's a lot better for me financially."

Scott wrote some notes on a pad. "What does a wine broker do?"

"He tries to match buyers and sellers of wine. Some brokers specialize in case goods from wineries and represent them to restaurants and retail stores. Others try to sell bulk wine or juice from a winery that might have excess supply to someone who needs it for blending or bottling. I haven't worked with a broker very often, but they can be useful."

"So you've had no contact with him since your meeting two days ago?"

"That's correct."

"Do you know whom the buyer was representing?"

"He didn't say. He told me his job was to find the wine. He knew me and said his client would pay well."

"We found a car we believe to be his in the parking lot of Prosser's Vintage Inn. The plates and registration match his name. We've impounded the car and we're getting a search warrant to examine it. Maybe we'll find additional information inside."

Eric looked at Scott for a moment before saying, "I don't know what to think. He didn't strike me as someone who would find trouble."

"I agree. I'll let you know if we find out anything else. In the meantime, keep your eyes open and don't mention this to anyone else as we continue our investigation. I'll be in touch."

Scott stood up and placed his empty coffee cup on Eric's desk. They shook hands and walked outside together. After saying good-bye, Scott got in his patrol car and drove slowly out of the parking lot.

Eric reflected on his meeting with Jeff Russell and the tasting as he headed to his office. Jeff really liked the wines, but Eric had told him repeatedly that he wasn't interested in doing business with him. He couldn't think of any unusual details though. His thoughts then turned to Walt and Susan. He'd give them a day or two to grieve and then drop by. As a father of a daughter himself, Eric couldn't imagine the pain and anger Walt must be feeling.

Ten minutes later, as he replayed the meeting in his head, he looked through his office window and saw Melissa's Subaru rolling into the lot in front of the building. He decided to honor Scott's request to keep their meeting to himself until he knew more.

4

November 1st

Walla Walla

A week had passed since Friday's apparent homicide in a vineyard near Prosser, followed by Sheriff Thompson's visit to Eric's winery. The day after their conversation, Scott called Eric to let him know that he had obtained an expedited warrant authorizing a search of Jeff Russell's car. He promised to let Eric know of any further results from the crime lab examination of the car and its contents.

The Cabernet Sauvignon was ready to press and Eric arrived at the winery early in the morning to prepare. A density meter showed the sugar level to be nearly zero, confirming fermentation was just about complete. Eric cleaned and sanitized the membrane press and the rest of the required equipment: pump, hoses, valves, and clamps. He was just finishing when he heard the office door swing open. Max and Ginger ran off toward the sounds. Eric looked over and saw Melissa appear in the doorway, followed by Max jumping up to say "hello."

"Good morning, Melissa," Eric said.

"Good morning, Eric." Melissa looked at him through piercing dark blue eyes as she kneeled down to say hello to the dogs. Her blond ponytail swept across Max as she played with him. "You ready to press?"

"I am. We only have two press loads, so we'll get out of here at a reasonable time."

Melissa had worked part-time for Eric over the past two-and-a-half years. He'd hired her on the recommendation of a friend who ran the wine education program at the local community college in Walla Walla, where Melissa had been a student in the Wine Sales and Marketing program. She had demonstrated keen interest and an aptitude for learning many of the winemaking tasks Eric gave her. Although she started out managing some of the office work, including billing and ordering supplies, it soon became evident that she excelled at the marketing side of the business. She kept the winery's website updated with photos and blogs from winemaking or harvest, and made sure the online order system was current. She also posted on Facebook and sent out weekly Twitter feeds about newsworthy events. Now, Eric found himself depending on Melissa. Besides being competent, she was always cheerful and enthusiastic, youthful traits that lifted his spirits during long days in the winery.

Even though she was dressed to work hard in torn jeans and a baggy sweatshirt, Melissa always looked clean and fresh, aware she was working in a place where a good first impression was always required. Her hair was neatly brushed and clean, her pierced ears accentuated by some tasteful studs, and her face appeared clean and makeup-free. Eric wasn't sure of her exact age because he'd never felt it appropriate to ask. Some casual comments made outside of work suggested some swimsuit modeling when she was younger. He thought she would look stunning at any beachside location.

As they stood together for a brief moment, he was reminded of an evening that past summer when she had attended a dinner party at his house. After the other guests left, she helped him clean up. They'd probably enjoyed one too many glasses of port, which is how he explained what happened next. In a moment awkward for him, and yet one in which she seemed completely at ease, Melissa suggested that they take their relationship in another direction. Though Eric found Melissa alluring, he assumed their age difference was considerable and any suggestion she found him attractive to be preposterous. He convinced himself that the alcohol was making her impulsive—much like going to a movie on a night when she should be studying. He was flattered of course, and perhaps a bit tempted, but he felt compelled to decline, albeit respectfully. He remembered telling her that their relationship should stay professional. They both let the moment pass and hadn't spoken of it since. She mentioned having a boyfriend that fall at the start of crush—a development he found reassuring.

After connecting the pump and hoses to the press, they started prepping barrels. Eric used only French oak barrels from his favorite cooperages: Demptos, Seguin Moreau, Gamba, and Taransaud. Most were new and the remainder used once to ferment white wine that fall. From experience, Eric found this combination added the right amount of oak properties to the wine. The night before, he had filled ten new barrels a third full with water to hydrate the staves: the thin, narrow, shaped pieces of oak that form the sides of a barrel. Hydrating helped the staves expand to seal the seams and prepared the oak to better interact with new wine.

Eric placed the partially filled barrels on steel racks by hand and then used the forklift to hoist a rack of two barrels onto the wash stand. Melissa rotated them over so that the bung holes in the side of the barrels were pointed toward the floor. Water came gurgling out and ran down the drain. Once the barrels used earlier for white wine were drained, he used the forklift to place them on the floor next to the press. They followed this process with all ten new barrels. Again using the forklift, he pulled out a rack of two clean barrels, used for white wine fermentation, and put them on the wash stand for a quick rinse. After being rinsed thoroughly, they too were ready to stack on the floor next to the press for draining. Melissa rotated the barrels by hand until the bung hole was at the top.

Eric parked the forklift and jumped off. He decided to test Melissa's knowledge of winemaking. "Melissa, what's the purpose of aging wine in barrels? Having lectured as a guest in some of your classes, I think you should know the answer."

Melissa accepted the challenge. "Well, I can think of three reasons off the top of my head. The first is to provide slow and controlled oxidation. Oxygen slowly permeates through the oak staves of the barrel into the wine, which softens the wine's tannins and increases red color intensity and stability. Second, oak provides phenols and flavor components which enhance and expand the wine's complexity. Third, alcohol and water slowly evaporate which increases the wine's concentration and flavor."

"Anything else?" Eric prodded.

"That's all I can remember."

"Extended time in a barrel gradually develops the wine's bouquet," Eric said.

"But isn't aroma the same as bouquet?"

"Not really," Eric said. "Aroma refers to the smells unique to a grape variety, like black currant in a Cabernet Sauvignon or lemon-grass in a Sauvignon Blanc. Bouquet results from the chemical processes in making wine, such as fermentation and aging, and can add new smells: notes of honey or vanilla, for example. A barrel's impact on wine decreases with use, which is why I use some neutral, or used barrels, along with new barrels. I don't want to overwhelm the aromas of the fruit."

"And how long do you keep the wine in barrels?"

"About eighteen months. Some winemakers age longer, but since I blend my Cabernet Sauvignon into my Bordeaux blend, I try to keep all the component wines on oak for about the same duration. If I were bottling a single varietal Cabernet, I might go as long as twenty-four months."

"Wow, that's a long time," Melissa said.

Eric got back on the forklift and made two trips back into the winery to retrieve the two stainless steel fermentation bins for the first press run. He set them by the press, and then Melissa pushed a hose with a metal screen on the end inside the bin toward the bottom. He used the forklift to lift the bin up high so that its wine would feed by gravity into the barrels. This method was a more gentle way to move wine than by using a pump.

Once the free-run juice had drained out of the bin, Melissa pulled out the hose, and Eric used the forklift to lift the fermentation bin up above the press. He poured the remaining wine and grapes into a large stainless steel funnel, which directed the contents into the press cylinder. Then he put the empty bin away and drove back into the winery to get a second bin. They followed the same process. When the second bin was empty, Melissa closed the doors on the press and using the controls on the side, keyed in and started the press program. Next, using the pump and a racking wand that were connected with hoses to the press pan, Melissa set to work filling up barrels as the juice began to stream out of the press.

By 2:00 p.m., they had twelve full barrels, each holding about sixty gallons, and two steel beer kegs, filled with fifteen gallons each. Over the next several months, Eric would use the two kegs as topping wine to replace wine lost from evaporation out of the oak barrels. It was important to keep barrels full to minimize any exposure to oxygen. The rest of the afternoon was spent cleaning.

Around 5:00 p.m., they walked back into his office and Eric invited Melissa to sit down while he fetched a couple of beers. Returning with two cold bottles and two glasses, he noticed Melissa had pulled off her wet sweatshirt and replaced it with a clean, long-sleeve, white T-shirt. Printed on the front was a quotation ascribed to Louis Pasteur: "A bottle of wine contains more philosophy than all the books in the world." Melissa had also taken off her boots and rolled up the cuffs of her jeans, wet from washing equipment.

Eric handed her one of the beers. They clanked the bottles together as Eric said, "Well done. To the end of harvest!" After taking a sip, he added, "I like your shirt. You know, Pasteur is responsible for our understanding of alcoholic fermentation in wine and beer, but it was another scientist who fully understood the benefits of the second fermentation most winemakers use today."

"You mean MLF—malolactic fermentation?"

"Yes. Before the chemical processes of MLF were well understood, wines would get cloudy in the spring as the ambient temperature in the winery rose. Warm temperatures can cause MLF to start spontaneously and give off carbon dioxide bubbles well after primary fermentation had completed, which was particularly unfortunate if the wine had already been bottled. Thanks to Émile Peynaud, we now intentionally start MLF in most red wines before bottling to increase their stability and enhance other characteristics of the wine."

Eric sipped his beer from a glass while Melissa drank directly from the bottle.

"So tell me Melissa, why are you so interested in winemaking? I'm guessing you grew up with parents who insisted you take ballet lessons, made sure you saw an orthodontist and dermatologist, and probably could have sent you to any college you wanted. I don't understand why your parents didn't convince you to study law or medicine. You know you have the mind for it."

"What's wrong, don't you think I'm doing a good job, Eric?" Melissa looked at him with a quizzical smile, and artfully ducked his question. "What about you? You manage the winery well, but I can easily picture you in an executive suite somewhere. From the number of tailored suits I noticed in the back of your walk-in closet, I'm guessing your old career was very different from this. I'll ask you the same question. Why are you so interested in winemaking?"

"I got tired of the corporate life. Sure, it paid well, and traveling all over the world selling airplanes gave me a unique opportunity to visit interesting places, but it felt like I was playing a small part in a larger corporate mission. I wanted to do something more personal, creative—something that would provide some happiness and satisfaction in people's lives. When I had the financial resources, I decided to start the winery. I haven't ever looked back." Eric smiled at Melissa. "When were you in my closet?"

"One day when I was taking care of the dogs while you were on a trip to Seattle. I went into your bathroom to look for some aspirin and happened to see into your closet. Hope you don't mind. I didn't take anything."

"My clothes wouldn't fit you very well anyway. And you haven't answered my question."

She took another sip of her beer. "I really haven't discussed this with anyone outside of my family, Eric." She paused for a few seconds and then continued. "I think you've got a pretty good read on my childhood. I knew my parents loved me. I was their only child and they wanted the best for me. But they also instilled a strong work ethic, insisting I not take things for granted. I was on the track team in high school—in fact, I set a school record in the 4-by-400 meter relay one year. I took honors classes and sat for several Advanced Placement exams. I even attended the University of Washington in pre-med. Honestly, I sometimes felt like an observer as my life went by. My parents orchestrated almost everything. But then things took a bad turn."

Eric observed Melissa's face intently. Her eyes glistened, suggesting she was near tears. He watched her young, innocent face become thoughtful and her eyes lose focus, as if she were deep in thought. One eyebrow arched upward. Feeling her sadness, Eric spoke gently, "May I ask what happened?"

"My father was a researcher at Hanford, the nuclear facility over in Tri-Cities. He'd majored in physics and was working on plans for the proposed nuclear waste disposal site in Nevada. When I was a freshman in college, he became ill. We weren't sure what was wrong, but he was later diagnosed with leukemia. He died about a year later. My mom was devastated, so I left school and moved back home to help her get back on her feet. That was ten years ago. I traveled a bit and worked at different jobs, including some modeling. Then a friend told me about the wine program here in Walla Walla. You know the rest."

"I'm sorry," Eric said. "I'm sure your father must have adored you."

"I think he did."

They sat in silence for a few minutes, finishing their beers. Then Eric spoke up: "I need to discuss next week with you."

"What's happening?"

"I'm going to Hawaii. While I'm gone, I'd like you to do the first racking of the fourteen barrels of this year's Merlot, off the gross lees and into clean barrels. This will be their first racking since the wine was pressed. Malolactic fermentation is complete, so in addition I also want you to add twenty-five parts per million of sulfur dioxide. And will you also take care of Max and Ginger for me?"

"Hawaii? Let me guess—Ashley is going with you. And yes, I'll take care of Max and Ginger."

"Good guess. Ashley and her two boys are meeting me there. I haven't seen her since last summer after she went back home to Houston. It'll be a good opportunity to meet her boys."

Ashley was the FBI agent Eric met in London. Without her efforts, Eric suspected he'd be in prison. While working together to solve the murder, they'd felt an attraction develop between them. A trip to Hawaii together was a big step forward in their relationship. He wasn't sure where it was headed; living in different locations seemed a huge impediment. It would be their first chance to see each other since harvest began three months ago in late August.

"I wish you were taking me to Hawaii."

He looked at Melissa and couldn't quite tell if her comment was made in jest. Learning of her father's death helped him to better understand her interest in him. He was likely a father figure to her. With added resolve, he planned to keep it that way. He had his own daughter, ten years younger than Melissa, and he was well aware of the special bond between fathers and daughters.

"Don't you have a boyfriend, an assistant winemaker somewhere? What's his name? I don't think you ever told me."

"His name is Kurt Hughes. If it's all right with you, I'm going to ask him to help me in the winery while you are gone. He's finished with harvest at the winery where he works so he can take some time off."

"Any chance I can meet him before I leave? I trust you, but I don't know him." Eric didn't want to let someone he didn't know have access to his wines. Besides, he was curious about the man Melissa was dating and a bit protective of her.

"I'd love that!"

"Why don't you both come over for dinner tonight? It won't be fancy, but I'll pull something together, and it'll give me a chance to meet Kurt."

"Sounds fun. We already planned to see each other tonight, so it won't be a problem to drop by. How does 7:00 p.m. sound?"

"Perfect. Let's get out of here. It's been a long day."

5

November 1st

Walla Walla

After locking up the winery and confirming dinner plans with Melissa, Eric buttoned up his coat and walked across the parking lot toward his truck. Max and Ginger were close behind. It was already past sunset, and the same cool wind that had blown all day bit at his face. He put the dogs in the truck bed and drove toward home. He was elated that the final pressing was done. It marked the end of harvest. Although plenty of work remained, three hard months of traveling to the vineyards, destemming, crushing, fermenting, pressing, and endless cleaning were over for that year's vintage. His hands were covered in scars and his back ached. Every muscle was tired, but he was happy. The weather had held, the fruit seemed solid, and none of the fermentations had become stuck, a condition that could occur for a variety of reasons when the fermentation stops and all of the sugar is not converted to alcohol.

On the way home Eric decided to call in an order for some takeout Thai because he was too tired to make dinner himself. He stopped off at the restaurant and waited a few minutes for the order to be completed, then continued his drive home. Once there, he fed the dogs and took them for a quick walk around the neighborhood.

While he was walking, his cell phone rang.

"Eric, this is Scott Thompson."

"Hi Sheriff, what's up?"

"I hate to bother you on a Friday night, but I wanted to let you know that we received the report back from the crime lab today. They finished examining Jeff Russell's car. I'd like to send you the summary."

"Okay. Email it to me and I'll take a look."

"It looks like Jeff was working for a company in Seattle named Honorable Wine Merchants. Ever hear of them?" Scott asked.

"Yes, the guy who runs it, Luc DuPont, has a very loyal, almost cult-like following. He claims to be a supertaster. Some think he's a bit of a charlatan, but he sells a lot of wine. He purports to scour the world for wines that are made with the least intervention. He does well with devotees of the artisanal and natural food movement and has built an impressive business."

"What's a 'supertaster'?"

"Humans can only taste five flavors: sweet, sour, salt, bitter, and *umami*—savory. Anything else, we actually smell. For example, spicy is not a taste. Most people confuse taste and odor. What some people think of as tastes are actually smells that travel up the back of your throat. This retro-nasal perception of odors is often confused with taste and is quite important in wine tasting. A supertaster is believed to occur in about fifteen percent of the male population and thirty-five percent of females. In theory, it relates to the density of taste receptors on the tongue. But it's actually more complicated than that."

"Well, from your description, I'm sure I'm not a supertaster. But I want to pay a visit to Mr. DuPont and I'd like you to join me."

"Why?" Eric asked. The prospect of getting involved alarmed him.

"Because you know wine and I know the law. Read the summary. I think the suspicious death of Jeff Russell is tied to wine, and I think Mr. DuPont may know something about it. But for now, I just plan to have a friendly conversation."

"I'd love to help, but there's a problem."

"What's that?"

"I'm leaving for Hawaii on Monday," Eric said.

"Then let's visit him before you go. We can take the early flight from Walla Walla to Seattle, visit Mr. DuPont, and then you can catch your flight to Hawaii as planned."

"Scott, I don't know . . ."

"Eric, I really need your help."

"You're the sheriff. How can I say no? Just promise I'll make my flight."

"Why are you going to Hawaii? Celebrating the end of harvest?"

"Yes. And I'm meeting someone there who believes in punctuality."

"Sounds important. Who is it?"

"Ashley," Eric said.

"Ashley? That FBI beauty from Houston who kept you out of prison?"

"That's the one." He knew Scott had admired Ashley's work as a Special Agent when she helped clear Eric of any suspicion he'd murdered his ex-wife that previous summer. He also assumed Scott was impressed she was joining him in Hawaii.

"Well, I wouldn't keep her waiting either. I'll make sure you get there on time."

"Good night, Scott. I'll look for your email."

Eric hurried his pace, walking the rest of the way back home in the now cold, still air. After letting the dogs scamper back inside, he glanced at his phone to check the time. Melissa and Kurt would arrive in thirty minutes. He headed off for a hot shower and a change of clothes.

Just after pulling on and buttoning up a clean pair of jeans and a long-sleeve shirt, the doorbell rang. Eric went downstairs, still in bare feet, and answered the door. He let Melissa and Kurt inside, went through an exchange of hellos, took their coats, and invited them into the kitchen.

"So you're the famous Eric Savage," Kurt said.

Eric pulled a bottle of wine from the refrigerator. "Guilty," he said, "but I'm not famous."

"Well, to hear Melissa talk, you must be," said Kurt, without a hint of levity.

"How about a glass of wine?" Opening the bottle, Eric poured everyone a glass of a local Sauvignon Blanc.

"Thanks for having us over," Melissa said.

"I'm glad you could make it on such short notice. I have to confess that I picked up some Thai food on the way home. I just didn't have anything around here to cook. I'm so tired; I'd probably screw it up anyway."

"That's fine," said Melissa.

"I hear you're going to Hawaii," Kurt said. "Must be nice."

"I like to take a week off after harvest," Eric said. "And recharge a bit. I'm usually exhausted and this year is no exception."

"Melissa says you make great wine."

"I don't know about great, but I try to make each year's vintage better than the last. As long as I work hard, continue to learn, and build a loyal base of customers, the rest will follow. I make technically solid wine, with a passion that I hope is apparent. But it's really about the fruit, and I've been lucky to source from some great growers. They're the stars." Sipping his wine, Eric decided to take the focus from himself and put it directly onto Kurt. "What about you, Kurt? I hear you're an assistant winemaker."

He noticed Melissa leaning back against the kitchen counter, taking it all in. He also noticed Max had come into the room and curled up on the floor near Melissa's feet. Smart boy!

"After I graduated from high school, I started working for a friend of my father's. He has a small winery out near the Walla Walla airport in some of the buildings the Port owns. He makes some pretty good Cabernet Franc. I bought a bottle if you'd like to try some."

"Thanks, let's have some with the food." Eric said. "In fact, let's sit down and eat." Eric knew Cabernet Franc wasn't best paired with Thai dishes, but that's what they had.

Kurt retrieved the bottle of wine while Melissa pulled some plates out of one of the kitchen cabinets. Eric removed the food containers from the oven and set them on the kitchen island. After he placed some red-wine glasses on the table, they served themselves and sat down. Kurt poured each of them a glass of his wine.

As he picked up the glass, the first thing Eric noticed about the wine was its color. It had a bit of a brick-red cast to it, signaling that it was older. But as he glanced at the bottle, he could see the vintage was only three years earlier. This suggested that the wine might have aged prematurely, perhaps due to some careless exposure to oxygen during production in the winery. The next thing he noticed was a bit of haze in the wine, which meant it probably hadn't been fined. Eric knew some winemakers didn't believe in fining, preferring a more natural approach to making wine, but he felt it greatly added to the clarity and brightness of wine and removed some astringency. He looked over toward Kurt, who was watching him intently.

"Looks nice," Eric said. He then took a quick inhale of the wine's bouquet, followed by a sip. He had two immediate observations: the fruit was subdued on the nose, confirming his assumption of premature aging as suggested by the color, and the wine tasted a bit flabby. "Do you acidify?" he asked. He knew most wineries added tartaric acid to grapes at fermentation to make up for the natural loss of acidity during the hot growing season in eastern Washington.

"No," Kurt replied. "The winemaker believes in making wine with as little intervention as possible."

"Have you gone to school to learn winemaking, or are you learning on the job?" Eric asked.

"I'm learning as I go. I've taken a few classes. That's where I met Melissa. I wish I had the luxury of retiring early from a well-paying career so I could focus on making wine and not have to worry about money, but I'm not so lucky," Kurt said, staring at Eric without smiling.

Eric didn't see any point in making more comments about the wine, as Kurt clearly had a chip on his shoulder. "It's nice," he said. "You did a great job."

Deciding to change the subject, Eric looked toward Melissa. "Speaking of wine, those maroon jeans you're wearing remind me of red Burgundy." He was routinely surprised when he saw Melissa outside the winery. Normally he saw her in work clothes, wearing wine-stained and ripped jeans, accompanied by a bulky sweatshirt in the fall and winter or a lighter top in the spring and summer. Tonight she was wearing skinny jeans, tucked into a pair of stylish leather boots. A black lace camisole peered out from beneath a wide-necked gray sweatshirt that hung off one shoulder. Her blond hair was brushed straight down, cut evenly at the back below her shoulders.

"Just something I pulled out of the closet," Melissa said. Eric guessed her clothing selection was anything but random.

He took a bite of Pad Thai, and they all sat silently for a few moments. He noticed Max was once again at Melissa's feet.

Eric broke the silence by saying, "Melissa, if you were a wine, you'd be a fine Grand Cru Chablis. With a color of yellow straw to match your hair, you'd be rich and luscious with vibrant fruit flavors. Of course you'd age well." He was intentionally playing with Kurt at this point, and Melissa decided to play along.

"Eric," Melissa said, wearing a big grin, "if you were a wine you'd be a Rhone Valley Syrah. Smoky, supple, and with a bold, complicated structure. And I'd drink every drop."

"That's it!" Kurt threw his fork down onto his plate, pushed back his chair from the table, and stood up. "I'm tired of these games, Melissa. Let's go."

Max jumped up from Melissa's feet and trotted out of the room. Eric stood and said, "Please stay; have some more wine and dinner. Kurt, we're just kidding around. We do this all the time at work. Don't be offended."

"I'm tired of hearing about you, your dogs, and your great wine. It's all she ever talks about. Melissa, I'll be out in the car." Kurt stormed out of the kitchen and Eric soon heard the front door slam.

"Melissa, I'm sorry. What got into him?"

"He knows how much I admire you, and I think he's a bit jealous."

"Jealous? He looked pretty angry. Will you be okay with him?"

"I'll be fine. I can handle him. But I should be going."

Eric walked Melissa toward the front door. He retrieved Melissa's and Kurt's coats from the closet and handed them to her. While holding the coats, Melissa turned toward Eric and wrapped her arms around his waist. Eric placed his arms around Melissa and held her tight. While she rested her head on Eric's chest, Eric caught himself enjoying the feel of her firm breasts pressing against him. Her hair smelled of fresh lavender.

He finally said, "I need you to tell your friend Kurt that I don't want him in my winery again. I know you occasionally brought him with you during harvest to help with punch downs, but after tonight's outburst, I don't trust him."

Melissa released Eric and looked up at him with wide eyes. Eric could tell she was hurt by his comment. "All right, I understand. I'll tell him. I'm sorry, Eric."

Melissa stepped outside and started down the sidewalk. She offered a slight wave back as she walked. Eric glanced toward their car and saw Kurt standing by the driver's side door. His face was illuminated by a brightening orange glow near his mouth from inhaling a cigarette.

6

November 2nd

Walla Walla

The next morning, Saturday, Eric slept in until 8:00 a.m., a rare luxury. After a leisurely breakfast of eggs, bacon, toast, and coffee, he took the dogs for a short walk around the Whitman College campus, about two blocks from his house. The well-respected liberal arts college was one of Eric's favorite places to walk the dogs and think. It was often filled with students walking between classes or dorms, and Eric found their youthful enthusiasm and laughter comforted him. The experience also helped him stay connected to his daughter, a sophomore at a college in Santa Barbara. He hoped that she looked as fresh and happy as these kids, although she would likely be wearing shorts and a sweatshirt instead of jeans and fleece. He looked forward to his weekly phone call with her on Sunday.

After returning from their walk, Eric put the dogs back into the truck and drove to the winery. He'd given Melissa the weekend off. He would take care of a few chores and write down some instructions for Melissa to follow while he was out of town the following week. By Sunday night, he planned to have his bags packed and everything in order to catch the flight with Scott early Monday morning.

His first task was to start MLF on the Cabernet Sauvignon he'd just pressed. This step, which is performed on almost all red wines, typically began during or after the alcoholic fermentation was completed. Its benefits include increased stability, reduced acidity, and an improved mouthfeel. The process of MLF is completed by a bacterial conversion of tart-tasting malic acid to softer lactic acid. To start MLF, Eric used a freeze-dried culture of malolactic bacteria which he kept in the freezer at the back of the winery in the lab area. Once the culture was added to the barrels, he stirred each one in a process called *batonnage*, and then gently rested a silicone bung in the hole on the top of the barrel.

After finishing his work inside the winery and cleaning up, Eric returned to his office to write instructions for Melissa covering the items she needed to handle during his trip to Hawaii. The instructions were straightforward. At the end, he added his request that Kurt not accompany her to the winery. If she needed help she should call a friend, Brad Smith, a volunteer who helped Eric on a regular basis and used to make wine himself. When Eric was finished with the instructions, he emailed them to Melissa and put a copy on her desk.

Eric then turned his attention to Sheriff Thompson's email, which was waiting for him in his inbox. Opening the email, he saw that it contained a coroner's report and other documents. He read the accompanying note:

"Eric, it looks like we have a murder on our hands. Review the attachments and I'll see you in the morning."

The coroner's report began with a description of the victim and cause of his death. It confirmed that Jeff Russell had been strangled, likely with a rope or cord, as indicated by the marks on his neck. The coroner determined the time of death to be six to eight hours before his body had been found in the vineyard, between 7:30 and 9:30 in the evening. The victim's car had been found in the parking lot of a popular motel on the interstate highway near Prosser.

Next, the report listed the items found in the car including a wallet, various articles of clothing, and a journal. The trunk also contained a cardboard box with seven open and re-corked bottles of wine, with several glasses of wine removed from each bottle, and a set of golf clubs.

Another attachment included photocopies of several pages from a journal. Eric's anxiety rose as he read the details of Jeff's week, including notes from the original call from "LD," who had a client named Wei looking for "50 BBLS" of a "Haut-Médoc style of Bordeaux blend," with a "$5K finder's fee and 5% gross commission." The wine was required to be "Merlot dominant, smoky oak, tannic, medium- to full-bodied, and ruby colored." Another entry described a round of golf one afternoon. A normal week and now the guy was dead.

Eric recalled Jeff Russell's visit to his winery and his compliments after tasting the wines. Eric didn't know that Jeff had decided Eagle Cap was the best, as he had noted in the journal, but he was positive he told Jeff he wouldn't sell in bulk. The journal also documented the meeting with Wei at the nearby hotel, giving him an opportunity to sample all of the wines Jeff had obtained. Why had Jeff gone ahead and held a tasting of Eric's wines with Wei? Maybe he thought Eric would change his mind. In any case, it had been a tragic mistake. It appeared that Jeff had been killed sometime after meeting Wei at the Vintage Inn.

He now understood why Sheriff Thompson wanted to meet with Luc DuPont. Based on the entry of the initials *LD* in the journal, it was obvious that DuPont had hired Jeff to find the Bordeaux blend. Eric wanted his wines to become well known, but he knew a story involving a sensational homicide and his Eagle Cap blend wouldn't give him the kind of publicity he wanted.

7

November 4th

Seattle

Eric arrived at the Walla Walla Airport on Monday morning at 5:30 a.m., an hour before his scheduled departure. He hadn't been in the waiting area more than a few minutes when he saw Sheriff Thompson arrive. He was surprised to see Scott dressed in a nice pair of wool slacks and a tweed blazer with a striped tie, as he was rarely seen out of uniform. The service weapon at his side made the sheriff's tall stature even more imposing. After exchanging pleasantries, they decided to search for coffee.

Back in the waiting area, Scott asked, "Did you get a chance to read the email I sent you?"

"I did. Now I know why you wanted me along," Eric said.

"I just hope to get some useful information out of Mr. DuPont. He must know something."

"I'm sure he does, but what makes you think he'll be willing to talk to us?"

"I'm not even sure he'll be at his office," Scott said. "I decided to take a chance that he's working, and if he's not there we'll run by his house. When I called last week, they said he planned to be in town. But if we are lucky enough to find him, I'm still not sure how willing he will be to talk. I want him to know that we are aware of the relationship between him and Jeff. I don't think it's a coincidence that the coroner estimates the time of Jeff's death to be within hours of his meeting with Wei. There must be a connection."

"So what role do I play?" Eric asked.

"I just want you to be my eyes and ears for anything wine related. Mr. DuPont could easily mislead me, so you can help me understand his comments about wine."

"Are you going to tell him who I am?"

"I think that's the best course."

"OK. The plane is boarding. Let's get on. I'm going to catch a bit more sleep on the way over." Eric settled into his seat and closed his eyes.

About an hour later, Eric woke up as the turboprop's landing gear extended with a thump on the plane's final approach to Sea-Tac Airport. He glanced at his watch. They were landing on time—at 7:30 a.m.

After Scott picked up a rental car, they left for downtown. Eric was quiet on the drive, mostly thinking about the impending meeting. He had a bad feeling about it and was already looking forward to arriving in Hawaii and what he hoped would be a romantic reunion with Ashley. But thoughts of sand, sun, and tropical breezes would have to wait until after the meeting. Scott drove past the baseball stadium south of downtown Seattle and over several sets of jarring railroad tracks. The map application on Scott's phone directed them to the correct building, an old warehouse adjacent to the tracks and jammed with trucks at loading docks on either side of the rough road. Old red bricks showed through a worn layer of asphalt.

After locating the sign for *Honorable Wine Merchants,* they walked up a short flight of metal steps and entered the building through an old wooden doorway that led them into the reception area. Wooden beams across the ceiling and the mixed period furniture scattered around the office attested to the building's history, while photos and posters of wine regions around the world suggested the nature of its business.

"Hi, my name is Gwen. May I help you?" asked the receptionist. She was a young woman with short dark hair who sat behind an old wooden desk with piles of papers neatly arranged. A tattoo of Chinese characters graced her neck. Eric stood by silently while Scott spoke with the receptionist.

"Yes, we are here to see Mr. DuPont."

"Do you have an appointment with him?"

"No, we don't."

"He's not yet in this morning. I'm not sure when he'll be in. He keeps a pretty busy schedule."

"Call him and let him know that Sheriff Thompson from Walla Walla County is here to see him. I think he'll want to come in. Here are my credentials." Scott pulled his identification badge from his pocket and showed it to Gwen.

"I see. I'll call him. Can I tell him what this is about?"

"Tell him I'd like to speak with him about Jeff Russell."

At that comment, Gwen's eyes grew wide. "I'll call him right away." She made a phone call, apparently to Luc, who must have said he'd be in shortly because she indicated they should take a seat. She brought them some coffee while they waited.

After about an hour, during which Eric took a short and cold walk around the warehouse under dark skies and wet drizzle, Luc came hurriedly through the doorway. Eric wasn't sure what he expected to see, but the man who now stood before them had the chiseled features of a movie star. He was about six feet in height with a slim build and a narrow face accented by high cheek bones. His long, silver and dark gray hair was swept back and ran down to his shoulders. He wore black denim jeans that implied wealth and style; a crisp white button-down shirt, untucked; and a calfskin leather jacket. On his feet were a pair of Ferragamo loafers without socks. Eric stood to introduce himself, feeling less than chic in his Eddie Bauer chinos and plaid sweater. Wine merchandising was apparently more lucrative than winemaking.

The sheriff introduced himself and Eric. They shook hands all around.

"Please, come in," Luc replied. He seemed very relaxed and confident as they followed him into his office. "Mr. Savage, you make excellent wine."

"Thank you," Eric said.

As they took seats, Eric quickly surveyed the interior walls of the room. He admired the many photos of Luc standing in vineyards, surrounded by leafy vines full of fruit, or near châteaux one might find driving along the famous D2 highway in Bordeaux.

"So how may I help you gentlemen?" Luc asked.

"Do you know Jeff Russell?" Scott answered.

"Yes, I do," Luc said, his face still confident. "He occasionally works for me as a consultant. Why do you ask?"

"We recently discovered his body in a vineyard." Scott said. After a short pause, he added, "It appears he was the victim of a murder."

Luc's face finally showed some emotion as it tightened a bit. "I read something about that in the paper. It's a tragedy. He was a great source of wines and grapes for me."

"I think of his death as a tragedy for his family and, perhaps, more of an inconvenience for you," Scott said.

"Right," replied Luc, "but what does this have to do with me?"

"We think he was working for you at the time of his death. We've examined some of his cell phone records and a journal, and it appears he met with one of your clients in the afternoon before his death later that evening. What can you tell us about your client?"

"I can't tell you anything. My clients ask that their names and our dealings be kept confidential. I really can't disclose who they are."

"Mr. DuPont," said Scott, "I'm more interested in finding out who killed Mr. Russell than I am in protecting your confidentiality agreements. Would you rather have this discussion pursuant to a search warrant or other court order?"

Eric was pretty sure he saw a flash of anger register on Luc's face.

"Sheriff, I run a respectable business and my reputation is everything to me. I can't be seen as untrustworthy. I'm sure you understand," Luc said.

"Mr. DuPont, I've looked into your business and from what I've read, your reputation is about all you have going for you. You buy mediocre wines that are often excess inventory and priced at a discount, and through your descriptive writing skills and an image of exclusivity, you sell them to your loyal clientele at a handsome profit."

"Nice summary, but there's nothing illegal about that," snorted Luc.

"Maybe not, but you also run a wine retail business and wholesale distribution business side-by-side in the same building. I happen to know the Washington State Liquor Control Board is leery of such commingling. They could make your life very difficult if they decided to put you through an audit."

There was an awkward silence for a few seconds. Scott finally broke it by asking, "Who is Wei?"

Luc stared back at Scott without showing a hint of surprise and then looked directly at Eric. "Wei was a representative of the client and was to approve any wine recommendation made by Jeff. He specifically liked your wine, Mr. Savage. You should have sold to him. If you had, maybe Jeff would still be alive."

"I'm a small producer," Eric blurted out with what he knew was probably too much emotion. "I need to sell my wines under my label. I don't have extra barrels to sell sitting around my winery. I've worked hard to build my reputation, just like you. I tried to explain that to Jeff, but he wouldn't take no for an answer."

"And I don't think my clients like taking no for an answer either. That's all I'm going to say without my lawyer being present. This friendly chat is over." Luc abruptly stood up. He walked toward his office door, opened it, and then waited. His calm and confident demeanor reappeared.

Gathering up their things, the two men walked past Luc on their way through his office doorway. Scott stopped and turned to say, "Mr. DuPont, I really don't care much about your business. I just want to find out who killed Mr. Russell. I think your client or even you may be involved. One way or another, I'm going to find out. Your reputation will suffer even more if you are seen as uncooperative. Here's my card. If you change your mind, please call. Thank you for your time."

They left the building and got into the rental car. "He seemed pretty cool under pressure," Eric said.

"Yes, he did. I was hoping he'd say more, but he was being very reticent," Scott replied. "What time is your flight?"

"Two o'clock."

"It's eleven now, so we have plenty of time to get back to the airport. My flight back to Walla Walla leaves about the same time."

"Scott, I didn't like what he had to say about me and how I should have sold my wine to this guy Wei. He sounded a bit threatening."

"I agree. I wish we could find Wei. My office tried the phone number we found on Jeff's phone, but it doesn't appear to be working. We tried searching for the number, but it's not registered to anyone and is likely a disposable phone for which he paid cash. It's among a block of numbers assigned for shipment to a large retail store. One of my detectives went out to the Vineyard Inn in Prosser. Jeff had reserved a conference room where we think he held the tasting with Wei, but there's no record of anyone named Wei staying there. Either he drove there on his own or he was using an alias. Without DuPont's help, we really don't have any leads."

"Can you think of any way we can encourage DuPont's cooperation? It's clear he won't talk to us unless he's forced."

"I was serious about the Washington State Liquor Control Board. I spoke with a friend of mine over there yesterday about DuPont. They'd like nothing better than to have a crack at his books. They suspect that he buys from producers through his distribution business and then sells retail through his online business without paying all the proper taxes."

"Can they just investigate him without cause?"

"Not without some higher level authorization, which I'm working on. But for now I think I'll suggest they just drop by and ask a few questions. That should show DuPont I mean business. Besides, I don't know why he'd be so reluctant to cooperate unless he really does have something to hide."

"Now I'm hesitant to go to Hawaii. This whole thing has me concerned."

"Hey, just remember what you have to look forward to. You and Ashley will have a great time."

Scott and Eric drove to the airport. After returning the rental car, they said their goodbyes. Scott walked towards the gate for his flight back to Walla Walla. As Eric checked in for his flight to Hawaii, he resolved there was nothing else he could do about Jeff Russell or Luc DuPont. Closing his eyes, he focused his thoughts on the pleasant prospect of getting reacquainted with Ashley in Hawaii.

8

November 4th

Maui

Eric settled into his window seat in coach and prepared for the six-hour flight. With a two-hour time difference, he'd arrive at the Kahului Airport around 6:00 p.m. Ashley and her two boys had departed Houston earlier in the day and they planned to meet him at the hotel. He'd reserved two rooms at a large family-style resort in Wailea and had a pretty good guess as to the room arrangements. He expected to take one room by himself while Ashley and her two boys stayed in the other. They'd just met at the end of summer, and this trip would be his first opportunity to meet the boys. It was only appropriate that their relationship appear to be platonic, although he hoped they'd find some private time together.

Ashley Hunter was a Special Agent for the FBI, stationed in Houston and assigned to the Criminal Investigative Division, where she investigated national or transnational criminal organizations and enterprises. Eric had met her three months earlier when he'd flown to London in an impulsive attempt to find out who had killed his ex-wife. Ms. Hunter was there investigating a State Department official suspected of insider trading. Eric and Ashley soon discovered their efforts were related. She came to trust him and helped him track down his ex-wife's killer.

Once the mystery was solved, they only had a few days together before she returned to Houston, her job, and her boys. He found Ashley to be a very attractive and capable woman. He was as attracted to her as she was to him, yet it wasn't clear to either of them how a long-distance relationship could work. They were both divorced with children and demanding careers. She couldn't move the boys from their home in Houston and proximity to their father any easier than he could move his winery from Walla Walla. Since harvest was about to begin, Ashley agreed to meet Eric in Hawaii once crush was over to see where their relationship might take them.

During the ensuing months while he was working nonstop, they spoke with each other occasionally, and looked forward to their time together in Hawaii. He was confident they'd have fun, but worried about where the future might lead. Truth be told, he wasn't sure what he really wanted anyway. He was still feeling the scars from a financially and emotionally painful divorce. Luckily his daughter was doing well at college in California, which left him with one less thing to worry about. Of course, as fathers tend to do with daughters, he found that he worried about her anyway. As he finished a glass of uninspiring wine amid his thoughts of Ashley, he fell asleep.

Eric awoke several hours later as the flight attendants began to prepare the cabin for landing. Eric looked out his window and saw in the distance the mountainous islands of Hawaii rising above the azure Pacific Ocean. Thin layers of clouds formed on the leeward sides of the peaks. He'd read that the islands span over 1,525 miles, from the island of Hawaii at the southeast end to Kure Atoll in the northwest.

After landing and deplaning, Eric found a nearby restroom where he changed into shorts and sandals. After changing his clothes, he picked up his checked luggage and headed for the rental cars. He picked out a Jeep, rolled down the top and side windows, and began the forty-five minute drive to the hotel. Driving down the two-lane highway, he soon forgot about Sheriff Thompson and Luc DuPont as the tropical, soothing air enveloped him. Along the way, the setting sun painted an orange backdrop for stunning views of pineapple fields and green shrouded mountains. He felt the magic of Hawaii begin to exert its power over him as his body and mind began to relax.

He arrived at the access road to the hotel and pulled into the *porte cochère* of the main building. Leaving his car with the valet, he walked to the registration counter to check-in. "I'm Eric Savage," he said.

"Good evening, Mr. Savage," said the receptionist. "Welcome back. I see you will be with us for seven nights. We've upgraded you to a one-bedroom suite with an ocean view. I think you will be very comfortable there." She smiled with a sincerity that suggested she'd been well trained in customer service.

"Thank you," he said, "it's great to be back."

"I also have a message for you. Ms. Hunter stopped by and said to call her when you arrive. She and her boys are down at the beach."

Eric took his bags and went in search of his room. He crossed the hotel's expansive lobby, its open floor-to-ceiling doors providing views of a restaurant, a pool below, and the blue ocean beyond. He took the elevator to the tenth floor and found his room. He threw his bags on top of the bed, changed into a swimsuit, and headed back to the elevator. From the lobby, he walked down several flights of wide marble steps and found his way to the beach. The sun was just dropping below the horizon, and many of the guests were sitting side-by-side on the beach, or in lounge chairs, watching the fabulous view.

He didn't have to look far before he found them. About twenty-five yards down the beach, he spotted Ashley on a towel-covered beach chair, wearing a wide-brim straw hat and over-sized black sunglasses. Two teenage boys frolicked in the water nearby, body-surfing and laughing as they were pitched by waves onto the sandy beach. Although he was confident it was Ashley sitting a few yards away, a quick survey of her lean, fit body in a white bikini removed any remaining doubts. He continued approaching her chair, his excitement surging.

"Welcome to Hawaii," he said.

Ashley looked over her shoulder toward him and then jumped up from her chair. As they embraced, she said, "It's so good to see you."

They held each other for a few seconds with their heads cheek-to-cheek. As he looked past her and toward the water, he saw the two boys he'd seen earlier stop playing and look in his direction. As much as he desired to kiss Ashley, he knew it was neither the time nor the place.

"Come, I want you to meet my boys." Ashley took Eric's hand and led him toward them.

"Elliott, William, this is Mr. Savage, my friend from Washington."

"Hello Mr. Savage," they each said in almost perfect unison.

"How do you like Hawaii?" Eric asked.

"It's beautiful," said Elliott, who was clearly the older of the two. "I love the water. It's so clear and warm."

William just stood and looked at Eric.

"I'm glad you like it. I hoped you and your mom would enjoy it as much as I do. It's one of my favorite places. How was your flight from Houston?"

"It was long," William said. "I fell asleep."

Eric knew they'd had a long day after first flying to Dallas and then taking a non-stop to Maui. "How about we get some dinner; I bet you boys are hungry."

"Can we play in the water a bit longer?" Elliott asked.

"Fine by me, but it's up to your mom," Eric replied.

"Thirty minutes more," Ashley said. "Eric, I'd like something to drink. How about you?"

Eric thought that was an excellent idea, so he set off in search of the pool bar. It wasn't long before he returned with the first two of what he hoped would be many tropical drinks. He pulled up a chair alongside Ashley's and sat down. Handing her the drink, he said, "Your boys are terrific."

"They're good boys. I can see they are going to love it here. Thanks for inviting us along."

"I've been looking forward to this trip since you returned to Houston in August."

"So have I, Eric. But I wasn't sure what to expect. Our time together in London and Walla Walla was so rushed, I don't think either of us had much of a chance to get properly acquainted. And then there are the boys. I didn't know what you'd think of them and—"

"Hey, slow down," Eric said. "We both just got here. Let's enjoy this evening together and take our time over the next few days. I'm going to like your boys; I can already tell. This will be the perfect opportunity for us to get to know each other a little better, without being interrupted by criminals or winemaking. Just step back and enjoy it here.

Hawaii is the perfect place to relax." Eric wrapped his hand around hers.

They were silent for a few moments while they enjoyed their drinks and watched the boys play in the darkening surf. The joyous laughs of the boys were regularly muffled by the roar of tall waves, crashing onto the sandy beach and then dissolving into foam.

Eric broke the pause. "Are you all right with the accommodations?"

"Thank you for putting the boys and me all in the same room. You understand how impressionable boys are and that we need to, well, set a good example. All I ask is for a second key to your room—for late-night visits."

9

November 5th

Maui

On his second day in Maui, Eric awoke early, pulled on his running shorts and a pair of shoes, then headed down to the lobby. He planned to run toward Makena and back. Even at 6:30 a.m., the sun was beginning to warm the air and his skin was moist from humidity.

Ten minutes later, he reached the main road and took a right toward Makena. After a slow climb, the road turned downhill and he picked up speed. Eric spotted a lone female runner in the distance coming toward him. As she approached, he recognized Ashley who waved at the same instant he did. They met and stopped on the road's shoulder.

"Heading for the clothing optional beach?" she asked.

"Where's that?"

"Little Makena. I read about it in one of the travel books I bought for the trip."

"Umm, no," he said, "unless you're planning on going with me."

"No, the only unclothed body I want you looking at is mine." She flashed a broad smile and started running up the hill back toward the hotel. "See you later for breakfast?"

"Sure, in about an hour," he said. He turned and started running back down the hill in his original direction.

After his five-mile run, he took a quick shower and headed down to the hotel's restaurant. He found Ashley and her sons waiting patiently for him. As always, both boys were very polite and respectful of their mother.

"I told the boys they couldn't attack the buffet line until you got here," Ashley said.

"Boys," Eric said, "no need to wait any longer. Go get some food."

The boys wasted no time jumping up and returning a few minutes later with plates heaped with pancakes, waffles, eggs, bacon, papaya, and strawberries. As they devoured their food, Eric enjoyed a cup of coffee with Ashley while they discussed plans for the day. They were still tired from the trip over so they decided to spend the day at the resort. He hoped the boys would find plenty to do at the beach, including snorkeling, paddleboarding, and more body surfing, and that he and Ashley would have ample time to talk.

Once breakfast was over, they went to the beach and found a place to set up four lounge chairs and towels. They all went back to their rooms and changed into their swimsuits. When Eric returned to their spot on the beach, he found the boys already back in the surf.

Eric's body relaxed even more as the tropical air coaxed away his tension. It was easy to suspend any thoughts about his troubles back in Walla Walla. Sitting in his chair with plenty of shade, watching the boys play, flipping through a magazine, and lazily chatting with Ashley, he found the day going by effortlessly in an easy rhythm. If he wanted a cold drink, all he had to do was ask. Should he need more sunscreen, there was plenty waiting for him at the beach activities desk. If he decided to try snorkeling, everything he needed was available. Life here was artificially carefree.

His conversations with Ashley were light and simple. She brought him up to date on her boys. Elliott was fifteen and had just started high school. William, who liked to be called Will, was thirteen and had just started seventh grade. One played basketball, and the other was a swimmer. They were doing well in school. Ashley said things were going well with their father, with whom they spent every other weekend. Hearing how Ashley managed the schedule of her two boys while working full time as a special agent with the FBI brought back memories of his own days as a divorced father with shared custody of his daughter. It reminded him of how glad he was that those days were behind him. Having a daughter in college was much easier.

He stared out at the water and was struck by its beauty. Nature inspired him. The color of the water nearest the beach was iridescent aquamarine. Fifty yards farther out, well-defined in a distinct line running parallel to the beach, the water's color changed to cobalt. Beyond that was a third distinct band of dark and uniform blue sapphire, stretching far out into the Pacific. This last band was disturbed only by occasional white-caps. Colors back home seemed so muted compared to the vivid presentation lying before him. Even though the temperature was in the mid-eighties, the trade winds kept the air comfortable. He became more euphoric by the minute.

He finished a page and turned to look at Ashley. At some point he wanted to tell her about the events of the past several weeks in Walla Walla, especially about the mysterious homicide in the vineyard and the meeting he and Sheriff Thompson had with Luc DuPont before flying to Hawaii. He decided it could wait. "Want to try paddleboarding?" he asked.

"Sure. Let's go!" replied Ashley, with her usual high level of enthusiasm. "Let me tell the boys and I'll meet you over by the equipment."

They spent the next hour out in the water with two paddleboards. Neither of them had tried it before, so they received a few minutes of land training. They learned how to balance and stand up on the board, proper use of the paddle and stroke technique, and beginning strategies for moving their feet around the board while maintaining balance. Ashley made it look simple. Eric had done some kayaking while living on Puget Sound and was confident those skills would help him become proficient without too much difficulty.

They both fell off quite a few times, but the board's ankle tether allowed them to easily recover the board and get back on. Early on, Eric paddled on his knees, but after a while he managed to stand and balance while he stroked. They headed out into the waters past the wave break. As he followed behind Ashley, he admired her balance and fitness. She stayed in shape as a requirement for her job and her body looked lean and muscular, just as he'd remembered it. Her blond hair was tied in a ponytail. A two-piece bikini in a flowered print accented her lithe figure.

They stopped paddling about a quarter mile off shore and sat on top of their boards, straddling them with their legs hanging over each side. Eric was amazed to look down through clear water, toward white coral below, and see a large school of at least one hundred yellow tang feeding. As their boards gently rocked back and forth, he casually reached for Ashley's board and slowly drew it closer. She detected the movement and looked at him expectantly. He leaned over to kiss her. Just as their lips touched, Eric's board turned over, throwing him on top of Ashley's board, which also rolled over, tumbling both of them into the warm water.

Laughing, they both surfaced and held onto their boards. The salt water made them extra buoyant. He pulled Ashley toward him, put his arms around her, and kissed her passionately. After he withdrew, Eric said, "I'm so glad to be here with you." Neither of them said a word as they locked eyes.

After their embrace, they climbed back on their boards and took a minute to admire the beach as they gently rocked back and forth in the clear water. Many rows of palm trees, with bright green fronds dancing in the wind, rose up from the rocky shore. Further inland, jagged, green valleys jutted upward toward the volcanic peak of Haleakala, masked in clouds ten thousand feet high.

"It's so beautiful here." After a pause, Ashley said, "I hate to say this, but I should get back to the boys."

They both climbed back on their boards and began the short paddle back to shore.

After returning all the equipment, and before heading back to the boys, Eric said, "There are some things going on at work that I need to tell you about. Do you think we can find some time this evening to talk privately?"

"Anything serious?" Ashley asked.

"I don't know. Maybe. I'd like to get your opinion."

"Well, it sounds serious. How about after dinner? I'll let the boys watch a movie. Maybe I can come over to your room for a drink."

"I'd love that."

"So would I. Let's go see what the boys are up to."

10

November 5th

Maui

Ashley, her boys, and Eric ate dinner under open skies on the out-side deck of the hotel's casual, Italian-themed restaurant. Eric, wearing board shorts, a muted Hawaiian print shirt, and flip-flops, felt elated as he watched the sun sink into the shimmering Pacific. Any re-maining tensions from his troubles at home had melted away. He shift-ed his gaze toward Ashley, who was dressed in a sheer, knee-length, turquoise cotton sundress with a white plumeria print. Her effusive smile suggested she also cherished the moment.

After dinner, they strolled together on the beach walk, which ran between the line of hotels and the ocean. Many people were out walk-ing and several kids and adults were still in the ocean, playing and jumping in the waves or trying to body surf. The boys asked to go in, but Ashley told them that they'd had enough beach time for the day.

As they arrived back at the hotel, Ashley said, "Boys, how about you go back to the room and watch a movie. I need to talk with Eric about his work, and I know you'd find it boring." Elliot and William both found the idea agreeable. Ashley said she'd meet Eric in the lobby bar thirty minutes later, after she'd gotten the kids settled.

Eric found his way to the lobby and located a table for two with a good view of the ocean. He decided to go ahead and order a glass of wine while he mulled over what he wanted to say to Ashley.

Ashley found him at the table about a half hour later. She leaned over and kissed him on the cheek before sitting down. "Now, tell me what's going on at the winery."

"Hey, before I get into that, I want to tell you how happy I am to see you." Eric took her hand into his. "I know our relationship has been a bit unconventional. Solving a murder together in London then having passionate sex at my house a week later isn't normal first-date material. I found it hard when you returned to Houston, but it's great to finally be together again."

Ashley's hand rested in Eric's. "Eric, I think you know I like you a lot. In so many ways, you are the perfect man for me: intelligent, sensitive, accomplished, and a bit of a romanticist, as shown by your love of winemaking."

"I think you left out *handsome.*"

"Yes, Eric, I do find you very desirable." Ashley's face didn't reveal any subterfuge.

"I think I hear a 'but' coming."

"Well, I have to be cautious. I have my two boys with me half the time, for one thing. For another, we live so far apart. Plus, I don't like having my heart broken. I know if I let my guard down, I could easily fall in love with you. Maybe I already have." With a warm smile, Ashley leaned back in her chair and took a sip of her Mai Tai, which had just arrived.

"That's reassuring," Eric said, fingering the wine glass on the table between them. "I've been consumed with the winery since you left and haven't had much time to think about us. Weekly phone calls have helped me feel closer to you. I'm drawn to you and I've found myself wishing we could have more time together. It's not just that you're beautiful and talented, which you are, but you have a kind heart beneath that tough-girl FBI façade you have going on. Do you always get your man?" He smiled, hoping to add some levity to what was developing into a pretty serious conversation.

"When it comes to the FBI, I've got a pretty good track record. When it comes to romance, not so much. At least I'm getting better at recognizing the good guys." They both laughed at that and she added, "So tell me about work."

As they finished their drinks and ordered another round, Eric told Ashley what had happened over the past couple of weeks. He started with Jeff Russell's visit to his winery and his request to buy Eric's wine in bulk and sell it under another label. He told of how Ricardo Álvarez, one of Walt Conner's crew, discovered Jeff's lifeless body in a vineyard, and pointed out that Jeff was Walt's son-in-law. He explained the connection between Jeff and Luc DuPont and described his meeting with Sheriff Thompson and DuPont before his flight to Hawaii.

As he was talking, Eric watched Ashley remove a small pen and notebook from her purse and start writing. He also noticed her brow furl as he recited the details.

"Eric, I'm concerned by what you're telling me. Is Scott looking into this while you're away?"

"Yes. He has some friends over at the Washington State Liquor Control Board in Seattle. They enforce the wine and liquor regulations in the state. Every wine reseller must deal with them. He's hoping the threat of an audit will put pressure on Luc, who flat out refused to tell us who his customers are. I think Luc knows more about this whole thing than he's letting on. I haven't spoken to Scott since arriving here on Monday."

"This sounds pretty serious. Tomorrow is Wednesday, I'd like to call Scott in the morning and see if he has any new information. He was a great help to us last summer. I think he's a stand-up guy."

"Whatever you suggest. You're the Special Agent."

"Don't ever forget it." Ashley reached over and squeezed his hand.

Eric looked at her radiant brown eyes. "Let's go to my room."

"I was hoping you'd ask," Ashley replied.

When he and Ashley entered his room, Eric noticed that turn-down service had already been completed. The bed was uncovered and glasses of ice water were on the nightstands.

"Expecting company?" Ashley pointed toward the bottle of wine that Eric had left chilling in an ice bucket.

"I was counting on it," Eric replied. He started opening the chilled bottle of French Rosé, a pricey wine that seemed to have lost some character in recent years, but the flavor and acidity of the Mourvèdre-based wine from Provence made it a pleasure to drink. He returned to Ashley with two glasses of the salmon-pink wine and offered a toast as he handed her one.

"To always getting your man," Eric said. They lightly touched their glasses together. Eric put his glass down and slid open the teak plantation doors. The sound of cresting ocean waves quickly filled the room and they enjoyed the feeling of warm tropical air coming through the patio door. Eric put his glass down on the table, then took Ashley's glass from her hand and set it next to his. He put his arms around her and drew her close. As he looked into her large brown eyes, he placed his lips on hers.

They kissed slowly at first while holding each other tightly. Eric felt warm as blood coursed through his body. He stopped kissing Ashley and leaned back. As they looked into each other's eyes, Eric reached around to the back of her dress and felt for its clasp. He undid it and slowly lowered the zipper. Most young men are taught that the words "please don't" might soon arrive at this juncture, but Eric didn't hear any protests. Once the zipper was down, she stepped away from him and slipped the dress from her shoulders. It fell to the floor with a soft rustle. Eric's eyes widened in surprise. She was completely unclothed.

Sensing his surprise, Ashley said, "Texas gals know how to keep cool."

"I'm getting hot," Eric stammered. He knew it was a lame response lacking in both originality and sophistication. He admired her tall, lean body glistening in the fading light coming from the sky outside the balcony. She was beautiful, and he wanted her.

"You still have your clothes on," Ashley protested. She wore an exaggerated pout on her lips.

Eric watched Ashley intensely as she walked to the table, picked up her wine glass, and glided over to the turned-down bed. She moved a pillow against the headboard and leaned back, seemingly relaxed and secure. Her confidence was another source of Eric's attraction. She took a long sip of wine.

"Right," Eric said. He unbuttoned and removed his Hawaiian shirt and then tugged at the button of his board shorts. They quickly dropped to the floor, exposing a tented pair of boxers.

"Now I remember what I liked about you," Ashley said.

He thought he detected both amusement and hunger in her eyes as he joined her on the bed, retrieving his glass of wine along the way.

"Stop teasing and finish the job," Ashley protested. She took Eric's glass of wine along with her own and set them both on the nightstand.

Eric leaned over and kissed her hard. Ashley slipped her hand inside his boxers and she heard an approving groan as she grasped him firmly. She reached down with her other hand and started to slide his boxers down. He helped her by arching his back up off the bed.

Ashley slid the boxers down past his knees and off of his feet before tossing them across the room. When she was done, Eric moved his hand down between her legs. His heart felt like it was beating for two as Ashley rolled on top of him. Unexpectedly, Eric thought he heard a soft knock come from the door. He tried to ignore it. Ashley, straddling Eric with knees bent and on either side of his waist, leaned down to kiss him. Eric heard the knock again. "Did you hear that?"

"Hear what?" Ashley replied. Just then they both heard a soft voice say, "Mom, are you in there?"

Eric panicked, slid out from under Ashley, and jumped off the bed. He grabbed his clothes and tossed Ashley's dress in her direction. They both dressed in seconds, as if the building were on fire.

"Yes, honey, I'm here," Ashley shouted. "Just a minute."

After finishing with their clothes, Ashley went to the door and opened it. Standing there was her oldest son Elliot.

"Elliot, what's wrong?"

"Mom, William is in the bathroom getting sick and his face is really red."

"Oh boy, too much sun," Ashley said. "Let's go take care of him." She looked at Eric. "I'll see you in the morning. I'm sorry."

Eric stood by the door as they left. He watched, in disbelief, as they walked down the hallway and out of sight.

Eric was so wound up after she left that he decided to drink some more of the Rosé and watch a movie. He really didn't pay much attention to the action-adventure film, but focused more on the sounds of the waves, and images of a very beautiful Ashley etched in his mind. He found her wild streak intriguing and concluded that she was likely a woman of many surprises. He fell asleep, thinking of how glad he was that she had entered his life.

11

November 5th

Walla Walla

Kurt looked at his watch: 9:30 p.m. He was growing cold and nervous while waiting in his car behind the Blue Mountain Cellars winery. He'd parked well out of sight from the main road. Where was Wei, he wondered?

In two more minutes he saw the answer. Wei's rental car, a blue Dodge, pulled into view and parked next to his. Kurt got out of his car and buttoned his shearling coat to protect against the cold wind. Wei, wearing a heavy wool coat over a dress shirt and black slacks, got out of his car and walked over to Kurt.

"The truck is right behind me," Wei said. "Go inside and open the winery doors."

Kurt did as instructed. Although the Chinese man was only about five-eight in height, he commanded respect. Kurt found the man's demeanor and apparent physical strength intimidating. He had come to learn that any abbreviated comments, spoken in near-perfect English, were usually serious. Wei didn't waste words on small talk. Kurt walked around the side of the building toward the front office door. He was thinking revenge felt sweet.

Melissa hadn't wasted any time in delivering Eric's request. On the drive home from that awful dinner at Eric's house, she'd said, "Eric asked me not to bring you to the winery while he's on vacation." Kurt remembered how angry he became, incensed that the great Eric Savage didn't trust him. He and Melissa hadn't spoken the rest of the drive home. In fact, they hadn't spent a single night together since.

Funny how life can serve up surprises though. It was only a few days before the dinner when Wei had contacted Kurt, offering to pay him for his help. After initial misgivings, Kurt viewed the opportunity to deal Eric a blow as perfectly timed. By the time Eric had banished him from the winery, he had already made the necessary arrangements.

Pulling on a pair of gloves, Kurt took the key from his pocket and opened the door. He walked quickly to the security system's panel, entered the code, and pressed the disarm button. The code was accepted and the alarm remained silent. He switched on the lights inside the winery and walked toward the large double barn-style doors at the far end. After undoing the latch, he slid the doors open a couple of feet. Just then, a truck trailer carrying a twenty-foot shipping container pulled across the gravel parking lot and stopped. As it began backing toward the winery doors, loud warning beeps sounded from its undercarriage. Wei was giving hand signals to guide the truck into position. When it stopped, the driver shut off the engine and climbed down from the cab. He landed on the gravel with a crunch.

Kurt looked at the scene before him and felt a shiver of dread. He started to worry he was in way over his head. After agreeing to do the job, he'd become increasingly suspicious that Wei was somehow involved in the death of his friend Jeff Russell. The discovery of Jeff's body in a vineyard made him worry that he too might be at risk. And then there was Melissa. He knew he loved her. Dating her was part heaven, part reminder of his personal failings. During their relationship these past three months, he always felt that he was out of her league. She appeared to like his being an assistant winemaker though. "Cool," she'd once said when he'd told her about his job. But he had never felt a strong sense of commitment from her.

In his ongoing internal dialogue, Kurt thought he was a pretty good-looking guy; in addition to being athletic, he had a good sense of humor. He more than kept up with Melissa when they went running and bicycling together, though it felt like she was just putting in time. Maybe it was his lack of pedigree, having been born into a blue-collar family of a factory supervisor and stay-at-home mom, or maybe it was that he'd never gone to college. He suspected Melissa was looking for a better ticket: someone who could give her more money and status. Maybe that was why he was convinced she had a thing for Eric. He was so tired of hearing about him, how smart he was, what a talented winemaker he was, how kind he was to his dogs. Kurt admitted he was jealous of Eric, a fact that helped make the task before him seem a bit more palatable. The promise of easy money and an opportunity to throw a wrench into Eric Savage's success made it easy to make up his mind the first time he met with Wei. Now he was eager to get this over with and then disappear.

"Clean the pump and start moving the barrels over toward the shipping container," Wei commanded.

Kurt found the wine pump and moved it over toward the drain. He located a large tub and cleaning supplies and began to circulate a sanitizing liquid through the pump, hoses, and racking wand he planned to use. It would run for twenty minutes and then he'd rinse it with a neutralizing acid bath followed by hot water. The pump would be ready in about forty minutes.

Kurt next went toward the back into the winery and found the forklift, which he started and drove toward the entrance to the cold storage room. The partition between the main area of the winery and the storage room was separated by heavy, vertical, clear plastic strip-curtains, which kept the cold in and allowed people and equipment to easily pass through. Inside the room, he saw racks of barrels marked *Eagle Cap*, stacked two barrels per rack, three racks high. They were just as he remembered them when he was out at the winery with Melissa a couple of days earlier.

He carefully picked up the first rack of barrels with the forklift and drove back toward the open doorway near the container. Using the control levers, he smoothly lowered the barrel rack and placed it on the floor. He knew Wei was watching closely and wouldn't tolerate any mistakes. Kurt backed up and returned to the cold room. He did this until he had eight barrels placed on the floor near the doorway. Then he shut down the forklift and attended to the pump. As he cleaned it, Wei watched him intently.

When he was finished, Kurt told Wei, "I'm ready to start filling the bladder."

"Then do it," Wei said.

The twenty-foot shipping container had been fitted with a food grade PVC bladder. It was designed to hold up to 16,000 liters of liquid. Kurt had read that shipping bulk wine this way had become increasingly popular. Half of wine shipments out of Australia were shipped in bulk containers. Kurt connected the output side of the pump's two-inch hose to the input valve on the bladder. He then connected the input side of the pump to a hose with the racking wand, which he inserted into the top of one of the wine barrels. The last thing he needed to do was add some sulfur dioxide to each barrel to act as a preservative during the upcoming long journey by ship.

Kurt had done the math and figured it would take about three hours to transfer the wine from the fifty-four barrels of Eagle Cap into the bladder. Each barrel took a little under four minutes to empty when the pump was running at full speed. He was in a hurry to get out of there. He worried about the possibility of some random person driving by, surprised by the sight of a container and crew working at the winery after midnight. Kurt began pumping while Wei went back to his car and fetched a thermos of coffee for himself and the driver. They watched and exchanged a few comments while Kurt worked.

While the pump ran continuously, Kurt used the forklift to move empty barrels out of the way and full barrels into position. He kept up with the flow and never had to stop. Three hours and fifteen minutes later, he heard the sucking sound of the racking wand as the last barrel went dry. He didn't even bother with draining the remaining wine from the hose. He just wanted to get out of there.

Wei saw that Kurt was done and alerted the driver who quickly disconnected the hose from the bladder and sealed its valve. He then closed the container doors, sealed the latches, and added a padlock. After exchanging a few words with Wei, the driver drove out of the parking lot toward town, less than ten minutes after Kurt had finished pumping the wine.

Wei then walked to his car, opened the trunk, and removed a large manila envelope. He returned to Kurt. For a second, Kurt thought this was probably the end, imagining the envelope contained a hidden gun. Instead, Wei simply handed the envelope to Kurt and said, again in perfect English, "Thank you for your service."

Kurt noted the envelope was sealed and decided not to open it there. He assumed it contained the fifty thousand dollars they'd agreed upon for his work. It seemed like good pay for the night's efforts.

"I suggest you leave the area soon, as you will likely be suspected of our activity tonight. If you ever say anything about this to the authorities, we will find you. It will not be pleasant. For now, you must learn how to disappear." Wei got into his car, backed up, and drove off in a hurry, following the truck toward town. Gravel pelted Kurt in the face as it flew up from under the spinning tires.

It was over, Kurt thought with a sense of relief. He looked at his watch and noted the time. It was a little after two in the morning. The whole thing had taken just over four hours. He then pulled a piece of paper and a pen from his coat pocket and wrote down the serial number on the container. He had memorized it as he was pumping the wine, thinking it might come in handy.

Kurt didn't understand why Wei was paying him so much to help steal several hundred thousand dollars' worth of wine, but he'd learned not to ask questions. He was certain of one thing: the loss of this much premium wine would be a major blow to Eric Savage.

Kurt closed and locked the sliding doors to the crush pad. Walking back toward the office, he surveyed the inside of the winery. It was a mess, with fifty-four empty wine barrels on racks scattered across the cement floor. The pump sat unwashed with its hoses on the floor, sprawled alongside a racking wand resting inside the last barrel. Kurt felt just a bit of guilt creep into the recess of his mind, but then he remembered the dinner with Eric and looked down at the envelope. Fifty thousand dollars was a great antidote to any feelings of guilt he might have.

After switching off the large floodlights in the ceiling of the winery, he walked toward the tasting room door. Once there, he found a refrigerator filled with bottles of wine. He helped himself to a bottle of Sauvignon Blanc. After finding a corkscrew, he removed the cork and took a long swig from the cold bottle. With the bottle in one hand and the envelope of money in the other, he rearmed the alarm system and slipped quietly out the office door into the cold, still night.

12

November 6th

Melissa's cell phone alarm woke her at 7:00 a.m. She normally woke up earlier, but she knew she had an easy day at the winery and could afford to go in later. When she opened her eyes, she saw Max and Ginger lying on the floor next to her bed. As soon as Max detected that Melissa was awake, he walked over to the bed and lay his head down on the sheets next to her face, waiting for some affection.

"Yes, Max," Melissa said, stroking his head, "I know it's time to eat. Come on, let's go."

Melissa padded off to the kitchen, rubbing sleep from her eyes, right behind Max, who enthusiastically led the way. Ginger, always the late sleeper, stayed behind. Melissa put a scoop of food into Max's bowl, which he ate as if it were the best food he'd ever tasted. Melissa started some coffee and put a bagel in the toaster. Soon Ginger appeared. Melissa fed her, too, and then put both dogs outside.

As she ate her bagel and drank her coffee, still wearing her flannel pajamas, Melissa contemplated the situation at hand. Here she was, taking care of Eric's dogs, while he was in Hawaii with Ashley. She recognized it was envy she felt and wished she was spending time in the warm sun with Eric instead of remaining behind by herself in the cold fall-weather of Walla Walla.

After tidying up the kitchen, Melissa dressed in her work clothes and prepared to go out to the winery. She was happy to be in charge. Eric had left on Monday. She'd taken Tuesday off and this Wednesday morning would be her first visit to the winery. The only thing she had to do was top some barrels, which she estimated would take a few hours. Eric's trust in her would not be taken lightly.

She loaded the dogs into her older model Subaru and then drove to the winery. Arriving twenty minutes later, she parked in front by the office and tasting room and opened the car's rear hatch. The dogs leaped out enthusiastically and ran around the outside of the winery. With their noses to the ground, they seemed to be taking an inventory of any new scents since their last trip out. She noticed they spent quite a bit of time over by the large sliding barn-style doors, near the crush pad, and ran around in seemingly random directions.

Melissa used the keys in her hand to unlock and enter through the office door. After turning off the alarm system and turning on the lights, she removed her wool hat and heavy coat and laid them over her chair. She walked over to the radio and turned on the National Public Radio station. When she was alone in the winery, she liked the sound of other voices inside the building.

Moving into the main building, she turned on the large ceiling flood-lights high above her head. As they warmed up and came to full bright-ness, she gasped, shocked by what she saw. Scattered across the floor were racks of wine barrels, some stacked in columns, others sitting by them-selves, two to a rack. When she saw the racking wand, sticking out of the barrel near the pump, she comprehended what might have happened. She walked over to the barrels and noticed that the silicone bungs were missing from all of them, lying scattered across the floor. She went and found a flashlight, pointed the beam inside the barrel, and peered inside. As she feared, it was empty. She walked over to the other racks and using the flashlight, peered inside those barrels too. They were all empty.

Melissa's mind was spinning as she contemplated what to do. Her first instinct was to call Eric. She looked at her watch and knew it would be around 7:00 a.m., Hawaiian time. She worried about waking him, but she knew she had to call him. She also knew she was now at a crime scene and she should probably first call Sheriff Thompson. She pulled out her cell phone and dialed 911. She told the dispatcher that she needed to speak with Sheriff Scott Thompson of Walla Walla right away because there had been a burglary at Blue Mountain Cellars winery. The dispatcher said he would send an officer to the scene and contact Sheriff Thompson.

Melissa walked to the back of the winery building and opened the sliding doors to let in some fresh air. Max and Ginger ran in soon afterwards, eager to get out of the cold. Her job for the day, topping wine, was now the least of her concerns; it would have to wait. She dreaded calling Eric and decided to wait until after she spoke with Sheriff Thompson.

She didn't have to wait long until her cell phone started ringing. "This is Melissa."

"Melissa, Sheriff Thompson here. I just received a call from the 911 dispatcher. One of my deputies is on the way over and I'll be there in twenty minutes. Are you all right?"

"Yes, I'm fine, but the winery is a mess. Someone stole a lot of wine." Melissa struggled to understand the scene in the winery.

"Stay there and don't touch anything. My officer will secure the area. I'll be there as soon as I can. Don't worry."

Melissa hung up and walked into the office and began to think through what had happened. As far as she knew, no one had been in the winery since Eric spent Saturday there, writing instructions for her and getting ready for his trip. It had been locked and no one should have been there since. She hadn't noticed any signs of breaking in or damage and the security alarm had been enabled when she arrived. It didn't make any sense.

She heard the sound of a car crossing the gravel parking lot and looked up to see a patrol car, emergency lights flashing, pull up to the building. A deputy, gun in hand, trotted up to the door. She opened it and instinctively put hands in the air.

"Are you Melissa?" he asked.

"Yes."

"You can put your hands down. Tell me what happened."

Melissa recounted the events of the morning since arriving at the winery.

"And you didn't see any signs of forced entry?"

"No. Everything looked exactly as I would have expected until I walked into the winey to turn on the lights. That's when I saw all the empty barrels."

"Can you estimate the value of the wine?"

"I didn't count but if it's all Eagle Cap, my inventory shows there were fifty-four barrels. Each barrel represents about twenty-five cases. Eric charges about $400 per case, so that's five hundred thousand dollars of inventory. This could wipe Eric out. Not only that, it was the best wine he's ever made. I know he hoped to get a lot of recognition for it." Melissa stared at the ground and felt she might cry.

They both heard another car pull onto the gravel lot and park. Sheriff Thompson got out and started walking toward the building. He hurried inside and immediately took over the conversation, telling his deputy to go examine the crime scene. He then asked Melissa to recount for him what had happened from the time she had arrived at the winery.

"I really need to call Eric," Melissa said. "It's going to ruin his vacation."

"I agree, but why don't you let me call? That way he can associate me with the bad news. I'll tell him what you found when you arrived this morning."

"I appreciate that, Sheriff, but I should really talk to him. He left me in charge."

"You can call me Scott. I understand. At least let me talk to him first. Then I'm sure he will want to talk to you. Do you know anyone who has the security code for the alarm system and a key to the building? From what you said, someone must have had access."

"I know. I can't figure it out. Someone must have a key. But who?"

"Do you know anyone else beside you and Eric who has a key? And what about the security system? Whoever came in here must have known the code."

"No one that I know of. I'm pretty sure only Eric and I have keys."

Scott called out, "Deputy!" Within seconds the deputy appeared in the doorway. "Call the alarm monitoring company and request an access report for the past two days. Tell them it's a priority."

"Don't you think they'll require a warrant?" replied the deputy.

"Tell the company to go ahead and prepare the report. We'll have Eric call them and authorize its release. We don't need a warrant. Is the forensics team on the way?"

"Yes," the deputy replied, "they'll be here within the hour to take fingerprints and photograph the scene."

"Melissa," Scott said, "you need to think hard about this. Do you know of anyone who could have had unauthorized access into the winery, other than you and Eric?"

"Scott, I'm confused. None of this makes sense. I don't know."

"Take a minute to think, Melissa."

"I came to the winery several times with my boyfriend, Kurt. It was during harvest and usually at night. I had to do some evening punch downs on fermenting wine. As a matter of fact, he helped me several times before Eric left for Hawaii. Could he have memorized my code from watching me?"

"He certainly could have watched over your shoulder and memorized the code."

"But what about a key?"

Scott was silent for a moment. "Do you think it's possible he could have taken your key and made a copy without your noticing it was missing?"

"I suppose. There were several times I spent the night at his place and didn't use my keys for a day. I suppose he could have done that."

"So let's say it was Kurt. Do you know of any reason he might have for doing this?"

"I don't know. Maybe."

"For what reason?"

"I suspect he might have been a bit jealous of Eric."

"Where is he now?"

"I don't know. I haven't seen him or spoken to him since Saturday. He was going camping up in the Wallowa Mountains over the weekend."

"All right, we need to get the report to confirm the time, and then we should try to find your friend Kurt. Let's call Eric and give him the bad news. Man, I hate to wreck his vacation with Ashley."

"I know," Melissa said. Even though she resented Eric for vacationing with Ashley in Hawaii, instead of with her, she really didn't want to ruin it for him.

13

November 6th

Maui

Eric awoke to the sound of his cell phone vibrating on the nightstand. He'd switched the ringer to *mute* the night before. He wondered who could be calling him and hoped it was Ashley. He answered the call with a sleepy, "hello."

"Eric, Scott Thompson here. I'm sorry to wake you, but it's important."

"It's fine, Scott. I should be awake anyway." He was surprised as he looked at the clock to see it was 8:00 a.m. "What's up?"

"I'm out at your winery with Melissa. She came in this morning and discovered that some of your wine is missing. She called me and I sent one of my deputies to come out and look around. I got here a few minutes later. I'll let Melissa give you the details, but it appears that during the past couple of days, someone stole some of your wine."

Eric sat up in bed searching for something to say. "May I speak with Melissa?"

"Of course, but I think this is an inside job, Eric. No signs of a forced entry. Melissa thinks it might be her boyfriend, Kurt Hughes. Whoever came in knew the security code and had a key. She says that only the two of you have the code and Kurt might have learned it while watching her enter it a couple of times when they came to the winery together. I put in a request to the alarm company for a record of entry, which you'll need to authorize. But I'm pretty sure it will show that Melissa was the only person entering the winery since you left on Monday."

"Do you think Kurt could be involved in this?"

"I don't know. I think it's related to the rest of the events over the past couple of weeks. I hate to suggest this, but you need to come home. It's not coincidental that Luc DuPont's customers wanted your wine, then there was a murder, and now your wine is missing."

"Scott, I'll try to get there as soon as I can. I'm not sure how I'm going to break this to Ashley. I expect she'll be disappointed. I'll look into flights and text you the details. Please put Melissa on now."

"Sure, here she is." Scott handed the phone back to Melissa.

"Hi Eric, I hate to ruin your vacation," Melissa said, trying unsuccessfully to quiet the tremor in her voice.

Eric could tell that she was upset. "Melissa, you aren't ruining my vacation. Tell me what happened."

Melissa gave him the details from the time she arrived at the winery. Eric did the math as she told him about the number of barrels of missing wine. He realized that he suddenly had a serious financial hole in his operations. Five hundred thousand dollars of revenue would be impossible to replace. And the costs of that wine, including fruit, bottles, corks, and labels, were already spent. Worse still, it was by far his best wine. He was confident that his Eagle Cap blend would receive a great score. Last year's vintage had scored well and he was confident the stolen vintage would have been even better. He had planned to bottle it in late spring and release it in the fall. He was stunned by this turn of events.

She finished a recitation of the details and went silent.

"Melissa, do you think Kurt could have done this? Did he come out with you to the winery?"

"Eric, I don't know who else could have done it. He came out with me a few times for evening punch downs, right before you told me you didn't want him out here. One of those nights he might have watched me enter the security code."

"What about a key?"

"Scott thinks Kurt could have taken mine from my purse and gone somewhere in town to have a copy made without me noticing it was ever missing."

"I didn't trust him. He made a bad impression that night at my house. In hindsight, I should have insisted that I meet him before I allowed him to help you."

"Eric, I'm really sorry. I never thought anything like this could happen."

"Melissa, I don't understand why you were dating him."

"Well, obviously it was a mistake, Eric." Melissa had raised her voice. "I didn't love him if that's what you're asking. Other than being nice to look at, he's not my type. I prefer someone who has more ambition. I don't know that much about him. Never met his family or anything like that."

"You've tried to contact him, right?"

"Yes, but he hasn't answered my calls. I sent him some text messages as well. Once we're done here, I'm going over to his place to see what I can find."

"Look, I think you need to be careful, but you can trust Scott."

"I know. Are you coming home?"

"Yes, I'll try to get there as soon as I can."

"What's Ashley going to say?"

"I don't know. I think she'll be as shocked as I am."

"I need you back here, Eric. I don't think I can handle this without you. I'm so sorry."

"It's okay, Melissa. I'll get back as soon as I can. Please put Scott back on."

Scott came back on the line. Eric promised he'd be in touch about the flights and said good-bye. Then he called the alarm company and authorized the release of the report. He headed to the shower, trying to make sense of what had happened.

After showering and returning to the lobby, Eric spotted Ashley at a table in the restaurant where she'd agreed to meet him.

"Good morning, handsome," she said. "I'm so sorry about last night."

"I understand completely, although it did take me awhile to fall asleep after you left. I was a bit agitated."

"That was obvious," Ashley said. "May I take care of you tonight?"

Eric ignored the question. "How's William?"

"He's fine. I gave him a cold bath and applied some calamine. He went to sleep pretty late, but this morning he looks as good as new. I told him he could only stay on the beach for a short time today, with a sun shirt and lots of sunscreen. He and Elliott are down by the pool now. So what's going on with you? When you called, I could tell it's something serious."

"I have to go back to Walla Walla."

"What?" Ashley's face tightened and her eyes narrowed.

"Scott just called me. Someone broke into my winery and stole fifty-four barrels of wine. Melissa discovered it this morning—I'm stunned."

"Do the police have any idea who did it, Eric?"

"Melissa thinks it might have been her boyfriend. There weren't any signs of forced entry. It appears someone knew how to disarm the security system and had a key."

"What are you going to do?"

"I'd like to try and fly back to Seattle tonight and then get back to Walla Walla in the morning."

Ashley frowned. "Eric, after what you told me last night, I'm worried. I think you need to go back and visit Luc DuPont. He's the key to this whole thing."

"I need to get back to Walla Walla and see what Scott has been able to piece together. Luc has no reason to tell us anything. I need to come up with some type of leverage. Until then I think I'd be wasting my time trying to talk with him."

They were both silent for a moment while Eric ordered a cup of coffee and some breakfast.

"Ashley, I'm really sorry about this. We just got here and now I'm leaving. We've looked forward to this trip for such a long time."

"Eric, there's not much I can say. It's a horrible turn of events, but our time together is the least of it. I know you must be devastated by the news. Would it be helpful if the boys and I returned with you?"

"I might like it, but I don't think it would be fair to them. It's their vacation too, and the weather in Walla Walla is pretty cold right now.

You should stay here and enjoy the sun. They will have a much better time."

"I know you're right, but I'm worried about you."

"I'll be fine. My biggest concern is the setback for my winery. The wine they stole was by far my best. There's no way to replace it."

"I want to help."

"Right now, the best way is to just stay here and have a good time with William and Elliot."

Eric's breakfast arrived, but he barely picked at the omelet and toast. His worries had destroyed his appetite.

"Hey," Eric said, "why don't we take the boys and go for a drive around the island today. There's a lot to see, and that way we can keep them out of the sun. You can drop me off at the airport tonight."

Ashley looked at Eric intently. She could see he was very upset. "I'd like to send the boys to the beach and go back to your room and finish what we started last night. I realize that wouldn't exactly be *Mom of the Year* material, plus the news you just received kind of ruined the mood. So I think a drive is a good idea. Meet in about an hour?"

"Perfect. I'll see you in the lobby."

Ashley rose from her chair, kissed Eric lightly on the lips, and headed toward the pool to collect her boys. Eric watched her longingly as she walked out of the restaurant. Her long and increasingly tan legs looked very fetching. He noticed other men in the restaurant looking in her direction as she passed by but did not mind. They couldn't help themselves.

Eric finished his breakfast and took a cup of coffee to go. He planned to go back to his room and finish his travel arrangements. What had started as such a promising vacation with Ashley and her boys was turning into a huge disappointment. He didn't feel great about leaving Ashley behind and he had no idea what he was going to do about the winery. A lot of valuable inventory and the great publicity he'd hoped to gain from his future release had simply vanished. His future suddenly looked very bleak.

14

November 7th

Walla Walla

After flying all night on Wednesday, Eric arrived back into the Seattle-Tacoma airport Thursday morning at 6:00 a.m. Although he was tired, he didn't feel like waiting for the next flight to Walla Walla at 1:00 p.m. He decided to rent a car and make the four-hour drive himself. The time on the road and expansive views of eastern Washington would give him time to think.

Along the way, he called Ashley in Maui but ended up in voicemail, where he left her a message. He then called Sheriff Thompson to leave a message that he was driving back to Walla Walla and expected to be home around noon. He was tempted to get in touch with Luc DuPont and ask him to reveal the names of his customers. He mused about that conundrum for some time. As Eric drove down the eastern side of the Cascade range, he had an idea. He picked up his phone and called his friend Jason Taylor, who answered after a few rings.

"Hi Eric, it's been a while. How's life in Walla Walla?" Jason was a close friend living in Seattle. They'd gone to college together and had both ended up working for his former employer, the aerospace company. In fact, Jason was the best man in Eric's wedding and was one of the brightest computer experts Eric knew.

"It's good," Eric said. "I sometimes miss the beat of the city, but country life does have its charms. And if I'm going to make wine, it's a great place to be."

"Hey, that reminds me, thanks for the case of wine you sent me a couple of months ago. It was excellent."

"Glad you liked it. You can always buy more," Eric joked. After a pause he continued. "Jason, the reason I'm calling is I need a favor."

"Name it."

"I hate to put you in an awkward spot, but this conversation needs to stay confidential. What I'm about to ask you is a bit questionable."

"Now you've piqued my interest. What do you need?"

Eric retold the story of the wine tasting, the murder, and the theft of the wine from his winery. "Jason, this could put me out of business. I suspect someone has information about the theft, but he won't talk to me or the authorities. I need a way to convince him to help me."

"What have you got in mind?"

"You're an expert at computer system forensics. I'm wondering if you might be able to probe his systems at work and determine if he's doing anything illegal, or at least questionable. If you find something, then I'd try to use that information to compel him to help me. If he doesn't, I guess I'd threaten to go to the authorities."

"Eric, that sounds a lot like extortion, which is a felony. Accepting for a second the illegality of your idea, it also sounds a bit dangerous. If you think the same people who stole your wine are somehow involved in this alleged homicide, why wouldn't you also be at risk?"

"It's a good point and one that I've thought a lot about. But I don't know what else to do. The local sheriff, a friend of mine, can't do anything because he doesn't have enough evidence yet linking the suspect to a crime. I may never get my wine back, but these guys need to be held accountable for what they did. It's a risk I'm willing to take."

"Do you have any idea of what I'd be looking for on his computer?"

"I'm suspicious that he's found a way to artificially increase his profits. I know that his wine-club business is good, but it looks to me like he leads a very rich lifestyle. I've read he lives in a beautiful house in an exclusive neighborhood. He wears expensive clothes. From stories in the social pages I suspect his wife is expensive to maintain. He has two kids in private schools, and he flies around in a private jet. It just doesn't add up. Plus, he strikes me as someone who's not concerned about breaking the law, especially if it means more money for him and he's reasonably sure he won't get caught. It's not a lot to go on, but it's all I've got."

"Have you told the sheriff about your plan?"

"No, I think it's best to keep him out of it for now."

"Eric, this is out of my comfort zone. I know you're desperate, but we could both get into a lot of trouble over this."

"Jason, I know I'm asking a lot. The last thing I want is for you to become complicit in my actions." Eric felt a twinge of guilt for making the call.

"Eric, we go way back so I'll help you, but you can't breathe a word about it to anyone. Send me an encrypted email with the email address of the suspect, as well as the website for his business. I'll get his IP address from them and poke around his system a little. Unless he's done something extraordinary, I should be able to get past his firewall and look around the company servers. You won't hear from me again unless I find something."

"Thanks Jason, I know I'm asking a lot."

"Send more wine."

Eric ended the call and thought for a minute. He debated whether to tell Scott about his conversation with Jason. He trusted Scott but also knew that deniability was important in keeping Scott out of trouble if his idea blew up. He decided disclosure could wait.

Eric felt a bit of an adrenaline rush from the phone call. His risky plan made him feel alive.

The rest of the drive back to Walla Walla was uneventful. Eric stopped once for coffee to help him stay awake. When he got back to town, he drove straight to the winery. He wanted to see for himself what had happened. He noticed Melissa's car in the parking lot when he pulled in. Max and Ginger came running up to greet him as he got out of his rental car. He spent a few minutes saying hello and petting them vigorously.

He passed quickly through the office and tasting room area and walked into the winery's inner space. He could hear the sound of the forklift moving around inside. He spotted Melissa, lifting a rack of barrels to the top of a stack of four more barrels, then backing up, lowering the forks, and driving back toward the wash area. That's when she saw Eric. She stopped the forklift, lowered the forks to the ground, and turned the machine off. By the time she jumped off, Eric had reached her.

She stepped toward him and immediately hugged him in a tight grip.

"Eric, I'm so sorry this has happened."

"Melissa, it's not your fault. You had nothing to do with this."

"I should have been more careful. Kurt seemed like a harmless guy, but if he did this then it was my fault. I should never have gotten involved with him."

"Lesson learned, I guess. Trust your heart, Melissa. You have a good one." Eric stepped back and surveyed the winery. "What are you doing in here?"

"When I got here yesterday morning, this place was a mess. Barrels were scattered everywhere, and wine was left all over the floor. After the forensic team finished taking photos, I started washing all the barrels with hot water and stacking them outside to dry for a couple of hours. Today, I planned to finish the rest and then fill them with sulfur gas and plug the bung holes, just as you taught me. After that I thought I'd wash the floors."

"I'm impressed. You're doing a great job."

"I had a great teacher."

"You keep working while I go to the office and call Scott. I assume we still need to do the racking of the Cabernet Sauvignon?"

"Yes, that's what I'd planned to do yesterday morning."

"It's already after one o'clock. How about we do it together tomorrow?"

"Sure."

Melissa hopped back on the forklift and continued working with the barrels while Eric walked back to his office. The first thing he did when he got there was send the encrypted email to his friend Jason with the information he'd requested about Luc. Then Eric used his office phone to call Scott. He reached him after a few rings.

"Hi Scott, I'm back in town."

"Eric, I'm really sorry you had to cut your vacation short, especially leaving Ashley behind. How did she take it?"

"She was supportive but disappointed. Probably the best I could hope for."

"You'll have to tell me more over a beer sometime. But now I want to talk to you about the theft of your wine. I've been doing some checking and I think we're getting close to finding out where it might have gone."

"What did you find?"

"The empty barrels and pump left scattered around the winery floor suggested that the thieves likely pumped the wine into a shipping container fitted with a bladder. The tire tracks left by a heavy truck in the gravel outside the winery doors confirm that idea. We did some research and found that shipping bulk wine this way is commonplace in the major wine growing regions of Australia, France, Italy, and California. We contacted a shipping company and they confirmed that a twenty-foot shipping container can carry a minimum of ten thousand liters of bulk wine. With fifty-four barrels of wine stolen, at two hundred twenty-five liters per barrel, they'd need to transport about twelve thousand liters of wine. One container could have worked easily."

"Is there any way to monitor truck shipments around town?"

"This morning we reviewed several archived video recordings from surveillance cameras located near downtown and major highways leading out of town. Based on the report I received from the security company that monitors your alarm system, someone came in and disarmed the system at 9:30 p.m. Monday, and then rearmed it at 2:25 a.m. Tuesday."

Scott paused, as if waiting for Eric to respond. Eric remained silent.

"The thieves used Melissa's code both times. It wasn't disarmed again until Melissa came in a little after 9:00 a.m. Tuesday. Based on that time frame, we only looked at video recordings made after 2:00 a.m. that morning, for a duration of two hours. We observed eighteen trucks that were heading into and then out of Walla Walla in the opposite direction, so they were obviously passing through town. However, we found three trucks leaving town heading west toward Seattle and one heading to the east. All of the trucks heading west were containers. The one heading east was a standard trailer and not likely to be carrying liquids. So we focused our search on the three heading west."

"What else?" Eric was impressed with what Scott had found.

"We contacted the state's Department of Transportation and asked to review their automated electronic screening data. They have twelve locations around the state where they electronically read license plates, weigh the truck while in motion, and confirm the truck's identification number if it has a transponder installed. If everything checks out, the truck is allowed to bypass the weigh station."

"So how does that help you determine the truck?" Eric asked.

"Trucks heading west typically take one of two possible routes: either through the Tri-Cities area heading toward Yakima on Interstate 82, or south of Tri-Cities heading down to the Columbia River and Interstate 84. The nearest weigh station heading west out of Walla Walla is near Grandview. The other one is south of Pasco. So after determining the amount of time it takes to drive from Walla Walla to either of those truck stops, we picked an hour window and found fifteen trucks passing through Grandview and three south of Pasco. We're in the process of trying to match any videos they have of those eighteen trucks with the videos we have of the three trucks originating in Walla Walla that morning. We should complete the screening later tonight."

"Scott, what can I do?"

"Nothing right now, Eric. But there's one more detail I need to tell you about. After we surveyed the scene at the winery, Melissa went over to Kurt Hughes' house. She has a key and she let herself inside. I couldn't go in because we don't have a warrant or any grounds for requesting one."

"What did she find?"

"Nothing. The place looks cleaned out. A lot of his clothes were missing, along with all of his toiletries, photos of Melissa she remembers seeing displayed in frames around the house, even some of his travel bags. It looked as if everything that someone might want to take on an extended trip was missing. Even the refrigerator was empty.

After she told me about this, I decided to check with some friends at Homeland Security. They had no records of him crossing the border, so I think he's likely still in the country. I asked them to put him on their watch list as a Person of Interest, related to the theft of your wine. I also put him on the State Patrol watch list."

"Scott, I'm going to go see Luc again. I'm convinced his clients are involved in this. It's the only logical explanation."

"I agree, but how are you going to get him to talk?"

Eric could hear concern growing in Scott's voice. "I'm working on something I can't discuss. It's best you don't know."

"Eric, leave law enforcement to professionals. I don't want to see something happen to you."

"Scott, everything important to me is at stake here. I could lose my winery, my reputation, everything I've worked for. I'm not going to just sit here while a couple of thugs ruin my life. And you've seen Walt Conner. He's devastated. The loss of his son-in-law has hit him hard. He's really worried about his daughter."

"I understand, but I think these guys are serious and won't hesitate to get people out of their way. You need to tell me what you have in mind."

"I should know something soon."

"All right. Just don't do anything stupid. Call me when you're ready to talk."

Eric hung up the phone and stared out his office window. At least it was sunny. He felt he should call Ashley and give her an update, but he just wasn't in the mood. He wished he was back in Hawaii with her. He decided to take the dogs for a walk instead.

15

November 8th

Shanghai

The elevator descended twenty-one floors and after its doors opened, Wei stepped out onto the forty-first floor of Shanghai's Jin Mao Tower. He turned down the hallway and walked toward the reception area of the Shanghai Star Industrial Group. Days earlier, tired and jetlagged after the fourteen-hour flight from Seattle, Wei had checked into the Grand Hyatt. The hotel was one of the highest in the world, located on floors 53 through 87 of the tower. He was glad he didn't suffer from acrophobia as he admired the view of the Huangpu River through floor to ceiling windows. To the north, he saw the mighty Yangtze River and to the east, the placid East China Sea, where the Yangtze ends its nearly four-thousand-mile journey.

A young and stylishly dressed receptionist said, "I am Zhao Xiaojie. May I help you?"

"I'm here to see Mr. Huang," Wei replied. As the receptionist made a phone call, he studied her large brown eyes and long, straight coal-black hair. She wore a knee-length dark wool skirt and a white blouse. Since she had used the term *Xiaojie*, similar to the English term *Miss*, it was likely she was unmarried. He appreciated that management hired not just competent office staff—most had attended university—but women who were also quite attractive and single. He guessed her age to be mid-twenties. He knew she probably lived at home with her parents and grandparents and, like most of the younger Chinese, was passionate about current Western fashion and music.

Standing by the windows, Wei admired the sweeping view. The tower's modern design and majestic height were symbols of the economic progress of the People's Republic of China. Once the tallest building in the country, it was eclipsed in 2007 by the Shanghai World Financial Center next door. An even taller building, the Shanghai Tower, was scheduled to be completed in 2014 with 128 stories. He remembered the day that the foolish French climber, Alain "Spiderman" Robert, had climbed the exterior of the Jin Mao without a permit and ended up in jail for five days before being deported. The government didn't appreciate anyone breaking the rules, especially when it came to violating their symbols of national pride.

Another attractive woman soon appeared out of a hallway and beckoned Wei to follow her. After turning down a few corridors, they arrived in an executive dining room with waiters dressed in tuxes and tables positioned along windows, set with pressed white tablecloths and red and white wine glasses. Wei was offered a seat at a table for two and sat down. Within moments a waiter appeared and placed a pot of hot tea in the center of the table. Wei knew to wait for his companion before pouring himself a cup. It wasn't long before Mr. Huang appeared. Wei stood up and bowed. "Hello, Father."

"Sit down, Wei." His father sat, too, as the waiter poured them both a cup of tea. "How was the rest of your trip?"

"It was fine. I returned two nights ago and have been staying in the hotel. I plan to return to Yinchuan in the morning."

"Did you secure the wine?"

"Yes, it should have left the Port of Seattle by now." Wei's face was paler than normal as he began the conversation with his father. Huang Cheng was a serious man. He'd risen far in the ranks of Shanghai Star Industrial Group and was now President of the Real Estate division, reporting directly to the chairman. This was to be his last assignment in the firm. Wei knew he planned to retire within the next two years.

"Why didn't you tell me that you had a problem?"

A waiter walked over to the table, and Wei sat quietly as his father ordered their lunch. Wei wondered how his father had heard. He knew it was pointless to lie. Such deceit would only lower his father's esteem even further.

"Mr. Russell tried to double-cross me. I met him at a warehouse to take delivery of the wine, and I tasted it. I knew immediately it was not the wine I had agreed to buy. He must have found wine from another winery in Walla Walla. When I confronted him, he said the winemaker would not sell me the wine in bulk that I tasted. The winemaker is a small producer and didn't have extra supply. I told him that it was the only wine I wanted to buy."

"What happened?"

"I told Mr. Russell that if he didn't complete the sale, I'd find another way to acquire it. I said I would not come home without it. He immediately threatened to go to the authorities. He must have suspected I might try to steal it. He abruptly left our meeting and walked outside toward his car. I followed him and when I got outside, I heard him making a phone call. He said something about speaking with a detective. I assumed he was calling the police."

"So you murdered him?" Cheng glared at his son. "You are a fool. You will bring shame to this family. Do you remember me telling you as a boy about the virtue of *li*?"

"Yes, Father."

"I used to say *'Let the emperor be an emperor; the father a father, and the son a son.'* You have violated every rule I have taught you about the propriety of family. You should have consulted me. "

Wei knew of the old ways, which meant so much to his father. He also knew he had made a grievous mistake, which may have put everything at risk.

Father and son sat quietly for a moment as a waiter arrived with their meal. Steaming hot dishes were placed on the table: bowls of a Shanghai delicacy called *xiaolongbao*, a type of steamed bun filled with soup and pork or minced crab, and Beggar's Chicken, a dish in which a chicken is stuffed, wrapped in clay, and then roasted. The waiter left and returned with bottles of red and white wines to pour. They both declined.

Cheng started eating his meal, with typical Chinese fervor, smacking his lips, slurping liquids in the small bowl placed next to his mouth, and tossing bones on the table next to his plate. He followed the common method of eating *xiaolongbao* by biting the top off of the bun, sucking out all the soup, then dipping it in vinegar before eating.

Wei used his chopsticks with as much restraint as possible. He still refused to use a fork, but he had become more accustomed to western manners. When Cheng was finished with his food, he pushed his plate away and drank some of his tea.

"How did you get into the winery?"

"Before Mr. Russell's death, he gave me the name of a friend who might help, a man named Kurt Hughes. Mr. Russell wrongly believed I'd spare him if he gave me the name."

"So what happens now?"

"The wine will arrive in Shanghai on one of the company ships in eighteen days. The container normally sits in the shipyard for at least a week in quarantine, but I think I can get it expedited. I used the custom print service in Seattle you recommended. They do excellent work and were easily able to prepare the necessary documents, including a shipping manifest, Customs forms, and a certificate of authenticity. I paid some of our workers an extra bonus to make sure everything went well. There should be no delay with the import and Customs officials."

"And what of Mr. Russell's body? What will keep them from linking the body to you?"

"I'm sure someone found the body, but I don't think that they will be able to trace it back to me. The only person who knows our identity is Mr. DuPont and I don't think he'll talk."

"Are you sure you can trust him? He's the one who called me and told me you had caused a problem."

"He's a smart businessman. He knows that if he doesn't keep our relationship confidential, we can make it difficult for him to do business in China. He is like us. Success is everything to him."

His father took off his glasses and stared out the window at the ground far below. "I am sorry I agreed to help you in your quest. When you came to me, I offered to help you negotiate a legal purchase and secure the services of the company's shipping division for you. Now, I fear that through your mistake and your ongoing failure to manage your temper, you will bring shame to this family. We could both end up working in rice paddies, like your grandparents before you. And all for your misguided notions of love."

"Father, she will love me for this."

"Are you so sure? She has rebuffed your advances in the past. Why do you think your plan will change her mind and attract her to you?"

"Because like most children of powerful men, she wants to please her father. Pride and success drive her. If I help raise her esteem in the eyes of her father, she will embrace me. I'm sure of it."

"You cannot influence the ways of a woman's heart, especially one who has been educated in the west and embraces individualism over collectivism. There was a time when a Chinese woman was expected to marry into an acceptable family before thirty years of age. It was assumed that she would put her own interests aside to enter into a permanent relationship, one acceptable to her family. This woman feels no such adherence to the old ways. I know this. I have worked for her father for over twenty-five years."

"I will prove you wrong."

"I hope so, my son, but if the truth comes out, her rejection of you will grow even stronger."

Huang Cheng signaled to the waiter. A plate of cut banana, pineapple and lychee was delivered to the table. Lunch was over.

16

November 16th

Eric spent a week working around the winery, performing some minor maintenance tasks and taking care of post-harvest cleaning. It was time to rack the Merlot and he wanted Melissa to do it. He spent time coaching her to make sure she understood the procedure. The rest of the wines were in good shape. The Cabernet Sauvignon, the wine he'd inoculated with malolactic bacteria before leaving for Hawaii, was progressing and secondary fermentation would be completed in three weeks' time. It would finish before Christmas.

Eric typically bottled his whites in early spring and the reds in late spring. Having lost his Eagle Cap blend, the late spring bottling would only include the Cabernet Sauvignon and Merlot harvested the previous year. He'd bottle the Sauvignon Blanc in early spring. About half of next year's inventory had been lost and he was running low on current inventory. He didn't know how to fill the hole. He'd thought of checking with other winemakers to see if they had any extra wine to sell that he could use to make a new blend and call it Rescuers' Blend, or something clever like that. His next Eagle Cap was now over a year off. Maybe he'd just have to tough it out. He hated the fact that he'd paid for all that fruit and labor, just to have it stolen. He'd been working with his insurance company but they reminded him that only the winery and bottled inventory were covered against loss, not wine in intermediate stages.

Devastated by the theft of Eric's wine, Melissa blamed herself and regretted ever getting involved with Kurt Hughes. She, of course, hated Kurt now and wanted nothing to do with him again. By 5:00 p.m. on Friday, Eric was downbeat and ready to spend a few days away from the winery. As he was preparing to leave, he decided to invite Melissa over for dinner and a movie. He thought she could probably use some company too.

Each day since returning home to Walla Walla, Eric had spoken with Ashley who was still on Maui enjoying her remaining days of vacation. She and the boys had continued to have a good time in Hawaii. "But it isn't the same without you," Ashley assured him. The wonderful image of Ashley standing undressed in his hotel room was etched in his mind. Not only was he pondering what to do about his wines, he also struggled with his thoughts of Ashley. He knew they had a future, but after their short connection in Hawaii, he resolved that long distance just wasn't going to work for him.

Eric got home and followed his usual routine of walking the dogs around the Whitman College campus. Afterward, he had an hour before Melissa's arrival. He had just started the shower when his cell phone rang. He turned off the water and answered the call. It was Scott. After the two men exchanged greetings, the sheriff went straight to the point.

"Eric, we finally got the report back from the Department of Transportation. They gave us a listing of all the trucks that passed through those weigh stations in the early morning after your wine was stolen, along with photos and descriptions."

"Find anything?"

"My staff worked on it all day. We had eighteen trucks we thought were candidates. Fifteen had passed through the northern route and the Grandview weigh station, and three went south through Pasco. We were able to compare the videos of the three trucks we found leaving west out of Walla Walla that morning with the data from the eighteen trucks recorded at the weigh stations, and we identified all three. Once we got the contact information, we started making calls to the companies that owned the trucks. We just got off the phone with the last one."

"Did you find the truck?"

"We think so. One container held canned agricultural products bound first for the Port of Tacoma and then by ship to Kuala Lumpur. Another carried wood pulp and cellulose shipped by rail to Utah, and the last container held bulk wine bound for China."

"You got the shipping manifest from each company?"

"Yes. We also requested that each company provide us with GPS data from their trucks. Most of them collect and record location information so they can provide real-time shipping status to their customers. Not surprisingly, each said they weren't able to comply without a warrant. I'm working with the prosecutor to get the warrant, but I'm convinced we have the truck that came to your winery. I'd like to have the GPS data as irrefutable proof that the truck was at your exact location, as recorded by the security system."

"So, do you know where the wine is going?"

"No, all we have is the name of the consignee in the Port of Shanghai. The container was turned over to a Port of Seattle freight forwarder at 9:30 a.m. the morning it went missing from the winery. That fits with the time it would have taken to drive over there. We requested the shipping documents from the freight company and they promised to send over what they have. They were circumspect about the nature of the contract to pick up the wine. I'm thinking it may have been off the books, but at least we have a container number and an approximate time of delivery to the Port of Seattle. If the wine did go to China as we suspect, there were two container ships leaving this week, one yesterday to Shanghai direct, and the other today to Shanghai by way of Hong Kong."

"With a wine shipment, I think they'd use the direct route," Eric said. "The temperature of wine in a bulk-shipping container remains much more stable than case goods because there is so much liquid mass to heat and cool. As they seem so concerned about quality, I'm sure they'd take the shortest route. Do you know when the ship will arrive in Shanghai?"

"Eleven days from now. But the wine will have to go through Customs. And being a food product, it will have to sit in quarantine for some time. My worry is that they have some sway with the authorities and can fly under the radar. Even if we have the container number, there's no guarantee we could find it in Shanghai. That port handles thousands of containers per day. There are probably six thousand containers just in that one ship. So if they bribed someone or used other forms of coercion, they could probably slip it out of the port and we'd never know."

"I still think the answer rests with DuPont," said Eric.

"I agree. Did that idea you said you were working on ever materialize?"

"No, I expected to hear something by now. It's complicated and might be taking more time than I anticipated."

"All right, let me know if you hear anything and I'll call you when we get the shipping documents from the freight company." Scott ended the call.

Eric was perplexed by the phone call with Scott. He was relieved to get some idea of where his wine was, but why would someone steal it and ship it to China? It didn't make any sense. He knew his wine was pretty good, but there was a lot of good wine in the world. Why his, he wondered? He looked at his watch. He needed to finish his shower and figure out something for dinner before Melissa arrived in thirty minutes.

When the doorbell rang, Eric was getting chicken breasts out of the freezer. Pretty lame he thought, but it was something. Max and Ginger ran to the front door with Eric close behind. They didn't bark because they recognized the sound of Melissa's car. Dogs were quite smart that way. He let Melissa in and took her coat. While shutting the door, he looked out and noticed it had started snowing.

"When did that start?"

"The snow?" Melissa asked, while unzipping her leather boots and slipping them off.

"Yeah, I just walked the dogs and it was cold, but I didn't see any snow."

"You ever listen to the news and weather? They've been predicting snow tonight for a few days."

"Nope, don't have time. It looks beautiful though. Come with me to the kitchen. You can open some wine while I get dinner started."

They went to the kitchen. Eric prepared the chicken breasts with a wine reduction and mushrooms to put in the oven. Melissa meanwhile opened a bottle of white wine and poured two glasses. Eric suggested they go to the den and watch a movie while the chicken was baking.

Melissa sprawled out on the large leather sofa and wrapped her legs in a wool blanket. While in the kitchen together, Eric had admired Melissa's black athletic tights and how well they emphasized her runner's legs. On top she wore a stretch fabric long-sleeve top in blue with pink accents. A three-quarter zipper was pulled down halfway, exposing just a hint of her ample cleavage. She looked ready for a long run.

Eric went to a shelf and returned with a DVD. As the movie credits started, Melissa turned to Eric and said, "Really?"

"You don't like Bill Murray?"

"I think you're a bit obvious, that's all."

"*Lost in Translation* is a great movie. You don't find the main characters believable?"

"Bill's character is an aging actor and I get his charm and accomplishments. But Scarlett's character is a sexy, confused, young bride who needs some direction. So they didn't get entangled, big deal. They were both married. I guess I'm glad they honored their vows. But I didn't quite believe it."

"But there was a huge age difference between them."

"Younger women have never fallen for older men before?"

Had Eric unwittingly chosen a movie that would send a message opposite to the one he intended? "Let's just watch the movie. Maybe we can learn something."

While the movie was playing and the colorful lights of Tokyo flashed across the screen, Eric decided to check email. He went to his office to retrieve his laptop and returned to the sofa.

As he opened up the computer, Melissa shot him a look and said, "I thought men waited until they were married to do that."

"Do what?"

"Ignore the person next to them."

Eric gave her a quick elbow in the side. "Just watch the movie."

He logged in and scanned his messages. He had about fifty, most of them spam, Facebook notifications, or notes from family. Then he saw what he was looking for: a message from his friend Jason. It simply read, *Call me—Jason.*

Eric looked at his watch and decided it wasn't too late to call. He excused himself, explaining he had an important call to make, and returned to his office. After he sat down at his desk, he picked up his phone and dialed Jason's number, who answered in a few rings.

"Hi, Eric. I was hoping it was you calling."

"Hi, Jason. I'm guessing you've found something."

"Yes, it took a while but I think I did. Ever hear of *zappers*?"

"When I was a kid I think spacemen killed monsters with them."

"Different kind. A zapper is also a piece of software that companies can use to hide revenue. I thought about your comments that Luc DuPont led a rich lifestyle and I did some research. Electronic sales suppression software is designed to work with point-of-sale systems and electronic cash registers. It can be used to select and delete cash sales from computer records to evade federal and state taxes. In some cases identified by the Washington State Liquor Control Board, companies have collected taxes from customers, suppressed sales records using this software, and not sent the taxes to the taxing entity as required by law."

"And you think Luc might be doing this?"

"I researched the leading developers of this type of software and built a list of the executable files each vendor provides and which might be found on systems set up for this kind of suppression. Each executable file has a well-defined signature. I accessed the Honorable Wine Merchant's server in Luc's office and searched for those files. It was pretty easy, really. Router firewalls aren't perfectly secure if you know how to get around them."

"Go on."

"I found a match. I also found a system log which shows that the software has been running consistently over the past nine months."

"That's great!"

"Well, not so fast. You can't let on that I've breached his system. I like to hack, but this is risky. As long as you don't say anything that would lead back to me, we'll be fine. But delete my emails and don't call again until I get you a new phone number. All of the hardware and software I've used is my own and not related to work in any way. If someone asks, I'll deny it. I've covered my tracks pretty well."

"Thanks Jason. I'll send you a case of wine. Your secret is safe with me, I promise."

"Glad to help. Good luck."

Eric sat back in his chair and stared out the window at the swirling snow, blown by a strong wind that buffeted the glass. He could barely see the campus across the street. A nearby streetlight illuminated the sky in bright white with streaks of snowflakes continuously streaming toward the ground. It reminded him of a snow globe of the North Pole he had as a boy. He decided to drive to Seattle the next day, provided the roads were open.

The timer on the oven starting buzzing, signaling his chicken was done. After turning it off, Eric peered into the den and saw that the movie was paused and Melissa was stretched out on the sofa lengthwise, apparently asleep. He watched her chest rise and fall in rhythmic breaths. Back in the kitchen he pulled out the chicken, mixed a salad, and set the table. He then went back to fetch Melissa. He gently woke her with a hand on her shoulder. "Dinner is ready."

As they ate, Melissa said, "You were on the phone?"

"Yes, with a friend in Seattle."

"Good news?"

"Intriguing."

"Want to tell me about it?"

"Can't."

Melissa gave Eric a quizzical look and pursed her lips. "I hate secrets." She looked even younger.

They finished the chicken and cleaned up the kitchen. Afterward, they took their glasses of wine and headed back to the den to finish the movie.

As the final credits rolled, Eric said, "See, they're still platonic friends. It can happen."

"That's how the movie ended, but I don't think it's really over."

During a moment of silence, Eric rested his arm on the sofa's cushion and looked at Melissa. She gazed at him with her brow furled in thought. "Do you find me attractive, Eric?"

Eric sighed before responding. "Of course, I do. I find you very desirable, if that's what you're asking."

"Then why don't you kiss me?"

Eric fumbled with the remote control as he prepared his response. He slid his hand underneath Melissa's and squeezed it gently. "Because if I did, I know there'd be no turning back."

"I wouldn't want you to turn back."

"I know."

Eric looked at her and smiled. "It's snowing really hard. I don't want you driving home. You take my bed, and I'll make up the sofa. I'm leaving early in the morning for Seattle and I'd like you to take care of the dogs for me."

"Okay. But if I can't sleep with you, I want to sleep in one of your shirts."

17

November 17th

Seattle

Eric got up early, which wasn't hard. He found the sofa uncomfortable and was happy to get off it. He folded the sheets and blankets and headed into the kitchen to make coffee. At first he was surprised the dogs didn't join him, but then he guessed they were in his bedroom keeping a watchful eye on their guest.

After dressing, he returned to the kitchen and filled a thermos with coffee and pulled together some food to take along. He put everything into a backpack, grabbed his heavy Mackinaw coat and gloves, and headed out the door. The snow had stopped. Quiet streets, empty sidewalks, and front yards covered with six inches of the white fluffy powder: it all looked stunning as the sun was just cresting the horizon.

He got in his old truck, kicked it to life, let it warm up a few minutes, and then backed out of the driveway and onto the street. His wheels spun slightly starting out but once he had a bit of momentum, he was fine. Soon he was on Highway 12, heading west out of town. The roads had been sanded and he expected a relatively easy four-hour drive to Seattle.

Thirty minutes into the drive he called Luc DuPont's house. The previous night he had found the address and phone number on the Internet. A woman answered. Eric assumed it was Luc's wife. After a bit of protest, she finally agreed to put her husband on the phone.

"Mr. DuPont, this is Eric Savage."

"The winemaker from Walla Walla."

"Yes."

"Why are you calling me so early on a Sunday morning, Mr. Savage?"

"I need to speak with you. I'm driving to Seattle from Walla Walla right now. I should be there around noon."

"But I don't want to speak with you, Mr. Savage. And as I recall, I think I told you and the sheriff that I have nothing else to say to either one of you without an attorney present."

"I need your help—off the record. It's important for both of us."

"You're interrupting a weekend I usually try to spend with my family."

"It will only take fifteen minutes. Do you know the replica of the Statue of Liberty on Alki? Meet me there at one o'clock. I promise it won't take long. I'm alone."

"As you wish, Mr. Savage. But you'd better not be wasting my time." Luc was clearly irritated by the call.

At 12:30 p.m., Eric arrived in the area known as West Seattle. He decided to drive past Luc's house on the way to Alki. He drove slowly down the street past the large Tudor-style home and pulled to the curb beyond. He was impressed by its size and location atop a bluff overlooking Puget Sound to the north and the downtown skyline of Seattle to the east. It was an exclusive neighborhood.

Eric continued down the streets descending the bluff until he found a place to park along the beach. He got out of his truck and buttoned up his coat. The sky was mottled gray and a cold breeze bit at his face. Few people were out. Couples with dogs walked by and a few kids played on the beach. Occasionally a lone bicyclist sped by. He remembered how in summertime the place was alive with beach volleyball, cookouts, and kids cruising up and down the street in cars with radios blaring. It seemed desolate now.

He walked to the statue and eyed the street. In a few minutes, a beautiful, dark copper Maserati pulled up, stopped, and then continued driving until it pulled into a parking spot. He watched Luc's imposing figure exit the car and walk toward him. Silver gray hair was again combed back, almost resting on his shoulders. He was stylishly dressed in a long, tan, wool coat and charcoal-gray pants. On his feet he wore shiny, lace-up, black European-style shoes. Both hands were in his pockets.

"Mr. Savage, this had better be worth my time."

"Mr. DuPont, I need your help."

"This isn't about my customers again, is it? Their identity is privileged and I won't tell you who they are. If you don't have a subpoena, I'm not talking. You must understand that."

"What I understand is that fifty-four barrels of my best wine were stolen last Monday night. I might go out of business because of it. I think your customers are responsible."

Luc didn't speak at first. Instead, he looked out at Puget Sound. Waves churned and seagulls cawed overhead. A ferry slid past silently off shore. He returned his gaze to Eric. "Mr. Savage, I'm sorry to hear about your wine, but I won't help you."

"Do you enjoy your business, Mr. DuPont? Because I think you do. You're good at it and it appears that it's given you a privileged lifestyle. But I question whether you are helping your customers, or taking advantage of them."

"What do you mean?"

"I've spoken with friends in the industry—distributors who know how you work. You buy wine at low prices, occasionally as excess inventory, and through the perception of exclusivity, sell to your loyal customers at a huge profit. Are you really serving them?"

"Look, you can't tell me that you don't also build a marketing perception of how great your wines are. You've seen the same results of blind tasting as I have. Most consumers can be fooled most of the time. Tasting is all about perception—the color of the wine, its bouquet, the ambience of the tasting room, the delicacy and shape of the wine glass, the image of the label, the imprimatur of god-like experts. It's *all* a bit of trickery, isn't it? Yes, I'm good at it, but as I told you before, there isn't a law against selling what people want to buy."

"But there is a law against hiding revenue and avoiding taxes."

Eric saw a familiar tightness arrive on Luc DuPont's face, the same as in his office during his visit with Scott. He fully expected a fist to rise up and punch him in the mouth, but he continued anyway. "All I want is for you to tell me who came to you for my wine. I have no interest in hurting you or your business."

"What do you know?"

Eric knew he was about to take a huge risk at this point in the conversation. He'd considered the possible outcomes, the worst of which would be Luc DuPont going to the authorities and accusing Eric of extortion. But he also knew that Luc was at risk for being an accessory to murder. As he felt his stomach tighten, Eric said, "I know that you are using point-of-sale suppression software, a Class C felony. It's a crime the state takes seriously."

"What makes you think something so outrageous?"

"I can't say but I'm confident it's true. I haven't spoken to the authorities, and I won't if you agree to help me."

Luc DuPont glared at Eric. After a moment his facial muscles relaxed and he said calmly, "Mr. Savage, I like your wines. You do have a talent for it. Maybe one day we can do some legitimate business together. I can move a lot of your product."

"Right now, I just want to catch the people who stole from me and likely killed Jeff Russell. Besides being a good guy, Jeff's the son-in-law of an important business partner of mine. As questionable as I find your business practices, I doubt you condone murder."

Luc stared out at the ferry again before looking Eric straight in the eye. "Mr. Savage, I'll tell you what. I like you but I think you are a bit naïve. I'll give you their business cards, but you must promise me you won't divulge how you came by them."

"You have my word," Eric said. He eagerly extended his hand.

Both hands still in his pockets, Luc said, "Wait here. I'll be back in fifteen minutes. Watch for my car. I'll hand you the morning newspaper." He turned and started walking away. Then he hesitated, and turned back toward Eric. "I'd be careful if I were you, Mr. Savage. These men are playing by a different set of rules."

It was 6:30 p.m. when Eric arrived back home. The sun had set, leaving behind clear skies and a temperature near freezing. The snow had melted somewhat but still looked fresh. When he walked inside the house, Eric was surprised that Max and Ginger weren't there to greet him at the door as usual. He looked around the house and found the answer. On the kitchen counter he saw a handwritten note from

Melissa next to a newly framed photo of him playing with the dogs. Based on the intensity of sunlight and the shorts he was wearing, he guessed it must have been taken in summer. He could tell by the scenery it was near the winery though he couldn't recall when she had taken it. Next to it was a note.

Eric, thanks for dinner and letting me spend the night in your bed. It smelled just like you. I'll drop the dogs by later tonight.—Melissa.

Eric was tired after the trip and just wanted to have a glass of wine and call it an early night. He'd call Scott in the morning. Just as he took his coat off, Eric heard the front door open. Max and Ginger came running into the kitchen and wasted no time in dancing around their food bowls. "Okay, I'll feed you," Eric said.

Melissa then appeared in the kitchen, removing her hat and coat. "How was your trip?"

"Successful." He placed a scoop of food into each of the bowls for the dogs and poured himself a glass of wine. "We need to talk about it but can we do it tomorrow? I'm beat."

Eric took a long sip of the wine. Realizing he hadn't offered a glass to Melissa, he poured her one too. "Thanks for the photo."

"You're welcome. I took it last summer. You love your dogs, don't you?"

"I do. They're loyal and they don't ask me difficult questions."

"They're lucky to have you." Melissa drained her glass. "Give me a call tomorrow when you want to talk. Sleep well."

Eric showed her to the door and then turned to the dogs. "Okay guys, let's go for a walk in the snow."

18

November 18th

Walla Walla

On Monday morning, Eric and Sheriff Thompson met in a crowded coffee shop in downtown Walla Walla. Both men wore jeans. Scott planned to change into his uniform after breakfast.

"What's up?" Scott asked as their coffee arrived.

Eric took two folded sheets of paper from his pocket and handed them to Scott. "These are copies of business cards I got yesterday."

Scott's eyes narrowed as he unfolded the sheets. "I assume these are from DuPont?"

"I can't say."

"How did you get them?"

"I think it best if I don't tell you."

"I appreciate you trying to protect me, but I need to know."

"Do you know anyone who can interpret the Chinese side of these cards? The English sides only have names."

"You're not going to tell me?"

"Scott, trust me, you don't want to know."

"I'll take these to the office today and we'll find someone who can interpret them for us. I should also receive the shipping documents from the trucking company today."

Eric took a sip of his coffee and looked at the menu. He was hungry. When their stout waitress came by, she gave Scott a squeeze on his shoulder and said, "What will you two fine men have this morning?" Scott wanted pancakes with eggs over easy, bacon, and whole wheat toast. Eric ordered the same. "I love it when you guys make it easy," the waitress joked, as she headed toward the kitchen.

Turning to Eric, Scott said, "So what are you thinking?"

"About going to China."

"To what end?"

"To find out who took my wine and why. I need to know."

"Eric, have you thought this through? What do you hope to gain? You won't get your wine back. Even if you find it, you can't ship it back. I doubt the Chinese would let you export something that had been imported improperly into their country without significant delay. By then, your wine would be vinegar."

"Come on, Scott. Don't you want to find who did this? And what about Walt Conner and the murder of his son-in-law? I owe most of my success to Walt. Don't we owe it to him and his family to figure this out?"

Scott stared at Eric and then began to smile. "I hate it when you try to turn the tables on me. Yes, I'd like to find out, but this is a bit out of my comfort zone and a lot out of my jurisdiction."

"So you won't help me?"

"I can't go with you, Eric. The county would rightfully have my ass. With all of our budget cuts, it would be unforgivable. But I'll do what I can from here."

Eric sighed. "I'll need some help."

"If you're determined to go, then we should find you some local talent in China, someone who knows the language and their way around a port."

"Let's get the translation done on the business cards and see what the manifests say. If you're right and the shipment left on Friday, we have about two weeks until the container arrives in Shanghai."

Their breakfasts arrived and they dug in. Scott changed topics. "So how was Hawaii?"

"Tough," Eric said. "Too many interruptions. And coming back early didn't win me any points with Ashley."

"But you had a good time with her?"

"I got to meet her two boys. They were delightful—well-mannered and inquisitive. Looked me in the eye. We had some great times on the beach. But Ashley and I never had any quiet time, if that's what you mean."

"Wow. Must have been hard to get the present but not unwrap it."

"I got to unwrap it. I just didn't get to play with it."

"Any plans to see her again?"

"Not yet. I'm calling her tonight. But as perfect as she might seem, I don't think long distance is going to work for us."

"Hang in there. She's worth the investment. As Shakespeare said, 'the course of true love never did run smooth.'"

"You should stick with police work. Therapy isn't your strength." They both chuckled and finished their breakfasts.

They paid their bill and walked outside. Scott said, "If you go, any chance you can get some help from the FBI?"

"I plan to discuss this with Ashley when I call tonight. See you, Scott."

Later that afternoon, Eric sat back in his office and called Ashley. "Aloha," he said when she answered the phone.

"Really lame, Eric. I hoped it was you."

"How was the trip back?"

"I hated to leave. It's a wonderful place. I felt really happy there."

"Even after I left?"

"Especially after you left."

Eric winced on his end of the phone.

"I'm kidding," Ashley said, to reassure him. "I think we need to go back, next time without the kids."

"If that's the next time I see you, you'll have your hands full."

"I'd love to have my hands full of you."

They were both silent for a moment.

"I need to talk about China," Eric said.

"Fascinating country."

"I'm thinking of going there."

"Why?"

"We've got a pretty good idea of what happened to my wine. Scott has done some great detective work and believes it's on a ship to Shanghai. It should arrive in less than two weeks."

"So you go to China. Then what?"

"I want to find out who stole my wine and who murdered Jeff Russell," Eric said.

"How's that going to help your winery? You're not going to get your wine back."

"You're starting to sound like Scott."

"He's a smart guy," Ashley said.

"I won't be satisfied until I understand what happened. It's not just about my wine. Someone murdered Walt Conner's son-in-law. I owe it to him to figure it out."

"I don't suppose I can talk you out of this?"

"I think it's the right thing to do."

"Can I help you in some way?" Ashley asked.

"I was hoping you'd offer."

Eric reviewed the events that had occurred since he got back to Walla Walla. He shared everything but left out his conversation with his friend Jason and his subsequent meeting with Luc DuPont. He concluded with a description of his conversation with Scott over breakfast.

"Eric, I'm worried about you traveling to China alone. I agree with Scott. You need someone to help you—someone local and knowledgeable. A single instance of wine theft, even if a murder is involved, isn't typically in the FBI's purview. Unless we can tie this to some internationally organized crime operation, or the crime is interstate, the FBI won't touch it."

"I understand."

"However, we do have over sixty legal attaché offices around the world, including one in the U.S. Embassy in Beijing. I can make some inquiries and see if they have any recommendations for contract investigative work in China. I'm sure they have to go outside occasionally for some tasks that might be considered delicate."

"Scott and I meet again tomorrow. We should have translations of the business cards by then and whatever shipping information Scott receives from the trucking company. I'm sure I'll have more questions."

"All right. Call me when you can."

"I will. I miss you."

"Me too."

Eric hung up the phone. He leaned back in his office chair, which creaked with every move. Outside his window, the sun melted the snow. Water dripped rhythmically down the clear pane of glass. His next challenge was figuring out what to do with the winery while he was gone. Asking Melissa to take charge again seemed his only option. He anticipated her response would be even less enthusiastic than Ashley's.

19

November 19th

Walla Walla

Tuesday morning at 11:00 a.m., Eric arrived at the Walla Walla County Sheriff's Office to meet with Scott. As Scott had hoped, a translation of the business cards had arrived from the King County Sheriff's office, which had jurisdiction in Seattle and maintained an East Asian language staff. He also had received some shipping documents from the freight company that had delivered the container to the Port of Seattle.

Scott handed copies of the translated business cards to Eric. "Take a look."

Business Card #1 Translation:

黄成
董事长 / 总裁
房产部
上海星工业集团有限公司
电话:+133-72718923

Huang Cheng
President
Real Estate Division
Shanghai Star Industrial Group, Ltd.
Phone 133-72718923

Business Card #2 Translation:
黄韦
设备经理
银川部门
上海星工业集团有限公司
电话:+150-61718924

Huang Wei
Facilities Manager
Yinchuan Division
Shanghai Star Industrial Group, Ltd.
Phone 150-61718924

"Are they related?" Eric knew it was Chinese custom to display the family name first followed by the given name. He looked at the English side of the cards. One had the name *Mr. Cheng Huang,* and the other was *Mr. Wei Huang.* "Wei's the one who met with Jeff Russell to taste wine."

"I think that's right," Scott said. "I've asked one of my deputies to research the company and see if we can find out more. I should hear back today."

"What about the shipping information?" Eric asked.

"There are some discrepancies."

"Such as?"

"All the individual documents are there, including Shipper's Export Declaration, Waybill, Commercial Invoice, Packing List, Certificate of Origin, and U.S. Export Certificate. But when I examined the Certificate of Origin, I saw the Alcohol and Tobacco Tax and Trade Bureau had stamped and signed it a week before the wine was stolen. I think they have a seven-day requirement to process, so it would have been filled out and signed a week before the theft, but that's not possible. It must have been forged so that someone checking the dates couldn't catch it. I've sent the whole stack out for analysis, but it wouldn't surprise me if the documents were falsified. They sure look authentic."

"Anything else?"

"The consignee is listed as a commercial Customs agent in Shanghai, the port of arrival. Care to guess who the listed buyer is?"

"Huang Wei?"

"You're getting pretty good at this. His address is a mail stop in Shanghai's Jin Mao Tower. My guess is the agent will handle arrival logistics from the time the ship has docked until Customs releases the container. Then they'll send it on to Wei."

"I should get to Shanghai next week, a day ahead of the ship. Ashley is checking with her FBI sources for a potential hire—someone with detective experience who understands Mandarin."

"You need to get going on securing a Chinese visa. I'd use an agent in San Francisco who can go to the consulate and speed the application along. It'll cost you, but otherwise it will be hard getting it in time."

"I'll start making some calls this afternoon."

"What are you going to do about the winery?"

"I'm planning to ask Melissa to watch both the winery and my dogs."

"Do you think she can handle it?"

"She'll have to rise to the occasion. I'll probably ask Walt Conner to help her. They get along well and Walt would enjoy some time in the winery after his devastating loss."

"I agree. He's a good choice. I can help out, too."

"Thanks, Scott."

"Let's talk this afternoon. I'll let you know what I hear regarding Shanghai Star Industrial Group, Ltd. and the analysis of the documents."

Eric said good-bye to Scott and left the Sheriff's office. He decided his next stop had to be the winery to have a talk with Melissa. He arrived early in the afternoon and found her working on her computer.

"What's up?" Eric asked.

"I'm just trying to catch up on some orders. We had several come in over the weekend, and I want to get them pulled, boxed, and ready for UPS pickup this afternoon. How about you?"

"Before you go home today, I'd like to talk to you about a couple of things. But finish that first. Customers are more important."

"I should be done in about an hour."

Eric went to his office to phone his travel agent. He told her just enough to convince her to prioritize his request for a Chinese visa and plane tickets. He then wrote a to-do list he needed to complete before leaving in a week, including a reminder to call his daughter in Santa Barbara and let her know of his plans. He then started on a task list for Melissa and the winery.

When the lists were completed, Eric put in a call to Walt Conner to ask him if he'd be willing to help Melissa while he traveled. Walt agreed enthusiastically. Eric suspected that the distraught farmer would look forward to Melissa's company. As he was finishing the call with Walt, Melissa strolled into his office and flopped down in a chair.

Melissa looked at Eric expectantly. "You're not going to Hawaii again, are you?"

"No, a bit farther this time. I'm going to China."

"You're really going to try and find your wine?"

"Yes."

"Won't that be dangerous?"

"Probably."

"Then why are you going? Forget the wine—let's just make more. We're a great team. I feel horrible this happened. The only way I can think to repay you is to help you recover. It'll be even better next year. I know this setback is huge, but you can still be a great success. Besides, it's not like you're going to get your wine back."

"You sound like Ashley and Scott. None of you appreciate how big of a deal this is. Half a million dollars is a lot of money. But it's not just the money. Whoever stole the wine likely murdered Jeff Russell as well. I owe it to Walt to find out what happened." Eric leaned forward and stared at Melissa.

"Maybe you should listen to Ashley and Scott and move on."

"Maybe I should but I'm pissed. Criminals shouldn't be able to murder someone then just walk into this winery, take my wine, destroy my business, and get away with it."

"Okay, so why don't you just take whatever information you've found, turn it over to Scott, then focus on the winery?"

"They'll never treat this as seriously as I will. I need to go over and start digging."

Melissa's shoulders slumped and she sank into her chair. "Eric, I don't want anything to happen to you. I've been doing a lot of thinking since this mess with Kurt. He was a poor substitute for you. I recognize that now."

"Melissa, we've talked about this. You deserve more than I can give you. Besides, I have Ashley in my life."

"What does Ashley have that I don't?"

"Maturity." He knew the word would sting but said it anyway. Had Ashley asked him the same question about Melissa while feeling as defensive as he did then, he likely would have replied, "Youth."

"Maturity? That's good for you? How? She lives in Houston, has two children who keep her from relocating, and I don't see you making wine in Texas."

They were fair points—the same ones he struggled with frequently.

They sat silently for a few moments. Melissa gazed out the window while Eric stared at her slumping posture. Her head had slipped down the back of the chair, and her legs stuck out straight. Her hands were folded in her lap. She broke the pause. "I'll take care of the winery and the dogs for you while you're gone, but when you get back you need to look for a new assistant."

"Why?"

"Because I want more than this, Eric." She sat up and leaned forward toward him. "We could be that great couple people dream of becoming. We could build this business into a successful and sustainable legend. Your wines are classic and honest. You make them with passion and artistry. And we could start a family."

Eric was stunned. *Did I really not see it coming? Have I been that naïve?* "Melissa, I don't know what to say. I don't see myself as a new dad again, which is why I've suggested you find someone who wants to build that kind of life."

"But Eric, you're such a great father. And just think how perfect our children would be."

That particular point was undeniable. "Can we talk about this when I get back? For now, I just need you to stick with me and the winery." He felt guilty for resorting to avoidance, but he wasn't ready to confront her head on, not now anyway. *But when?*

"*If* you get back."

"I'll get back."

"OK, but when you do, we need to talk about my future." Melissa abruptly stood up and left the room.

Eric finished up his documents at his desk and then put in a call to Scott.

"Scott, find out anything?"

"We've found out quite a bit. The shipping documents were forged. We checked with some of the agencies who should have a record of them. The originals don't exist. They are of very high quality, so whoever printed them locally is very good. True, they do have incorrect form numbers and a minor typographical error, but most office staff would never notice. Also, we tracked the container and found it on a ship heading directly to Shanghai—just as we thought. It'll arrive Tuesday, a week from today."

"What about Shanghai Star Industrial Group?"

"We haven't uncovered anything yet, Eric. It's a large corporation with divisions in real estate, construction, shipping, and some heavy manufacturing. Huang Cheng is the President of the Real Estate Division, just as his business card states. And we confirmed that Huang Wei is the Facilities Manager of the Yinchuan Division. We haven't been able to find out what that division does. Yinchuan is the capital of the Ningxia Hui Autonomous Region, located in northern China, west of Beijing, and not far from southern Mongolia. The region is mostly high desert near a mountain range. Population is around two million. Commerce is agricultural, with some large coal production."

"Sounds hard to reach," Eric said. "If you find out anything else, let me know. My travel agent is working on my trip. I'll fly to Shanghai on

Saturday and arrive on Monday because of the international dateline. When I get there, I'll follow up on Ashley's recommendations for a private investigator to help me, and then get ready to watch the port in Shanghai. I've spoken with Melissa and she's agreed to manage the winery with help from you and Walt."

"Are you okay with leaving it in her hands?"

"Scott, I don't have a choice. Melissa is very competent and she'll do her best. The worst that can happen is everything gets screwed up and I have to close." Eric tried levity, but he remained concerned. "But I think that may happen anyway."

"Come on, Eric, it's not that bad. You'll bounce back from this."

"I hope so, Scott."

Eric finished up the call and got ready to call it a day. He noticed Melissa's Subaru was already gone from the parking lot. He locked up the winery and drove home.

Part Two

Love many things, for therein lies the true strength, and whosoever loves much performs much, and can accomplish much, and what is done in love is done well.

Vincent Van Gogh

20

November 25th

Yinchuan

Lily Kwong ascended the marble double-helix staircase to the third floor of the château. The heels of her black leather pumps clicked loudly on the Italian stone with each step. It didn't matter though. No one could hear her; the administrative offices were mostly empty at that early hour. She hated the uncomfortable shoes and wore them only on business trips. She'd much rather be in the winery's lab, wearing flats and a lab coat, while running tests on wine samples. At the top of the landing, she turned and walked through massive, hand-carved, wooden doors that opened into her office.

"Good morning, Miss Lily," her assistant said. "All packed and ready for your trip?"

"Yes, Ling, I am. What time does my car depart for the airport?"

"At eleven. A little over two hours from now."

"Thank you. I will be in my office."

Lily wasn't looking forward to the trip. It wasn't that she didn't enjoy the company of her father, but she was worried about the quality of her wines. Her father's corporate offices were located in Hong Kong, and she had agreed to meet him there so they could discuss her recent performance. She also planned to help host a number of wine tastings with several of his best corporate clients. She predicted they would rave about her wines, but she also knew that they would never say anything to offend her father, Chairman of Shanghai Star Industrial Group, Ltd. She couldn't expect them to be completely honest in their assessment.

For the truth, she needn't look much further than her desk. She hung her long wool coat on the antique wood and brass coatrack and walked around the massive oak desk to the chair behind it. She pulled it out and sat down, while glancing at her mail. Ling had already arranged it in neat and prioritized stacks, as was the case every morning. Adjacent to the mail was a red leather portfolio, which she knew from prior experience contained all of the necessary travel documents and an itinerary for her trip. She admired Ling's proficiency but always suspected that her assistant, a long-term employee in her father's firm, had been assigned to the position as one more way for her father to keep a watchful eye on his daughter.

Flipping through the mail, she found what she had anticipated: the latest edition of the *London Wine Times* magazine. She eagerly turned to the *Tastings* section, where she found her wine's score and tasting notes:

Red Star Winery, Celestial Blend, 2010. *Mid-crimson color. Sweet, dense tannins with some astringency. Lots of barrel influence, mostly new oak. Reasonably ripe, with decent nose and acceptable balance, though no great fruit intensity or character. Fresh, robust, just a bit rustic. Drink by 2016. 88 Points.*

Lily closed the magazine and pitched it in the direction of the rubbish bin. She leaned back in her chair and bit her lip. She felt capable of so much more. She knew what the problem was: the quality of the grapes. She stared out her window high above the vineyards and admired the rows of vines running into the horizon. Now dormant, the trunks of the vines were buried in dirt to protect them from the harsh winters of the Ningxia wine region. Ningxia, located at the foot of the Helan Mountains, near the Gobi desert and south of the Mongolian border, sat at an elevation of 3,600 feet. Summers provided excellent weather for growing grapes, including warm daytime temperatures and cool nights. The region was receiving acclaim as one of the best viticulatural areas in China. But winters were often cold, and with an average daytime temperature near freezing, the vines sometimes froze. Burying them took additional labor, which really wasn't a problem. Labor was generally cheap and easily available. Because of the cold weather, many vines didn't survive, even with burying, and were replaced each spring. In some years grape quality was uneven.

The other challenge was with the farmers who had been growing grapes for less than a decade. Tending a vineyard required new skills and expertise to control volume, measure humidity and acidity in the soil, and provide the proper amounts of water and fertilizer, concepts that took time to learn. Even compensation was a problem. The winery oversaw two hundred farmers working on ninety-five acres. Historically, farmers were paid by weight of product produced. To increase revenue, some farmers had gone to the trouble of injecting water into the grapes before delivery. The result was the opposite of what winemakers wanted: a higher ratio of skin to juice to impart more tannins, color, and flavor. Lily knew achieving excellence would take time. As her father liked to tell her, "It does not matter how slow you go as long as you do not stop."

Her thoughts of grapes and vines were interrupted by a sound at her door. As she wheeled her chair around to see who was knocking, she instinctively grimaced. It was Wei.

"Hi, Lily. Have a minute?"

"Just a few. I have to leave for Hong Kong soon."

"Yes, I heard you will be gone for a week. Is that right?"

"Yes, I'm going to visit father and do some wine tastings with a few of his clients. I'll be back next Monday."

"I'm sure your father must be very proud of you."

"Wei, we've discussed this. He knows how hard I'm working, but he will accept nothing less than greatness for his wines. Here in the Yinchuan division, our goal is simply to make the best wine in China. We're not there yet."

"As facilities manager, have I failed you in any way?"

"No, the winery is excellent, and we have the best equipment available. Barrels from France, press equipment from Italy, scientific instruments from America—anything I've asked for you've procured. We lack nothing as far as I can tell. At least that's what all the consultants tell me."

"I'll do anything I can to help."

"Thank you, Wei. You've been very responsive."

"When we graduated together from high school, I knew you would accomplish great things, Lily."

"I'm not as confident anymore. High school and the university were straightforward, and I felt accomplished working in an investment firm after graduating. I may understand international finance, but none of my schooling prepared me to become the president and head winemaker here at Yinchuan."

"You're a smart woman, Lily. You'll figure it out. You always do."

"I just hope my father doesn't give up on me. I couldn't face him."

"He won't. Have a good trip. I'll see you when you get back."

As Lily watched Wei walk out of her office, she wondered if she could have him transferred to another division within her father's company. He was a bit like a puppy dog, always hanging around, looking for a treat and a pat on his head. They had dated briefly in high school, but she felt no attraction for him and let him know it. Besides, he wasn't that bright and he had a quick temper. Several times in high school he had been suspended for fighting. When she started running the winery, her father had insisted that she hire Huang Wei, the son of a loyal company executive. Family and business were everything to her father.

At the university, Lily had dated infrequently, preferring to focus on her studies. Although she was petite and not unattractive, she knew she would never receive attention from men for her looks alone. She'd never really tried to increase her appeal—not then, not now. Back then she had worn modern rectangular-framed eyeglasses and spent little time on her hair or makeup. She had a few forgettable dates during those years, but she'd suspected the invitations came only after her suitors learned of her father's power and wealth.

Lily returned her focus to her desk and its stack of papers. Soon she'd leave for the airport and board her father's jet for the five-hour flight to Hong Kong.

21

November 25th

Shanghai

Eric stepped from the China Eastern flight at 6:15 p.m. and into the Shanghai Pudong International Airport. He'd flown business class, which had made the nearly fourteen-hour flight almost tolerable. He hated flying.

After passing through immigration, where his new visa was authorized for a thirty-day visit, Eric and his single carry-on bag moved through Customs without a hitch. He found his way to the taxi queue and caught a ride to his hotel. Staring out the window of the small taxi during the hour-long ride into the city, Eric noticed the densely spaced houses and tenements passing by on either side of the car. He felt subdued and began to wonder why he'd considered this trip. Shanghai, with twenty-three million inhabitants, was the largest city in China and showcased the complexity of this emerging world power. With its financial, manufacturing, and military might, the country seemed unstoppable. Yet, he couldn't help but think of all the people, invisible behind those walls, living in such density.

His taxi finally arrived at a modern, glass-lined tower, which housed his hotel. The hotel catered mostly to business clientele and was located in the Bund, a few blocks from the famous promenade along the Huangpu River. Eric knew this part of Shanghai well, as he had stayed at the same hotel during his previous career selling airplanes. Lined with dozens of historical buildings, the area had once included numerous banks and trading houses from around the world.

Initially a British settlement, it was later combined with the American settlement to form the International settlement.

When he arrived at the hotel's front desk, Eric was required to relinquish his passport, which made him nervous. In his room he pulled out a journal that contained his notes from his last conversation with Ashley. He had written down the name and phone number of a private investigator who was highly recommended by her contacts at the FBI station in the U.S. Embassy in Beijing. This PI was known to be discreet and well-connected to government authorities in Shanghai. Eric dialed his number. Although it was late, around nine at night, he wanted to make contact right away.

"This is Jiao Ming. Who, may I ask, is calling?"

"Mr. Jiao, my name is Eric Savage. I just arrived in Shanghai. Your name and number were given to me by a friend with the FBI in the United States. I need some help."

"It's rather late, Mr. Savage. However, I've been expecting your call. Perhaps we can talk in the morning face-to-face."

"Yes, I would appreciate that," Eric replied.

"Tell me where you are staying and I'll meet you in the lobby, shall we say around noon? We can have lunch."

"Okay, how will I recognize you?"

"Don't worry, Mr. Savage, I will recognize you."

Eric gave him the name of his hotel and hung up the phone. Had Ashley notified Jiao Ming of Eric's plans to come to Shanghai? It would be like her to do so. He was extremely tired, but didn't feel like going to bed. It was one in the afternoon Seattle time, so his body clock wasn't ready for sleep. He decided to walk down toward the river to find a drink.

Eric walked out of the hotel and turned east down a side street toward the Bund, which he remembered was a few blocks away. Soon he found himself shoved along by fellow pedestrians and yelled at by bicyclists riding on the sidewalk. Moving along with the mass of people, he squeezed past dozens of squatting street vendors, selling everything from fake Rolex watches to strange-looking creatures deep fried on sticks. After passing through all of the pungent food smells and smoke, he arrived at Zhongshan Road, the majestic boulevard adjacent to the Huangpu River. Flowing from his right to his left, this busy waterway was filled with ships of all kinds, including dozens of small dilapidated wooden boats with laundry hanging from makeshift clotheslines. The Huangpu captured time and separated the old from the new.

Eric decided to return to one of his favorite places, the Long Bar at the Waldorf Astoria at number 2 Bund. The Long Bar, as it was aptly named, was at one time the world's longest bar. Measuring 110 feet in length, it was built as part of the Shanghai Club, the premier gathering spot for British men. The club's heyday was in the 1920s and 1930s. While placing his cheek on the unpolished mahogany bar, Noël Coward reportedly said that he could see the curvature of the earth. It was a haven for the rich and powerful *taipans* and bank managers living in Shanghai. Their place in society dictated their location at the bar: the higher their status, the closer they stood near windows overlooking the Bund.

As Eric walked the last block toward the bar, he remembered having conversations as a boy with his grandfather, who had served in the U.S. Navy on a gunboat. He recalled that the *USS Sacramento*, nicknamed the Galloping Ghost of the China Coast, had patrolled the Yangtze River in 1936. His grandfather, only twenty-four at the time, had told Eric vivid stories of shore leaves in Shanghai. One such leave included a brutal fight in which his grandfather almost died. Missing from the tale had been facts about whom he'd fought and why, but Eric suspected that the adventure involved some heavy drinking with other sailors. With the outbreak of war in the Pacific in 1941, the Shanghai Club was closed and occupied by the Japanese forces until the end of the war. The building was expropriated by the new Communist government of Shanghai in 1949 and converted into the International Seamen Club, which catered to foreign sailors.

Stepping into the bar, Eric took a seat near the windows and ordered a Scotch on the rocks. As he took his first sip, he admired the view of the river. He was thinking about the Shanghai his grandfather had encountered. In the 1920s, living in Shanghai would have been both exciting and dangerous as the excesses of the time—music, theatre, opium, prostitution, and gambling—gave way to fighting between the Nationalists, the recently formed Communist Party, and the Japanese. He took another long sip of his Scotch.

"Hello, may I join you?"

Eric turned toward the voice on his right and met the eyes of a beautiful Chinese woman, dressed in a traditional Shanghai garment known as a *Cheongsam*. The tightly fitting yellow dress, made from a floral pattern out of silk, had a slit in the fabric from her feet to just above her knee. Her long, coal black hair was in a tight roll on the back of her head and held in place by a comb.

"Of course." Eric stood, and offered the woman the high-back chair next to his. As she sat down, Eric admired the attractive and well-shaped leg that appeared as the slit in her dress parted.

The woman extended her hand and said, "My name is Grace."

Eric told her his name as they shook hands.

"Eric, I'm hoping you might help me with speak English. I sometimes like come to bar and find Americans like you for practice with."

Eric knew this was one of the oldest scams in Shanghai. First, it would be practicing English. Then they'd have a few drinks. Before long, she'd be asking him to pay an exorbitant bill, as one or two toughs waited nearby to enforce the transaction should he try to skip out. It usually wasn't about sex, although it could be, but about money, a national pastime in China.

"Sure, what would you like to talk about?"

"What do you do?"

"I'm a winemaker, visiting China while on vacation."

"Wine very popular in China. Especially red wine. It bring good luck."

"Yes, I've heard that. Most wine consumed in China is red."

The woman leaned toward Eric until her shoulder touched his. "Would you like to buy me a drink, Mr. Eric?"

Eric signaled to the bartender. "I'll have another Red Label, and she'll have—"

"I'll have Champagne."

Now Eric knew he was being set up. As he expected, a full bottle appeared. "Shall I open it?" the bartender asked.

"Sure," Eric said. He wondered where this was heading.

"Thank you, Mr. Eric."

"You're welcome. So what do you do?" Eric watched the Champagne flute filling with straw-colored liquid, its delicate bubbles rising to the surface.

"I work in an office and take English classes two nights a week. I hope to go to America someday."

"I hear it's hard to emigrate on your own. Are you married?"

"No, not yet. I would like to marry, but I haven't, how you say, find right man." Grace then put her hand on top of Eric's and said, "You married, Mr. Eric?"

"No, but I have a girlfriend."

Grace removed her hand and reached for her flute. A single jeweled ring on her middle finger tapped the glass as she picked it up. She took a sip and turned toward Eric. "Is she serious girlfriend?"

"Yes, very serious."

Grace finished the first glass and motioned for another. "I'm wondering, Mr. Eric, would you like to go to your hotel and practice English there?"

Eric studied Grace's mouth. Her red lips were full and turned down slightly. They begged to be kissed. *It all seems so obvious.* "Thank you, Grace, but no."

"You don't find me attractive?"

"You're very attractive, but I have a girlfriend."

"She lucky girl."

Eric nodded in agreement and raised his Scotch to his lips. He knew it was time to go. Exhaustion and the effects of the drink were starting to take hold. "I should go," Eric said.

"Let me go with you."

"No."

"You sure?"

"Yes."

"Miss Ashley lucky lady." Grace looked at Eric, smiling as a cat might before it ate the mouse.

Eric's forehead furled at the name. "How do you know her name is Ashley?"

"Don't worry, Eric. I'm with the FBI. Ashley and I are good friends. We met many years ago during classes at Quantico. She asked me to keep an eye on you in Shanghai." Grace reached down into her bag and produced her badge. Her full name was Grace Chin and her title was Special Agent, just like Ashley's.

Eric didn't know whether to be angry or to start laughing. "How did you know where to find me?"

"Jiao Ming called me after your phone conversation tonight. I had you followed to the bar and came here to meet you."

"Was it Ashley's idea to test me like this?"

"No, it was mine. I wanted to make sure this great boyfriend she's been raving about was trustworthy."

"What if I wasn't?"

Grace put her hand back on top of Eric's. "When I saw you sitting at the bar by yourself, I asked myself the same question. I'm not sure what I would have done."

Eric looked into Grace's eyes and thought about Ashley. "I do need to go. I'm getting tired and I expect a long day tomorrow."

"Here's my card. Jiao Ming is a trustworthy private investigator. The Agency has used him a number of times while I've been employed here. He's very discreet and resourceful. But if you find you need help, please call me."

Eric paid the rather large bill for the drinks and got up to leave.

Grace stood as well, and offered her hand. "Ashley's a great woman, Eric. Take good care of her."

Eric left the bar, laughing at the ploy. As he stood at the curb, he watched the mass of pedestrians with curiosity. The crossing signal still showed a red hand, yet herds of people crossed the street, oblivious to traffic. Cars ignored red lights, bikes swerved through traffic, and pedestrians dodged in-between cars, whizzing past them in every direction. Eric picked his way across the street along with the others, hoping for the best.

22

November 26th

Shanghai

The next morning, Tuesday, Eric sat in his hotel's lobby watching people come and go. After about fifteen minutes a trim-looking gentleman in slacks and a button-down shirt walked toward him. As Eric watched, he observed the subtle indication of a limp. The man stopped in front of Eric and said, "Mr. Savage?"

"Yes, and you must be Jiao Ming." Eric stood and they shook hands.

"Let's go have lunch. And please use my first name, Ming."

After arriving in the hotel restaurant, they ordered several dishes and drank some of the tea that had been placed on the table.

"So how may I help you?" Ming asked.

"First, I'm wondering if you have any official identification, perhaps a private investigator's license."

Ming opened his wallet and produced a certificate, issued by the city of Shanghai. "I don't blame you for being cautious, Mr. Savage. I can assure you that I'm legitimate."

"Thank you. Please call me Eric." Eric looked at the card and noticed that the English spelling of Ming's last name was Jiao. But when he heard Ming pronounce it, the name sounded like Chow. It was a quick reminder for Eric of *pinyin*, the official phonetic rules for transcribing Mandarin pronunciations of Chinese characters into Latin.

Eric then retold the events of the past several weeks and handed Ming copies of the business cards he had received from Luc DuPont. He explained that his wine was in a shipping container scheduled to arrive in the Port of Shanghai that day. "I want to follow the container and learn who stole my wine. I hope that will also help determine who murdered Jeff Russell."

Ming looked at the copies of the business cards and said, "You think this somehow involves Shanghai Star Industrial Group? They are a very respectable and well-connected company here in China. Even if we do find any evidence, it will be a challenge to get the authorities to take action without some irrefutable proof." After a pause, he added, "Are you aware of the nature of the Yinchuan division?"

"No, all I know is that Wei works there and insisted on buying my wine."

"The Yinchuan division is a winery and vineyard. It's located in one of the best grape-growing areas of China. The legend is that the Chairman of Shanghai Star Industrial Group traveled extensively while he was building his business. Over dinners and business negotiations with other corporate CEOs and politicians in Europe and Australia, he learned to appreciate good wine. As he grew older and richer, he saw that China's economic boom was raising living standards, so many Chinese could afford to purchase fine wines. Convinced that China could be first in anything, he thought the country should learn how to become a world-class producer of fine wines in an old-world style. He purchased several hundred acres of land near the city of Yinchuan in the Ningxia region. He even built a château there, which looks like it might have been lifted from France and dropped onto the high plains of China. I haven't seen it, but I heard no expense was spared in its design and construction."

"If Wei is the facilities manager at Yinchuan, then who runs it?"

"Now that's the most interesting part of the legend. The Chairman put his daughter, Lily Kwong, in charge."

"What does she know about winemaking?"

"Initially, not much. He assigned Lily to the job when she was twenty-six, about four years ago. She had received her master's degree from the London School of Economics, after graduating from Purdue with honors. She worked for an investment house in London for a time before her father asked her to become CEO of the Yinchuan winery.

Since then, she has studied winemaking and viticulture extensively in Europe and Australia. She has hired several traveling consultants, who give her advice. She is a determined young woman."

"I'd like to taste her wine."

"That can be arranged. But first we need to establish what we are going to do. Eric, have you thought this through? Have you considered just going back home?"

"Yes, I've thought it through. I'm sure it seems impulsive, but I won't rest until I figure this out. I doubt it was intentional, but the theft of my wine could destroy me financially. And if the same person committed a murder, then I'm right to find out who did it."

"I understand. Your sense of justice seems quite rare to me. I am willing to help you, but at my standard rates, of course."

"Of course. What are they?"

"For this type of work, I charge $125 per hour plus expenses. I'd like a retainer of $3,000 now, and we can settle the rest later."

"Fine, I'll get you a check tomorrow. So how do we get started?"

"Give me the shipping information, including the container number. Normally food products must sit in quarantine for at least a week before being released by Customs. But as I mentioned earlier, Shanghai Star Industrial Group is well connected. Since they also own the shipping line, it wouldn't surprise me if they are able to circumvent the normal procedure. I know someone inside the port who can give us regular updates on the disposition of the shipping container. Once it is released and removed by truck or by rail, we'll be on our own. We must be ready to leave on a moment's notice and simply follow it. I think we both know where it might be going."

As Eric wrote down the shipping information for Ming, he asked him, "What can I do until then?"

"Get some rest and see our beautiful city. The container will likely be off-loaded from the ship within twenty-four hours after arrival. They double cycle at the port, which means that the cranes move down the ship row by row, unloading then reloading, at the same location. The ship will then set sail for its next port of call within a day."

"One more day and I'll be over jet lag."

"Give me your mobile number. I'll text or call you with any updates. Check out of your hotel tomorrow morning and be ready to go. I'll pick you up at eight."

Eric jotted down his number and handed it to Jiao Ming. "Thanks, Ming. I appreciate your willingness to help me."

"I hope you get what you want, Eric. As you travel the city, beware of scams. Don't trust any strangers you haven't known longer than twenty-four hours. And watch out for people asking you to help them learn English. It's the most popular con in town."

"So I've heard. See you tomorrow."

Eric said good-bye to Ming and walked over to the concierge desk. When he asked for a recommendation for a shop selling wines made in China, the staff told him that Just Vines, a wine shop and tasting room not far from the hotel, was the best one around. Eric retrieved his coat from his room and headed out into the mass of people walking by the hotel. Wishing he had brought warm gloves and a hat, he put his hands in his pockets and started off in the direction of the shop. Located only half a mile away, it took Eric thirty minutes to wind his way through the traffic, bicycles, and pedestrians clogging all the surface streets. Fighting his way to the shop's front door, he nearly tripped over a man squatting on the sidewalk, selling what appeared to be cheap tablet computers. Eric was happy to get inside.

Entering the shop, Eric surveyed the long display cases of wines, organized by country of origin, and highlighted by placards indicating style: *fresh*, *smooth*, *rich*, or *special*. Some wines had multiple stickers indicating a combination of characteristics. Several smartly dressed, young Shanghainese men and women were also looking at wines, mostly those from Europe, Australia, and California.

"May I help you?" asked a male clerk in halting English.

"Yes, I'd like to sample some Chinese wines."

"Come with me to the tasting bar. Are you looking for something specific?"

"Do you have anything from Red Star Winery?"

"Yes, of course. They are one of our better-known Chinese wineries. Would you like to start with whites, or just try the reds?"

"I'll just try the reds, thanks."

The man went behind the bar and picked up a wine glass. He polished it with a towel and set it down in front of Eric. "We have a tasting fee of ¥120. Is that all right? It's refundable with purchase."

"Sure," Eric said.

"We have three Red Star wines available: a Cabernet Sauvignon, a basic Bordeaux blend made of Cabernet Sauvignon, Merlot and Cabernet Franc, and their best blend, the *Celestial Red*, which sells for ¥480."

Eric did the currency conversion in his head and figured the bottle was around $75 in U.S. currency.

"I'll start you with the Cabernet Sauvignon," the clerk said. He placed Eric's glass under a tap on the Enomatic system, which used nitrogen to keep an opened bottle of wine fresh for up to four weeks, then pushed a button. An automatically measured ounce and a half of dark wine filled his glass.

Eric examined the wine. When he first inhaled from the top of the glass, he discerned very little fragrance but didn't detect any faults. He swirled it and inhaled again. No improvement. In one sip, he knew he was done with that particular wine. It was thin and didn't have any real varietal character. Eric poured the remainder of the glass into the spit bucket, signaling he was ready to move onto the next wine. As he waited for the clerk to refill his glass, Eric asked, "What wines do your customers prefer?"

"Mostly those from France, Australia, and California. Our customers are just now learning about wine. We try to educate them about the varieties and styles that are available." He finished pouring the second sample and placed it on the counter in front of Eric.

"Do they buy mostly red or white wines?" Eric asked.

"Mostly red—about 90 percent more red than white wines. Chinese people think red is good luck. And they don't like cold beverages, so whites just don't sell. I don't think many appreciate that while the U.S. has become the leading wine-consuming nation, China has now surpassed the U.S. as the third-largest red wine-consuming nation. And Chinese love to buy Bordeaux."

Taking a quick inhale of the second glass, Eric detected a nose of ripe red fruit and some spice. The taste was a bit earthy, the mid-palate hollow, and the finish short. Still, it held out hope for the last wine, the *Celestial Red*. Eric took a few more sips before pouring the rest into the bucket.

Eric looked around the shop as the last glass of wine was poured. It seemed many people were buying one or two bottles of wine each. "I'm curious; do you have much trouble with counterfeit wines here?"

Placing the last glass in front of Eric, the clerk said, "Not in this store. We have several locations and our owners are very proficient at spotting fakes. It's at some of the smaller and less scrupulous stores, outside the main shopping areas, where you can find inexpensive knock-off bottles of French wine. Some people are just as impressed by the name as they are by the wine inside. I recently heard of an Australian winemaker who came to China for a conference. As he was walking through a wine shop, he spotted a display with one of his wines. The only problem was that no one had been authorized to distribute his wines in Shanghai. He looked at the bottle closely and detected some minor flaws on an otherwise excellent forgery of his wine label. And this was for a $300 dollar bottle of Australian wine."

"What about collector wines?"

"I could easily walk a few blocks and find a counterfeit bottle of Château Lafite for $160, while the real one might go for $8,000. Impostors take empty bottles of expensive brands and fill them with inexpensive wine. Here in China, an unsuspecting buyer might not be able to taste wine well enough to know it's fake. In fact, I've heard there are bottling lines afloat in Hong Kong harbor. You can pick a well-known label of your choice from a catalog. They print it up, and then you deliver a container of bulk wine to the barge with the bottling line. They bottle and label it right there. The importers then take the cases of wine to shore and distribute them at great profit."

Eric had heard some of these stories and wondered if they might contain clues as to why someone would steal his wine. Surely his brand wasn't recognizable and wouldn't justify creating a counterfeit. And if someone wanted to sell fake bottles of his wine, it made no sense to steal it. He had read about the bulk wine flooding into China. They could easily copy his label, buy some bottles identical to his, and fill them with the other stuff. Stealing his wine still didn't make any sense.

Eric tried the third wine. The color was dark ruby and the nose evident, but not very aromatic. The taste was balanced and full of dark fruit. He was surprised at the suppleness of the tannins and the dry finish. It was by far the best of the three he'd tried, but he still didn't think it great. Overall, he was impressed that the grapes were grown domestically and the wine showed solid winemaking skill. The Chinese were quickly learning to master the basics.

Eric paid the clerk the required tasting fee, thanked him, and left the shop. It was now about three in the afternoon and he decided to go for a walk along the Bund. The weather wasn't too bad, and he had nothing better to do for the afternoon.

After finding his way back to Zhongshan Road, where he had been the night before, he crossed over to the pedestrian walkway along the bank of the Huangpu River. He headed north among the throng of other pedestrians, squeezing past various carts selling foods and souvenirs, each featuring similar orange umbrellas. He admired the colonial buildings on his side of the river, constructed in various architectural styles, including Romanesque, Gothic, Renaissance, and Beaux-Arts. Across the river, he studied the newer financial district of Pudong, complete with modern skyscrapers rising into the smoggy sky above. Pudong, established as a Special Economic Zone in 1993, was once an undeveloped area of rice fields and old dockside warehouses. It now represented the financial strength of China. Eric especially liked the modern tiered-pagoda architecture of the Jin Mao tower.

Looking downriver, Eric saw the famous Waibaidu Bridge. He remembered his grandfather telling him the role the bridge played in the battle of Shanghai in 1937. Japanese occupiers were on one side, and the freedom of the unrestricted International Settlement was on the other. Bayonet-adorned Japanese soldiers demanded respectful bows from the Chinese as they crossed the bridge. Then with the attack on Pearl Harbor in 1941, the Japanese occupied the International Settlement, and their rule over the whole of Shanghai was complete.

Eric was considering a river tour when his cell phone starting ringing in his pocket.

"Eric, this is Jiao Ming. We need to move up our timetable."

"Why, what happened?"

"My friend who works for the Port of Shanghai gave me credentials to log onto its administrative services, and I've been tracking the container number you gave me. I just saw a notification in the logistics system that the freight forwarder has requested your container. It's scheduled to be unloaded and placed dockside late this afternoon. Once the request has been approved and scheduled, it could be just a matter of hours before the container is loaded onto a truck trailer and moved to the quarantine area. But there is a possibility it could bypass quarantine altogether, depending on the shipping manifest."

"What do we need to do?"

"I'll pick you up tonight around eight, and we'll drive over to the port. It could be a long night. You should go back to your hotel, pack, and check out. I'll meet you outside the lobby. Hope you brought some warm clothes."

"Okay, Ming, see you then." Eric headed off in search of a bank to have a check drafted from his account back home to pay Ming his retainer.

23

November 26th

Shanghai

Eric was standing outside the portico of the hotel at 8:15 p.m. when he saw Ming drive up in a dark blue SUV. Ming's vehicle had been made by Great Wall Motor Company, one of China's largest national auto manufacturers. It appeared to be about ten years old and had a few dents and scrapes. Eric picked up his bag and met Ming by the car.

"Put your bag in the back and we'll be on our way," Ming said.

"How far is it to the port?" Eric asked.

"About half an hour drive, depending on traffic."

The drive to the port was stressful, as Eric watched Ming avoid the occasional car coming at them the wrong way on a divided road. Eric noticed that some of the errant motorists had intentionally turned in their direction after crossing though a gap in the barrier.

"What are they doing?" Eric blurted.

"Typical Chinese driving technique," laughed Ming. "The multi-lane roads are divided by fences, separated by occasional gaps. Drivers don't want to drive far to find a proper intersection to make a U-turn, so instead, they just drive a few blocks in the wrong direction until they can cut through the barrier and start driving with traffic in the same direction. Saves time."

"Many accidents?"

"Not really, but you must remain vigilant. The other worry is Chinese drivers don't like to drive with their lights on. Combine that with pedestrians' tendency to wear dark clothing and cross in the middle of the road, and you have a real obstacle course. I think it's a bit like playing a video game. You just have to be alert."

"I'm glad you're driving."

"I always warn visitors not to drive at night." Just as Ming spoke, Eric watched several cars run through red lights at the next intersection, causing cars in their lane to slow down or brake to avoid collisions, even though they were freely moving along in the proper direction with a green light.

"Another time saver?" Eric asked.

"Yes, if drivers think they can make it across, they just ignore red lights, stop signs, and crosswalks."

Forty stomach-tightening minutes later, they pulled up to a road and stopped at the curb. Eric could see a well-lit area across the street which looked like a toll booth plaza.

"There's the port," Ming said.

"What's our plan?"

"Have you heard of GPS tracking?"

"Of course."

"We just sit here and wait until the container is loaded onto a truck." Ming took out his laptop and connected it to the port's wireless network and then logged into the logistics system. After a few clicks of the keyboard, he was soon presented with a long list of container numbers. He scrolled through the list and said, "There it is. It's been off-loaded and is now stacked quayside. It's in block fifty-six, bay four, row seven, tier three. That's too bad."

"What's too bad?"

"After the container is off-loaded from the ship by the quay crane, it's placed in a temporary storage area to await transfer by the straddle crane, a mobile crane that moves it among the rows of stacked containers for transfer to another area, a train, or a truck. Your container is stacked three high, which means it will be hard to reach from the ground."

"Why does that matter?"

"You're about to find out."

Ming pulled out his cell phone and dialed a number. He then spoke in what Eric assumed was Mandarin. After a string of high-pitched and rapid sounds that meant nothing to Eric, Ming hung up. Next, he reached around and pulled a small backpack from the row of seats behind them. Putting the bag in his lap, he zipped it open and pulled out a small plastic device. It measured about seven inches long, three inches wide, and an inch thick. He then reached in and pulled out a small tube of what looked like toothpaste.

"What's that?" Eric asked.

"This is an electronic identification tag. It's used for asset tracking anywhere around the world. Your military used these frequently on containers in Afghanistan. This particular model uses satellite phone technology to successfully transmit location data from anywhere. Other models use cellular networks, but coverage is spotty where I think we're headed. I felt having uninterrupted satellite coverage was best."

"That's it? It can do all that in a package that small?"

"Yes. The trick is going to be getting it affixed to the container."

"How are we going to do that?"

"I think you mean, 'How am I going to do that?'" Ming looked at Eric with a grin.

"Me!" Eric said.

"Yes, I can't go into the port. If I got caught, the authorities would be most difficult to deal with and would likely suspend my license. If you get caught, you'll get better treatment because you're American. Besides, you won't get caught."

"What makes you so confident?"

"My friend inside is pretty good. He should be here in a few minutes. What you need to do is use this tube of adhesive to attach the device to the top of the container. You have to make sure it is facing the sky. Just spread the adhesive on the base and press it onto the metal frame."

Eric studied the device and the tube of adhesive, doubtful that anything so potentially dangerous could be easy. "It looks simple enough," Eric said.

After a few more minutes of sitting in the car, Ming again reached around to the seats behind them and pulled out a thermos and some paper cups. He put two cups in the cup holder between their seats and filled them with a steaming hot liquid, which Eric assumed was tea. After putting away the thermos, Ming reached into the glove compartment and produced a leather-covered flask. He opened the top and poured a pale yellow liquid into his cup, paused over Eric's cup and said, "Would you like some brandy?"

"I'll pass," Eric replied.

"Suit yourself. It helps with the pain in my leg."

"I noticed you have a slight limp. What happened?"

"Some bad luck, I'm afraid. I was tailing someone for our mutual friends at the Embassy and he gave me the slip. I jumped over a fence, thinking he had gone over it, and came face to face with a rather surprised and angry-looking dog. I headed back the other way but before I could clear the fence, he had his jaws into my leg like a bear trap. I beat him off with my hands, but not before he'd damaged my tendon. The doctors tried to repair it, but I've had some sharp pain ever since, which causes me to limp when it's too intense."

"I'm sorry."

"It's all right. I was amply remunerated for the job and we finally caught the guy."

Soon a small sedan came out from the truck plaza and pulled up next to the curb behind their car. A smallish man in a security uniform got out of the car, slipped into the seat behind Eric, and closed the door. Ming and the man spoke in Mandarin for a few minutes while Ming referred to his laptop. Eric guessed he was reciting position information for the container. When they were done, Ming handed the backpack to Eric and said, "Good luck. Go with him and follow my instructions. You'll be fine."

Things were happening so fast that Eric didn't have time to grow concerned over what he was doing. He just got out of the SUV and into the car behind them. The security employee started the car and pulled away from the curb. As they approached the entrance to the port, the driver signaled Eric to crouch down in his seat. Eric could see out of the corner of his eye that they had approached a gate with a cross arm. He watched the driver swipe a passkey over the gate's front panel. As its arm swung upward, the car began moving again into the dock area. Eric wiped sweat from his brow.

The driver tapped Eric on the back, which Eric assumed was a signal that he could sit back up. He was amazed by what he saw. Stacks of brightly colored containers, sometimes six containers high, rose up on either side of him for as far as he could see. Eric noticed the man was driving on through the stacks without his headlights, prompting a near collision when a large straddle crane passed directly in front of them, carrying a forty-foot container in its frame. The crane had appeared suddenly from behind the stacks on the right and then disappeared behind the stacks on the left. The man continued driving the sedan several hundred yards before braking hard and turning to the left. He slowed down as he looked at Chinese characters painted on the ground. Eric assumed they were labels of positions on the quay. He referred to the notes he had written during his conversation with Ming and took a right into the next row and stopped. He gestured to Eric to get out of the car.

As they stood together looking at a stack of containers five high, the driver signaled to Eric with his fingers, lifting one at a time until three were opened, and pointed at the stack. Eric knew he was telling him that his container was the third one high in the stack. Eric studied the containers and didn't see an obvious way to ascend to the top to affix the tracking device. He tried to climb up on the locking bars on the door of the bottom container, but from there he didn't have a way to lift himself up to the second container. He jumped back to the ground. The man then signaled him with his hand to wait. Eric watched as he trotted off around the end of the row and out of sight.

As Eric waited, his body shuddered several times as his nerves began to take hold. He didn't like being left alone in such a foreign spot. In the distance, he heard what he thought was another straddle crane moving through the stacks of containers. Instead, a small vehicle appeared from around the corner and pulled up next to him. It was the driver, but this time he was operating a forklift, again without lights.

Eric noticed a wooden pallet was on the forks as the man signaled him to get on. He stepped onto the pallet and sat down. The man drove forward and turned the vehicle to face the stack. Soon Eric heard and felt the hydraulic forks begin to rise upward. When he was next to the doors of the third container, they stopped. Eric stood and removed the backpack and got out the tracking device and the adhesive. He quickly spread the gel on the back plate of the plastic housing and tried to reach up to the top of the container. He couldn't quite reach it. He signaled the man below with his hand, and the forks started going down.

Eric yelled, "Up, not down," motioning frantically upward with his hand. He'd forgotten the need to be quiet. The man understood Eric's signal and soon Eric was rising upward again. He came to a stop at a height near the top of the container. Eric put the device, adhesive side down, on the top of the container in the two-inch gap between it and the bottom of the next container in the stack. After firmly pressing it into place, he sat back down on the pallet and signaled that he was ready to come down. His stomach felt like it was rising into his chest as the pallet dropped back down at a fast rate, stopping inches from the ground. He hopped off and ran back to the sedan, relieved to be finished with the improvised elevator.

The driver quickly backed up the forklift and then drove it around the corner and out of sight. Within a few minutes, he came trotting back to the car and signaled Eric to get in.

They retraced their route through the containers and back toward the truck plaza. Eric hunched over again as they drove through the gate and back onto the street outside. He released an audible sigh of relief as they arrived back at Ming's car. While Eric returned to the passenger seat, the man jumped into the back seat behind Ming and started speaking with him in rapid Mandarin. Ming pulled a wad of money from his pocket and handed it to the man, who wasted no time getting out of the car and back into his own. Eric watched him drive back through the gate and back into the port.

"He said you did well," Ming said.

"I'm just glad it's done. Now what?"

"We wait."

Eric settled back into the passenger seat of Ming's car and glanced at the paper cup of cold tea, sitting in the holder. "If you have any more of that tea, I'd like a cup. And you can add some brandy, too."

Ming retrieved the thermos and refilled both of their cups. He then topped them off with his flask. Once that was done, he opened his laptop and checked if the transmitter on the container was working. Eric looked over and was elated at the sight of a flashing icon on the screen's map of the port.

"It looks like everything is working perfectly," Ming said. "According to the scheduling system, the container could be moved any time. Hmm, that's interesting."

"What?" Eric said.

"The last time I checked the site, the schedule request from the freight forwarder had an indication from the Shanghai Customs Authority that the container would have to go through quarantine. Now, it's unchecked."

"So you were probably right; Shanghai Star Industrial Group must have been able to expedite the release of the shipment."

"Looks like it. I'm not surprised."

Eric took a sip of his tea and appreciated the warmth of the brandy. He was beginning to relax. As he watched the truck entrance, he was amazed at the continual stream of trucks pulling containers into and out of the port. He had read somewhere that the Port of Shanghai handled 2.7 million twenty-foot equivalent containers annually. He did the math in his head and figured that if all the containers were forty feet in length, about four thousand containers per day traveled through the port via train, truck, or transfer to another ship. He'd never seen anything of such magnitude.

"If I were you, I'd take this opportunity to get some rest. If we're right and this shipment is headed to Yinchuan, we have a long couple of days ahead of us."

It was about 4:00 a.m. the following morning when Eric heard Ming say, "Wake up. The container is moving."

Eric looked over at the display on Ming's laptop and saw a flashing icon going slowly across the screen and leaving a trail of dots behind it.

"Here, take these binoculars and watch the truck plaza for the container number on the trucks as they come out."

Eric took the binoculars and every few minutes, as a truck came out of the plaza, he scanned the side of the container for its number. After six trucks had passed through the gate in a twenty-minute period, he said to Ming, "I think it's coming out now."

Eric saw a truck come through the gate and pull onto the street. It was unlike container trucks he'd seen in the U.S. The flatbed behind the cab was designed for one twenty-foot container and much shorter than those he was used to seeing back home. As it passed by, he confirmed that the number on the container was the same as the one carrying his wine. He felt excited to see it, suddenly aware that he was one step closer to figuring out what had happened.

"Let's go," Ming said. He started the car and pulled out behind the truck. In a couple of blocks, it went through a red light. Ming hesitated momentarily before deciding to follow the container through the intersection. Since it was so early in the morning, traffic was light. No cars came through from the crossing road.

"If he's driving to Yinchuan, he should follow this route," Ming said, handing Eric a map with a highlighted path through a maze of highways. "Nanjing is a little over three hours from here. We'll stop for breakfast there."

"What's Nanjing known for?" Eric asked.

"It's the provincial capital of Jiangsu and has a population of around seven million. It sits on the Yangtze River Delta and contains several economic zones where petrochemical, steel, auto, and electronics businesses are located. It used to be called Nanking. Sadly, it's remembered for the abhorrent occupation by the Japanese in December, 1937. Up to three hundred thousand civilians were killed in what has become known as the 'Rape of Nanking.'"

As they followed the container through the maze of highways, they were soon surrounded by farms and fields of crops, interspersed with small villages. Everything was quiet and few cars were on the road.

"I think it's time to talk about what's going to happen once we get to Yinchuan," Ming said. "Have you given that any thought?"

"Yes, I have. Let's assume that you are right and my wine is headed for Red Star Winery. I'm hoping that once we get there, we can figure out what they plan to do with it."

"Then what?"

"Go to the authorities."

"I'm not sure how helpful the authorities will be. Why should they take our word for any of this? In fact, how would they know that the wine is even yours? Do you have any proof? It appears it was easy for them to get your wine out of Customs—which tells me they have well-placed friends in the government. I think we need to put some external pressure on them. Otherwise, I don't see them cooperating."

Eric spent the next few minutes thinking about Ming's comments. He was right. He thought maybe Ashley, through the FBI, or his friend Scott, at the sheriff's department, might help in some way. He looked at his watch. It was about 5:00 a.m. his time, which meant it would be about one in the afternoon in Walla Walla. When they got to Nanjing, he would call Scott.

24

November 27th

Walla Walla / Nanjing

Sheriff Thompson answered his phone on the second ring.

"Hi, Scott," Eric said.

"Eric, is that you? Are you in China?"

"Yes, got here two days ago. I'm with the private investigator Ashley recommended. He's been very helpful."

"Making any progress at finding your wine?"

"We're at a truck stop in Nanjing and I can see the container holding my wine across the parking lot."

"Well done. What's your plan?"

"Jiao Ming is the private investigator. He knows that Wei and his father are well connected within the People's Republic of China. Because of their contacts, he suspects it was easy for them to have the container quickly released from the port. It wasn't even quarantined, which is required of most food products."

"I'd say he's right to be suspicious."

"With Wei being so well connected, Ming thinks we probably won't have much luck with the local authorities. We'll need some cooperation from someone higher up in the People's Republic of China."

"I agree. I've been thinking of talking to the Walla Walla Prosecuting Attorney to see if there is enough evidence to charge Wei with First-Degree Murder. If the prosecutor agrees, he'll request the court to issue a warrant. Since Wei is a non-resident Chinese national, I think the Justice Department and the State Department would become involved."

"Do you think you have enough evidence to establish probable cause with the prosecuting attorney?"

"Maybe, but it could be a bit stronger. I'll give him a call and see what he thinks. Can I call you back?"

"Yes. For at least the next day, we expect to be following the truck. Can you call Ashley and give her an update? I haven't spoken with her since leaving home."

"Of course. I'm happy to call Ashley anytime."

"No doubt. Thanks, Scott. Good bye."

Eric looked out at the gray sky and noticed drops falling on the car's windshield. He wished he were back at home in Walla Walla. As he stared out the window, the running lights of the truck and container switched on. Ming turned on the windshield wipers of the car. The wipers' electric motor made a rhythmic hum while the blades moved back and forth across the windshield, the container coming into and out of focus with each successive pass.

"It looks like we are about to get going again. Care to drive?"

"Sure." Eric got out of the car and changed places with Ming. He didn't have a Chinese driver's license, which could mean big trouble if he got pulled over, but he felt that risk was the least of his concerns. Once he and Ming were both settled in, Eric started the engine, engaged the manual transmission, and zigzagged past the other cars and trucks that were parked haphazardly around them. He pulled onto the highway behind the truck.

Eric decided to pass the time by learning a bit more about his companion. "Ming, did you grow up in Shanghai?"

"I was born there but then moved to Hong Kong when my parents fled the arrival of the Communists in 1949. My mother had been a movie actress in Shanghai in the thirties and my father feared the Communists would consider them to be counter-revolutionaries. I remember my father telling me frightening stories about the Canidrome."

"What's the Canidrome?"

"It was a greyhound racing track built in 1928. It held up to fifty thousand spectators, mostly Shanghai's Western cultural elite, for sporting events, like soccer, music performances, and other pastimes. When the People's Liberation Army marched into Shanghai in 1949, they outlawed gambling. The race track became part of the newly named Shanghai Cultural Plaza."

"What happened there?"

"Most official texts of this period have been censored, but the Communist Party held mass executions, sometimes as many as five hundred per day. My father told me the Shanghai police, along with the Communists, arrested twenty-four thousand Chinese in a single night and placed them in concentration camps on the outskirts of Shanghai. Those arrested included school-teachers, Christian religious members, non-Communist union leaders, property owners, newspaper workers, and students. My parents were lucky to escape."

While they spoke, Eric noticed Ming occasionally taking short sips directly from his flask, not bothering with the dilutive effects of hot tea. "So how did you get back to Shanghai?"

"I attended British schools in Hong Kong and did well on my final exams. I decided to enlist in the military. They valued someone with Mandarin skills and I showed aptitude, so I made a career out of it. After my parents died, the Chinese military offered me a position in the Shanghai Intelligence Division. The Cultural Revolution had passed and the country was opening up. I decided to go back to my home."

"You've experienced a history I've only read about."

"We were lucky. Surviving that period was tricky, and I've had a good life. After I left the Intelligence Division, I became what you might call a consultant. And that's how I met our mutual friends."

That was the end of the conversation about Ming's past. Eric sensed that Ming wouldn't volunteer much more. At least he now had a better understanding of the person whose fate was now tied inextricably to his own.

Eric and Ming drove for another ten hours, switching off driving duties, until they reached the town of Xi'an. They followed the truck and container as it turned into a large parking lot outside of town, near a motor lodge. Eric thought the hotel could have been one of many similarly boring and nondescript multi-story buildings, if not for what looked like half a decorative pagoda bolted onto the building's facade to provide a culturally authentic entrance.

"I think our driver is about to get some sleep and so should we," Ming said. "I will set the alarm on the tracking software to alert us if the truck starts moving again. Even if he gets a head start, we will know where he is. I'm quite sure that he's headed to Yinchuan. Let's give him a few minutes to get settled in and then we'll get rooms ourselves."

Walla Walla
Sheriff Thompson dialed Ashley Hunter's phone number at work.
"Special Agent Hunter," she said when she answered the call.
"Agent Hunter, this is Sheriff Scott Thompson of Walla Walla."
"Hi Scott, I'm so glad you called."
"I spoke with Eric earlier today and he asked that I get in touch."
"Is everything all right?"
"Seems to be. He's with Jiao Ming, the detective I believe you recommended. They are following the container of wine from the Port of Shanghai. Eric and Ming believe it's headed to Yinchuan, in north central China."

"What are they planning to do once the container reaches its destination?" Ashley asked.

"That's what Eric and I discussed this morning. We agreed it would be helpful in dealing with the Chinese government if there was an official request from the U.S. to arrest Wei for the murder of Jeff Russell. I contacted my prosecuting attorney and he didn't feel we have enough evidence to clearly substantiate probable cause."

"What do you have?"

"I have identified an employee at the hotel in Prosser where Jeff met with Wei. He can testify to seeing them together the afternoon of the murder. I have Jeff's notebook, which documents his meeting with Eric, followed by the meeting with Wei. We have the theft of the wine, but no evidence to tie its disappearance to Wei. And we have documentation indicating that Wei is the customer who will take delivery of the wine in China, but that's circumstantial as to the theft. We need evidence linking Wei directly to the murder—a weapon, fingerprints, or a witness."

"What about DNA? Did you test Jeff's corpse for the presence of any DNA besides his own?"

"Yes, the coroner's report did indicate the presence of foreign DNA, but I need a way to tie it to Wei and I don't have a sample."

Ashley thought for a moment. "There must be something."

"I agree, but I came up empty at the hotel and at the winery."

"It's too bad Melissa's boyfriend Kurt disappeared," Ashley said. "I suspect he'd be helpful." She went silent for a second before saying, "Scott, I think Eric and Ming will also need some evidence that the wine in the container was made by Eric. They have to deal with the Chinese authorities who won't cooperate without proof that the wine was stolen. Doesn't Wei have some paperwork that shows he purchased the wine legitimately from another source in Washington State?"

"Yes, but we believe it's forged. My deputy is researching the purchase and is contacting the winery that purportedly made the sale. I'm requesting that they submit an affidavit stating they've never sold wine to Wei."

"Good idea," Ashley said. "I'm going to do some research on my end and see if we can prove that the wine in the container that turned up in Shanghai is Eric's."

"Thanks, Ashley. I'll call you when I have something." Scott ended the call.

Xi'an

It was about 6:00 p.m. when Eric and Ming checked into the hotel on the outskirts of Xi'an. The experience was a bit of a fiasco as Eric realized the staff didn't speak English and kept asking for his passport and visa. Finally Ming came to his rescue and translated the request. As they waited, Eric took note of the electric self-playing piano in the lobby with its keys dancing up and down and the sounds of pop tunes like "Tomorrow," from *Annie*, and "Eye of the Tiger," from *Rocky III*, emanating from loudspeakers. After what seemed like a long wait, during which the front-desk staff was likely making copies of Eric's passport, Eric and Ming were finally assigned rooms.

On the way to the elevators, Ming said, "I think I'm going to turn in. It's probably fine to eat at the hotel if you're hungry. You'll stick out around here, so stay alert. Keep your phone handy in case I need to get ahold of you."

Eric and Ming said goodnight and entered their adjacent rooms. Eric threw his bag on the bed and surveyed the room. The air was stuffy, the bed hard, and the comforter thin and stained in places. It reminded him of some old budget hotels he had stayed at during college skiing trips. At least the floor looked clean. He grabbed a jacket and took the elevator back down to the lobby. He knew he wouldn't be able to sleep so he decided to go for a walk around town in the early evening.

At the front desk, he bought a map and a guidebook of the area, written in simple English. After some quick research, he decided to go see the historic wall around the old city and the ancient Wild Goose Pagoda. He also picked up a Chinese address card for the hotel, so if he needed a taxi back he could just give it to the driver. He headed out the door.

After walking for fifteen minutes, Eric arrived at the Pagoda. Built over a thousand years earlier, it was created during the Tang dynasty in 652 A.D. to store Buddhist texts and figurines brought back from India. Despite having been through several major earthquakes and a number of remodels, it remained an impressive structure. Next to it was a fountain described as the tallest in Asia. Its water rose and fell in concert with traditional instrumental music.

After spending half an hour admiring the Pagoda and the fountain, Eric walked on toward the wall. It had originally been built as part of the imperial palace of the Tang dynasty and then reconstructed by the Ming dynasty during the fourteenth century. As Eric sat nearby and read more about the history of the city, he learned that Xi'an was the starting point of the Silk Road and also home of the Terracotta Army of Emperor Qin Shi Huang. Had it not been closed, Eric would have gone to visit the collection as well.

Eric sat quietly and admired the wall. He considered his impressions of China. The guidebook said Xi'an had a population of eight million and was home to over one hundred universities. He'd heard somewhere that these universities produced up to three thousand computer graduates per year, most of whom found employment. Overall, China was producing undergraduates in science, technology, engineering, and math at the rate of 500,000 per year, compared to 150,000 per year in the U.S. Even though the official numbers might be inflated, Eric accepted that it was only a matter of time before China surpassed the United States as the greatest economic power in the world. Napoleon once wrote: *Here lies a sleeping giant; let him sleep, for when he wakes, he will astonish the world.* Eric knew that not only was China awake, it was poised to take center stage. He believed that as personal incomes rose and demand increased for fine wines, China would expand its domestic production out of necessity.

Tired, Eric took a taxi back to the hotel. The trip back was uneventful. He paid the fare and as he walked back inside the hotel, he noticed that the piano was still playing without a guest in sight. He took the elevator back to his room and wasted no time going to bed. Even the hard mattress didn't prevent him from falling asleep.

25

November 28th

Xi'an

Eric awoke disoriented, not realizing where he was. As he opened his eyes and looked around the small hotel room, it all came back to him. He was surprised to see light coming from around the cheap fabric curtains on the window. He looked at his watch and saw it was 8:30 a.m. He was surprised because the truck should have been back on the road then and Ming should have awakened him. He got up from his bed and looked out his window to see if the container was still parked in the hotel lot. It wasn't.

Eric pulled on his pants and rushed out the door and down the hall to Ming's room. He pounded on the door. No response. He started pounding again, then stopped and waited. Finally, the door opened a crack. Ming's face appeared and wore an expression of confusion. Eric pushed the door open and went inside. Ming stood motionless as Eric walked to the windows and pulled open the curtains.

"Look, the truck is gone," Eric said, agitated.

Ming walked over to the window and peered out as he rubbed sleep from his eyes. He looked startled and went over to his laptop. "I don't understand," he said. He typed on his keyboard. Clicking sounds pierced the room's silence. He studied the screen for a moment and then said, "It left at 6:43 a.m. I must not have heard the alarm from the tracking software."

Eric glanced around the room and noticed a decorative white ceramic bottle and a shot glass on the nightstand. He guessed Ming must have had a few drinks the night before and slept through the alarm. "What is that?" Eric asked, pointing at the bottle.

"Baijiu. It's liquor that has been made in our country for over five thousand years. It's the most popular beverage. This one is made from wheat sorghum and is distilled over many steps. I believe you would call it strong."

"You should take a shower and wake up. We need to go."

"Yes, sorry, Eric. I had bad pain in my leg again." Ming headed to the bathroom.

Eric poured a small amount of the clear liquid into a plastic cup he found on the dresser. He knew Baijiu was often used in ceremonies and state meetings. He took a sip and noticed the warmth of its alcohol. It tasted sweet—not at all bad. But what he really wanted was coffee. He left Ming's room, returned to his own, and took a hot shower. After dressing, he threw his clothes and toiletries into his bag.

Ming and Eric went downstairs to check out and when Eric finished, he fetched coffee for both of them from a self-service counter on the side of the lobby. He didn't care that the coffee carafe was almost empty and the coffee smelled burnt. He put two sugars and a small tub of creamer into each cup and then met Ming at the front door. "Come on, let's go," Eric said. He felt a sense of urgency which he could tell Ming didn't share.

"Don't worry, Eric. The truck is only about two and a half hours ahead of us. From studying the map, I think we should catch it before it gets to Yinchuan."

"How far is that?"

"About seven hours away. We'll make it."

Houston

Ashley was curious as to whether the FBI had any techniques on how to prove the authenticity of wine. After her discussion with Sheriff Thompson, she made some calls to the FBI's Science and Technology Branch. One of the Branch scientists told her that the lab had been involved in numerous investigations to determine the provenance of various food products and had even played a key role in the Chinese milk scandal of 2008.

The scientist explained that during the scandal, FBI scientists helped confirm accusations that infant formula manufactured in China had been adulterated with melamine, a chemical used in making durable plastics. Two Chinese conspirators were sentenced to death and executed after the government's investigation. Other food products the Branch had studied included orange juice and wine. At the end of the conversation, Ashley received the name and contact information for a scientist at a research organization in Western Australia who had pioneered the technology. After exchanging several emails, she scheduled a phone call with Dr. Simon Fletcher, the institute's chief scientist.

At 7:00 p.m., Houston time, which she calculated was 9:00 a.m. in Perth, Ashley made the call.

"This is Professor Fletcher. Is that Agent Hunter?"

"Yes, Professor, please call me Ashley."

"No worries, you may call me Simon."

"Simon," Ashley said, "I'm contacting you because I need your help in establishing the provenance of some wine produced in Washington that is now in China. I understand you can provide this type of analysis."

"Yes, we're a leading research institute in the use of technology we call 'wine fingerprinting.' Several scientists have taken some of our research and started a commercial lab. We are the provider of such forensic services to the Australian Federal Police. We've also worked with a number of other law enforcement organizations in Asia, and with Scotland Yard, your CIA, and FBI. Tell me more about your situation."

"I'm working on a case involving wine theft," Ashley said. "We suspect fifty-four barrels of wine were taken from the U.S. and transported by container ship to Shanghai. The container of wine is now being transported by truck. I have a detective on the ground following the shipment by car and once it arrives at its final destination, we plan to ask local law enforcement authorities to help prosecute the thieves.

However, to receive their cooperation, I believe we'll need proof that the wine actually came from the U.S."

"I think you're right to want proof," Simon said. "Do you have any idea why someone would go to the trouble of stealing this wine? It must be valuable. After all, bulk wine is readily available if they simply wanted some for a counterfeit bottling. I often see New Zealand and Australian wines offered in bulk for as little as four dollars per liter for ten thousand liters, freight included. Australia is now shipping over half its wine in bulk containers that have been fitted with 24,000-liter bladders. It makes good economic sense to recapture a third of a container's volume lost to bottles and cartons and then bottle the bulk wine nearer to where it's consumed. I was gobsmacked when I first found out how much wine is bottled illegally from such international bulk shipments."

"Why they stole the wine remains a mystery. That's another question we'll try to answer once we make contact with the principals in China. We believe the wine is headed to a Chinese winery in Yinchuan."

"Interesting," Simon said. "Well, I can try to help you, but I think it may be a bit tricky."

"Why is that?"

"To accurately fingerprint the wine, we need to have samples from the vines and soil in the region where the grapes were grown. We normally take samples from about eight plants over half an acre. For every vine, we sample at the surface then every ten centimeters down, to a depth of about seventy centimeters. We measure the concentration of metals in the soil and determine the extraction of these metals by the vine."

"I don't understand," Ashley said.

"What we do is measure the concentration of any number of elements in the wine. We've been mostly working with sixty elements, all stable isotopes. We then use mass spectrometry to analyze the presence of these elements in the wine. We've used this technology on wine and even tea. If a tea is labeled 'Darjeeling,' for example, we can identify the actual tea garden from which the tea was taken. That helps us identify fakes. Same with wine, but there is a problem in your case."

"Which is?"

"We have been building a database of vineyards here in Australia for some of our more popular growing regions, like Margaret River and Yarra Valley. We are working on collecting data from several hundred sites in Western Australia. For this to work in your case, we'd need vineyard samples from the area where the grapes were grown for your wine."

Ashley's heart sank and her mind started to race. "Simon, I think there is a slight chance that we might be able to come up with something. I know there is a viticulture research facility in the grape-growing region around the winery. It's possible that they would have soil samples from around the area. If you can give me a description of what you need, I can try to get in touch with one of the soil scientists there and see if they have built their own database of vineyard samples."

"Where did you say your wine was produced?"

"Washington State—in a town called Walla Walla."

"Oh yeah, now I remember. I think I might know the bloke that runs that research facility. It's part of one of your large universities over there. In fact, he worked and studied in Australia for many years and he would easily understand our processes. There's something else we're going to need to perform the analysis."

"What is that?"

"We'll need a sample of the wine from the winery there, certified as to its origin, and then a sample of the wine that is now in China. That way we can demonstrate that they are indeed from the same source."

"Simon, you've been very helpful. Once I receive the list of the datasets you need, I will start working to acquire the plant data and samples."

"Good on ya, Ashley. I'll email the dataset definitions to you by the end of the day. Let's tee up another call after you find out if the data is available."

"Thank you."

"Cheers."

On the road to Yinchuan

Eric and Ming took turns driving. Like most interstate highways in the U.S., the divided highway was multi-lane in both directions in the cities and with limited, sometimes dangerous, uncontrolled access in the rural areas. Eric frequently found himself speeding along the highway, faster than the posted limit, expecting that cars waiting to enter the highway would wait until he was clearly past them. He often had to slam on the brakes, or quickly move to another lane, to avoid a collision. The other challenge was slowly moving farm equipment. Ming just chuckled at Eric's occasional burst of profanity.

Ming continually checked the GPS position of the container on his laptop and after four hours, he determined that they were closing in. With luck, they'd catch up with it well before Yinchuan. Eric hoped the driver would soon stop for lunch. Before long, Ming mentioned the container had stopped a short distance ahead. In half an hour, they arrived at a small industrial area with a truck stop, including a gas station, hotel, and restaurant. Eric looked ahead and saw the container parked ahead on the right in a large paved lot.

"Let's stop and eat," Eric said.

"OK, but I think we should probably get food to go. He may leave at any moment."

Eric got out of the car and immediately reached for his jacket. The landscape was arid and a cold breeze blew. Looking down the road, he saw a mountain range in the direction of Yinchuan. As Eric and Ming walked across the parking lot, Eric was surprised to see that the restaurant was a McDonald's. He was curious to find out what was inside.

"I feel sort of dumb going into an American fast-food restaurant," Eric said.

"Believe it or not, McDonald's is viewed as having healthy food because of the industrial processes they use. Most Chinese believe the chain's food is safe from spoilage and contaminants. Local restaurants are viewed a bit more warily."

Inside, they joined the line of customers. Eric eyed the menu, which included a number of usual items, as well as some regional foods he thought he'd try. With Ming providing the translation, Eric ordered what looked to be a pork wrap with cabbage and rice in a green tortilla, a bowl of Miso-like soup, some French fries, and a Coke. As Ming ordered his food, Eric looked outside the restaurant's large windows, which faced the parking lot, just in time to see the container pull onto the highway.

Eric nudged Ming and said, "Look."

"Let's get our food and go," Ming said.

They headed back to the car with their containers of food. Ming drove while Eric began to eat. The food tasted great because he was so hungry, having missed both dinner the night before and breakfast that morning.

As they crossed over the mountain pass, Eric was impressed by the view of the valley below. The Yellow River ran through the city of Yinchuan and the Helan Mountains rose up behind it. Terraced crops carved into the sides of the mountains looked like random layers of earth-colored steps. The contrast was striking, between the muted colors of the desert and the green trees and brown winter crops of the valley below. Ming continued driving faster than the speed limit, passing cars at a frenetic rate, until he spotted the container ahead of them near the bottom of the hill. They pulled in behind it and slowed down. Eric peered up at the top of the container and could see the GPS unit that he'd installed only thirty-six hours earlier. That night of riding the forklift seemed long ago.

"I'm positive he's going to the winery," Ming said. "It's at the bottom of the pass and down by the base of the Helan Mountains, about a half hour away. We'll find out soon."

After turning off the main highway, the truck followed several local arterials and then turned onto a long paved road. As they followed the truck in the fading daylight, Eric observed a large masonry wall and cast-iron gate come into view ahead. What he saw next startled him. It was a large château of a scale and design that suggested it could have come straight from the Loire Valley of France.

The gate at the front of the château's property appeared closed and the truck turned to the right onto an access road. As Ming followed in his car, Eric continued to stare in awe at the château. He saw that it even featured its own *jardins du château,* complete with a long linear pond and a fountain with two bronze-winged horses spraying water high into the air. The road turned back left, as if they were following the layout of a large rectangle. They followed behind the truck and along the fence for about a mile. On either side of the road were rows upon rows of dormant grape vines and trellises. The vines were covered with soil to protect them from damage by the cold winter weather. Finally, the truck turned left around the fence at the back of the property. Ming pulled off the road as the truck pulled up to what appeared to be a delivery entrance. The truck sat for a few minutes until a man walked up, looked at some paperwork, and then waved the truck in.

Ming pulled back onto the road and drove slowly past the gate. To their left, they could see a large flat building, two stories high, with a loading dock and what Eric immediately recognized as a crush pad, where grapes were processed during harvest. Inside he expected they'd find the usual array of harvest equipment like a press, fermentation tanks, and barrel storage. Ming drove past the gate and pulled over to the road once they were out of direct sight of the building.

"What do you want to do now?" Ming asked.

"I want to see what they do with my wine, but it doesn't look easy to get in," Eric said.

"I agree. I noticed security cameras along the walls. Given that it's near the end of the day, do you think they'd actually do any work tonight?"

"I don't know," Eric said. "I think the first thing they'd want to do is empty the container and rest the wine, to see what kind of shape it's in. We're pretty sure they added sulfur dioxide when they took the wine. Sulfur dioxide acts as a preservative and antioxidant. When the sheriff's detectives surveyed the crime scene, they found enough empty chemical packaging for the thieves to have added about twenty-five parts per million. Since the wine didn't travel through hot weather, I assume it's in pretty good shape. I'd like to smell and taste it."

"I don't think we'll do any tasting tonight. Too risky. Come on, let's walk back to the delivery entrance."

After leaving the car and walking several yards back toward the gate, they could see through to the crushed gravel lot that ran to the back of building. The truck was backed in until the container nestled up against the loading dock. They watched as the driver uncoupled the truck's cab from the flatbed trailer holding the container. After removing a few fittings, he cranked down the legs on the trailer so it would stand on its own when the cab pulled away. "He's planning to leave the container behind," Ming said. "They won't empty it tonight."

A man came out of the building, climbed down some metal steps, and walked toward the driver. He appeared to be short and powerfully built like a football running back. While Eric continued to watch the activity in the gravel lot, Ming began searching through his coat pockets. Eric saw the stout Chinese man take a clipboard and sign several pages. He handed them back to the driver, who returned to the truck, climbed inside, and started the engine.

"Come on," Ming said, "he's leaving." They walked together toward Ming's car and as they approached it, Ming handed Eric a folded piece of paper. "Take a look at this."

Eric got back inside the car and stared at the piece of paper. At the top of the page was a photo of the man he immediately recognized as the one signing papers near the loading dock. Below the photo was information about him, including his name and title. At the bottom of the page was an official-looking symbol of the FBI office in Beijing.

"Where did you get this?" Eric asked.

"From our friends at the Embassy," Ming said.

According to the report, the picture was of Huang Wei, who was Facilities Manager of the Yinchuan Division of Shanghai Star Industrial Group.

Eric looked up from the paper just in time to see a small pickup truck with flashing emergency lights pull up in front of Ming's car and stop, blocking their path. Two men dressed in security uniforms got out and approached their car. Eric was relieved to see they only carried batons and not guns.

Ming instructed Eric to remain quiet until he directed him to talk.

26

November 28th

Yinchuan

Eric and Ming got out of the car as the security guards approached. The older guard started speaking to Ming in Mandarin. Eric had no idea what was being said as the guard started pointing at him. The other guard walked slowly around Ming's car, surveying the interior through its windows. Eric thought about what was inside the car and couldn't come up with anything worrisome.

"Eric, please show this man your passport," Ming said.

Eric reached into the back seat of the car to access his travel bag. The younger guard watched him intently. He returned to where Ming and the older guard were standing and handed it over. The guard flipped through it and stopped at the page with his Chinese visa and entry stamp. He seemed satisfied, but then pulled out a cell phone and took photos of several pages of the passport. Eric felt uneasy as the guard handed it back to him.

The guard directed a few more stern comments toward Ming before motioning to his companion it was time to leave. Both guards returned to their truck and got in. They backed up, made a U-turn, and drove away.

"What was that all about?" Eric asked.

"He wanted to know why we were here and why we were watching the winery," Ming said.

"What did you tell him?"

"I said you were a friend from the United States, liked wine, and wanted to see a Chinese winery. He made sure I understood that this is private property, and off-limits to the public after business hours. He said if you want to see the winery, you should take a tour."

"That's actually a great suggestion," Eric said.

"I agree. He said the first one is at ten in the morning. He said he'd put your name on the reservation list."

"Why did he want to see my passport?"

"Standard procedure," Ming said. "Chinese officials want to know the whereabouts of foreigners, especially if there is any suspicious activity."

Eric and Ming got back into the car.

"It's almost dark, so I think we should go find a hotel," Ming said. "You should take the tour tomorrow and see what you can find out. For now, we should just keep a low profile."

"What do you think he's going to do with my passport information?" Eric asked, worried about the possibility that Wei might be made aware of his chance meeting with the guards.

"They will likely file a report with the local police department. I wouldn't worry about it."

Instead, Eric immediately started to worry about the encounter. The last thing he wanted was for Wei to know he was in China. It had been the first bit of bad luck in a successful trip, thus far.

Ming drove them into town to find a place to stay for the evening.

Port Angeles

Kurt Hughes was spending the last of four nights on the Olympic Peninsula at the Royal View Motel in Port Angeles. According to an advertisement in the local paper, the accommodations were "perfectly adequate" and "at a good price." As for the view, he could only see the parking lot through his room's window. With his imagination, he could visualize Vancouver Island twenty miles across the Strait of Juan de Fuca, the body of water that separated the U.S. from Canada and connected Puget Sound to the Pacific Ocean.

He'd stayed close to the hotel while in Port Angeles, even though the room was a bit depressing. The comforters were shabby and the microwave oven looked ancient. At night, he frequently heard the ice machine next door dispensing ice with a loud rattle as it cascaded into plastic buckets. He spent his time drinking cheap beer and watching too many reruns of *Murder, She Wrote* and *Everybody Loves Raymond*, which were occasionally punctuated by the sounds of moaning and grunting coming through the thin walls between the motel's rooms.

The day before the heist at Eric's winery, Kurt had stolen a set of Oregon license plates off a car he'd spotted in a long-term parking lot in Walla Walla. He then put them on his car because he felt they would give him cover for a few days while the police looked for him. He'd also packed most of his belongings from his rental house in Walla Walla and planned to stay away for a while. He actually thought he might never return. After leaving the winery with his envelope of cash, he'd driven over to the Seattle house of a friend, who had agreed to let him lay low for a while.

The next step in his plan made him the most nervous. Since Kurt wanted to go to Canada, he had found someone in Seattle to provide him with falsified identification in the form of an enhanced driver's license. Washington residents could travel into Canada with such a license or with a passport. He had purchased the authentic-looking license in Seattle for three thousand dollars before leaving for Port Angeles.

Now in his Port Angeles motel room, Kurt reviewed his plan for the following morning. He would take only one bag of possessions and walk onto the morning sailing of the Black Ball Ferry Line's *M.V. Coho*, a ferry that crossed to Victoria twice per day. He'd leave his car behind on the streets of Port Angeles. Since it wasn't worth much, he wasn't concerned about the loss.

At around eleven that evening, Kurt sat on the bed and drained the dregs of his last can of beer. He decided his preparation was done. Now he needed only to wait until morning. He tossed the empty beer can in the direction of the recycling bin, overflowing with dozens of cans just like it. The airborne can bounced off the heap with a clank and fell onto the floor, taking a few other cans along with it. He didn't care. He decided to buy another six-pack. He grabbed his keys and walked out the door, stumbling as he stepped over the threshold.

Kurt got into his car and drove along Highway 101 to the outskirts of town, toward a small liquor store he'd been frequenting during the week. As he left the city proper, he didn't notice the stop sign at the intersection ahead. Fortunately, no cars crossed through the intersection from the side street as he drove through. Less fortunately, a Washington State Patrol officer, driving along the highway in the opposite direction, witnessed the infraction. Kurt didn't even notice the patrolman make an abrupt U-turn, illuminate his emergency lights, and pull in behind him. It wasn't until Kurt weaved his car into the parking lot of the liquor store and parked that he noticed the flashing lights of the patrol car.

Kurt squinted in the rearview mirror and saw an officer get out of the patrol car and walk toward him. After some fumbling, he located his wallet and rolled down his side window. As the officer shone a flashlight in his face, Kurt's dulled mind suddenly registered that he had a big problem—his new forged driver's license was back in the motel room, and his wallet contained his legitimate license with his legal name.

Houston

On the morning after her conversation with Professor Fletcher, Ashley searched online to find contact information for the Director of the Department of Viticulture and Enology at a large public university in Washington State. Realizing he wouldn't be in his office yet, as it was only 7:00 a.m. there, she sent him an email requesting him to call. She next turned her attention to her inbox where she noticed an email from Professor Fletcher in Perth. He had sent her the viticulture dataset required for the analysis they had discussed. Glancing at her watch, she calculated that the time in China was 11:00 in the evening. She really wished she could speak with Eric. Well no, she wished they were both back in Hawaii sitting on the beach—or better yet—in his hotel room…

The shrill ring of Ashley's phone brought her back to reality. The Director of the Viticulture and Enology program was calling to tell her that he typically came into his office early and had seen Ashley's email right away.

She spoke with him for about fifteen minutes. She explained her interest in wine fingerprinting and asked him if he might have any soil data from the vineyards where Eric had sourced his fruit. She read him a list of the vineyards for Eric's Eagle Cap blend, taken from the winery's website.

The director was confident he had data from some of the vineyards she'd read from the list, but not all. He was familiar with Professor Fletcher's research and surmised that with only a subset of vineyard data, Professor Fletcher could ascertain a match between the wine in China and a sample from Eric's winery in Walla Walla, provided they knew the blend fractions. When Ashley asked him to explain what blend fractions were, he described them as the percentages of varietal wines, such as Merlot, Cabernet Sauvignon, Cabernet Franc, and Petite Verdot, that had been used to construct the blend. He asked Ashley to send him the dataset definition, along with Professor Fletcher's email address, and promised to have one of his graduate students find whatever data they had and forward it to Professor Fletcher by the end of the day.

As she thanked the director and ended the call, Ashley felt a shot of energy—a typical response for her as she made progress on a case. Over the years, it was what kept her motivated, despite all the routine and rather mundane paperwork in the Bureau. Once she had worked for seventy-two hours straight on a case, filling in clues like a jigsaw puzzle, until she uncovered critical financial records required to break up an organized identity theft ring in Sudan. The thrill of the chase had kept her going without sleep or food.

Ashley's next step was to call Melissa and ask her to send a sample of the Eagle Cap blend to Professor Fletcher. Melissa confirmed there was some remaining wine, wrote down the shipping address, and promised to get it out that day. Noting that Melissa's attitude on the phone seemed rather brusque, an observation she chose to file away for the moment, Ashley decided to call Sheriff Thompson to bring him up to date and find out how close he was to issuing an arrest warrant incident to Jeff Russell's murder. She also hoped he might have some news about Eric.

When Ashley called Sheriff Thompson's office, she was told that he had been called away and she should contact him on his cell phone. When she tried that number, he didn't answer. She left him a message asking that he call her back.

Somewhere over Washington State

Sheriff Thompson sat in a small twin-engine plane flying from Walla Walla to Port Angeles. At 2:00 in the morning, he'd received a call from the shift supervisor at the Clallam County Sheriff's office in Port Angeles, informing him of the arrest of Kurt Hughes two hours earlier. During the flight, Scott considered his strategy.

The shift supervisor told Scott that a state patrol officer had observed Kurt driving through a stop sign outside of town. The patrolman initiated pursuit and observed Kurt driving erratically before pulling into the parking lot of a nearby liquor store. When the officer made contact with Kurt, he detected the smell of alcohol. The officer had Kurt perform a field sobriety test which Kurt failed. He then arrested Kurt for driving under the influence of alcohol. Kurt was taken to the Clallam County Sheriff's Office where he voluntarily submitted to a Breathalyzer test. The test confirmed a blood-alcohol level above the legal limit. Following standard procedure, Kurt was searched, photographed, fingerprinted, and booked into the Clallam County jail, with his car impounded. He was offered a phone call, which he declined.

After the arrest, the shift supervisor had checked the state patrol's *persons of interest* register. Law enforcement agencies commonly used the phrase "person of interest" to identify people involved in a criminal investigation, without using the legal terms of suspect, witness, or accused, as those terms might imply an unsubstantiated level of involvement. Scott had listed Kurt as a person of interest in the burglary of wine from Eric's winery. After seeing a listing for Kurt Hughes, the shift supervisor had called Scott at home.

Upon learning that Kurt was awaiting arraignment in the Clallam County jail, Scott arranged for use of a Washington State Patrol airplane. The plane, which had been ferried to Walla Walla from Spokane earlier that morning, was now taking him to the far western side of the state. Scott was in a hurry because the shift supervisor had said he would only be able to keep Kurt in jail for a short period. Once he was arraigned and had posted bail, Kurt would be free to leave while awaiting trial. Scott knew the arrest represented a huge potential break in the case. As he carefully considered what strategy to take with Kurt, the plane began its descent.

After Scott's plane landed at the William R. Fairchild International Airport in Port Angeles, a Clallam County sheriff's officer drove him to the jail and courthouse complex. Within fifteen minutes, Scott was standing at the shift supervisor's station. He was in luck because the deputy prosecutor had not yet been able to locate an available district court judge for the arraignment proceeding. Scott was then escorted to the holding area and led into a small conference room. He and the shift supervisor spoke for a few minutes. The shift supervisor reported that while searching Kurt, they had found a key to the Royal View Motel, where he was presumably staying. The motel was located on a bluff, above the waterfront and ferry dock. Scott asked if he could read a copy of the booking report, which he hoped would include an inventory of any items Kurt had on his person at the time of arrest.

Nodding, the shift supervisor went to a filing cabinet and opened a drawer. After thumbing through it for a few minutes, he withdrew a file and handed it to Scott. As the shift supervisor watched, Scott opened the file and scanned the report. Just as he'd hoped, he found a section entitled "Personal Possession Inventory." It contained a list of items found on Kurt's person: the aforementioned motel key, some car keys, various coins, a cell phone, and a nylon wallet that contained the rest of the items on the list: currency, assorted credit cards, a library card, a driver's license, and a small slip of paper with the characters CNNU183784422G1 written on it. Scott was curious about the number and wondered what it referenced. He wrote the code down in his notebook and returned the file to the shift supervisor. After returning the file to the cabinet, the shift supervisor escorted Scott back to the conference room and asked him to wait.

In about five minutes, the door opened and an officer escorted Kurt into the room. His street clothes were rumpled, and judging by his red and swollen eyes, it looked as if he hadn't slept much. His tousled hair, stubbled face, and sullen demeanor added to his pathetic appearance.

"Mr. Hughes, I'm Sheriff Scott Thompson from the Walla Walla County Sheriff's office."

"What do you want?" Kurt's face had registered no surprise at seeing Scott, suggesting he had been told who he was and why he was there.

"I'd like to ask you a few questions about some events in Walla Walla two weeks ago. First, I need to tell you that you have the right to remain silent, and that anything you say will be used against you in court. You have the right to consult with an attorney and to have that attorney present during questioning. If you cannot afford an attorney, one will be provided at no cost to represent you. Do you understand each of these rights as I have explained them to you?"

"I'm not talking to you," Kurt said defiantly.

Scott repeated the question. "Do you understand each of these rights as I have explained them to you?"

"Yes."

"Do you know Eric Savage?" Scott asked.

"Look, I don't need to talk to you. You just said so."

"Mr. Hughes, I'd just like to know where you were on the night of November 5th."

Kurt's jaw set. He glared at Scott. "I want an attorney."

"Mr. Hughes, we're just having a conversation here. If you are involved in a burglary and theft, then charges will be brought against you. But that's not my main interest. I want to identify and charge the person responsible for the murder of Jeff Russell. I think you can help me. I can't guarantee it will make a difference, but if you will work with me, I promise to address the court on your behalf and ask that your cooperation be considered at sentencing. Trust me, I've been at this a long time, and I'm confident that charges will ultimately be filed against you. The facts are out there somewhere; sometimes it just takes a while to uncover them."

"Guard!" Kurt shouted.

Kurt and Scott sat quietly for a moment, until the conference room door swung open, and a guard appeared.

As Kurt stood to leave he said, "Sheriff Thompson, I'm in jail for a DUI, nothing more. I don't need to talk to you." He followed the officer out the door and turned down the hallway.

Scott followed them out the door and returned to the shift supervisor's station. "When is he going to be arraigned?"

"In about thirty minutes. The judge is finally available and the prosecutor has a deputy on the way. Mr. Hughes signed an affidavit stating he doesn't have funds to hire a private attorney, so a public defender will be assigned by the judge. On duty for the court's session today is Neal Becker, the attorney who will likely be assigned to Mr. Hughes. I expect he could be out of here within the hour. He'll need a bail bondsman."

"Can I attend the arraignment and address the court?" Scott asked.

"Sure, but it's really up to the Deputy Prosecuting Attorney. Head down to the Clallam County District Courthouse, and you can brief her. Follow the signs outside."

Scott walked along the sidewalk until he found the courthouse. It was a little after 1:00 p.m., and a cool and damp fog chilled him. He buttoned up his coat as he walked. He glanced at his cell phone and saw that he had a message from Ashley Hunter. He decided he'd return the call after he finished in court. In the meantime he sent a text message to his deputy in Walla Walla, requesting him to research the meaning of the number he'd found in Kurt's wallet.

Inside the courthouse, he found the Deputy Prosecuting Attorney outside the court room. After introductions, Scott explained his interest in Kurt and asked that he be permitted to speak before the District Court judge assigned to hear preliminary motions that day. "No problem," she said. "Let's go." They walked into the courtroom, which was in session, and Scott took a seat on the bench behind the prosecuting attorney's table. He only had to wait a few minutes before the judge reached Kurt's case in his docket. As expected, Kurt was assigned to public defender Neal Becker and given a few minutes to confer with the attorney. They then approached the bench on one side, with the Deputy Prosecuting Attorney on the other.

During the arraignment, Kurt acknowledged his name, address, date of birth, and confirmed that he understood the charges against him, namely of driving under the influence with a .14 level of alcohol. When the judge asked for a plea, Kurt responded, "Not guilty." Upon entering Kurt's plea, the court set a trial date of February 15th. The court ordered Kurt to be released pending trial, upon posting of a $1,000 bail. After the paperwork was completed, the Deputy Prosecuting Attorney announced to the judge that Sheriff Scott Thompson of Walla Walla County was in attendance and would like to address the court.

"Welcome to Port Angeles, Sheriff. What's your interest in this case?" asked the judge.

"Your Honor," Scott said, "Mr. Hughes is a person of interest for a crime that was committed two weeks ago in Walla Walla."

"What's the nature of the crime?"

"Burglary and theft of wine valued at over $500,000, Your Honor."

"Have any charges been filed in the case?"

"No, Your Honor. Our investigation is ongoing. We have been trying to locate Mr. Hughes since the crime was reported, and we have been unable to locate him at his home in Walla Walla. I came over this morning, having been notified of his arrest. I'm hoping to speak with him, with his permission and that of his attorney. As a condition of his release, I'm requesting that he not be allowed to travel outside the state. Mr. Hughes should be counseled that travel to Canada is prohibited for persons with either a DUI charge or conviction. He'll be turned away."

"Request granted," the judge said.

She turned her attention to Kurt. "Mr. Hughes, Sheriff Thompson is correct about travel to Canada. It would be a grave mistake to attempt it. They have little tolerance for driving under the influence up there." The judge amended the conditions of Kurt's release per Scott's request.

The judge then addressed Kurt. "Mr. Hughes, you are free to go upon posting bail while awaiting trial. Until then, you are not to leave Washington."

"Thank you, Your Honor," Scott said. The arraignment was over in about five minutes. Scott watched as Kurt was escorted from the courtroom and back to jail, where he'd presumably arrange for bail and be released. The judge then called the next case in her docket.

Scott left the courtroom and located Kurt's public defender, who sat on a bench browsing through some file folders. "Mr. Becker, may I speak with you for a moment?"

"I have another case in a few minutes. What do you need, Sheriff?"

"I need to speak with your client, Kurt Hughes. I met with him briefly over at the county jail before his arraignment, and I read him his rights. He refused to talk to me without his attorney present. I thought maybe the three of us could have a quick conversation."

"He did the right thing in refusing. What do you want to speak with him about?" Becker continued to flip through his files.

"As I just mentioned, I'm investigating a burglary and theft of valuable wine in Walla Walla a few weeks ago. I think Mr. Hughes has some information that might be helpful."

"Is he a suspect in either the burglary or the theft?"

"I consider him to be a person of interest. He may have been involved; I'm not sure. But my primary interest is related to a murder that occurred prior to the burglary and theft. I believe Mr. Hughes knows who may have committed it."

"Why do you think that?"

Scott recited the relevant facts and the events surrounding the murder, burglary, and theft. He also explained that two individuals, including a private detective, were following a container of wine that had left Seattle and was now in China. That container had been consigned to the suspect in the murder.

"So if my client was involved, I assume you'll charge him with burglary and theft? What about the murder?"

"I don't believe he was involved in the murder. The timing doesn't work out. I think Mr. Hughes was involved with the suspect after the murder. If he can show he was elsewhere at the time of the murder, then clearing him will be straightforward. As for the burglary and theft—given his clean record, I think any sentence handed down after a guilty plea would be manageable, especially if he cooperates with me."

"I don't see any reason why he shouldn't at least hear you out. Let me take care of this next arraignment, and I'll meet you over at the jail."

Scott was pleased with the interaction. The public defender seemed to have an open mind. If only he could get Kurt to see it his way! He walked back to the jail in weather that could best be described as awful. The gray fog had given way to curtains of pelting, cold rain. He was glad he lived on the drier side of the state.

Back inside the jail, Scott only had to wait fifteen minutes before Mr. Becker arrived. He spoke with the receptionist to arrange a meeting room for the three of them and ask that he be permitted to speak privately with Kurt first. Scott agreed and took a seat outside in the lobby. Just as he sat down, his cell phone chimed, indicating a new message had arrived. He pulled his phone from his overcoat and read the message:

The number you sent is in the std. format used to identify shipping containers. I checked our records & it's the same number of the container that we tracked on the ship from the Port of Seattle to Shanghai. The first 4 letters, CNNU, indicate it's owned by China Intl Container Leasing in Shanghai.

Scott smiled broadly as he read the message. He knew he had Kurt right where he wanted him. A few minutes later, he was invited back into the same room where he'd sat earlier with Kurt.

"My attorney says I don't have to talk to you, but he suggested I listen," Kurt said.

"Mr. Hughes, I believe you've ended up involved in something that you might now regret. I've looked at your record, and I don't see a pattern of breaking the law. I can only assume you made a mistake, and now you're on the run."

"The only mistake I made was falling in love with a woman who didn't love me," Kurt said. "My judgment has been screwed up ever since."

Scott had suspected as much. He had heard from Eric that Kurt and Melissa were in a relationship, but Eric didn't feel it was one that was very important to her. "What do you know about the removal of wine from Blue Mountain Cellars?"

Mr. Becker looked at Kurt and shook his head, advising Kurt not to answer the question. Kurt remained silent.

"Do you know Huang Wei?"

Kurt looked nervous and started pulling at his hands, then glanced at his attorney. "Do I have to answer?"

"Sheriff Thompson," Mr. Becker said, "I'm going to advise my client against answering any questions. Unless you have direct evidence that he was involved in a crime, I think we should wrap this up."

"Mr. Hughes," Scott said, "I think you were present the night wine was stolen from Blue Mountain Cellars. Furthermore, with your expertise in winemaking, I think you helped Mr. Huang remove the wine from the premises. In this state, burglary in the second degree and theft of property valued in excess of $5,000 are each Class B felonies, subject to a prison term of up to ten years, or a fine of up to $20,000, or both. While I think the burglary and theft were terrible offenses, and could put Mr. Savage out of business, my main interest is in the murder of Jeff Russell, which occurred a few days before the theft. If you can document your whereabouts during the time of the murder, I think you will have a solid defense against a charge of murder."

"Murder! I didn't have anything to do with murder. Jeff Russell was my friend." Kurt's voice trembled as he leaned toward Scott and spoke. His hands pressed hard on the tabletop, and his fingers turned white.

"I don't think you did, either," Scott said. "But I also think you would be better off cooperating with me than continuing to run."

Kurt remained silent. Mr. Becker said, "Is that all?"

"One more thing," Scott said. "Right now, a private investigator and Eric Savage are in China, tracking a shipping container that we believe contains the wine removed from Mr. Savage's winery. It turns out that container bears a serial number identical to one written on a piece of paper found in your wallet after your arrest last night. I believe it won't be long before we have proof that Mr. Huang is in possession of the wine, and you'd better hope that when we apprehend him, he doesn't turn on you."

Kurt fell back in his chair, an expression of shock covering his face as the full impact of the situation hit home.

Scott reached into his pocket and pulled out a business card. He handed it to Kurt. "Call me if you change your mind about cooperating." He stood up to leave.

"Sheriff, may I have a moment with my client?" Mr. Becker asked.

"Take your time," Scott said. He left the room.

Within a few moments, both men emerged from the conference room. Mr. Becker said, "Mr. Hughes declines to cooperate at this time. We'll be in touch if he changes his mind."

"I think you're making the wrong choice, Mr. Hughes," Scott said. "It's only a matter of time before all the facts come out. You'll be better off if you cooperate now."

Kurt and Mr. Becker walked back toward the lobby. Scott watched from the conference room doorway. He assumed that Kurt's mind was likely spinning from the conversation. He hoped that when the spinning stopped, he would cooperate.

Kurt posted bail and signed discharge papers committing him to appear in court on February 15th for his trial. The bail bondsman offered Kurt a ride back to his motel, so Kurt could pay the bond premium. When they arrived at the Royal View Motel, Kurt asked the bondsman to wait in the car while he ran inside to get the money. After he entered the room, he walked over to the small sofa in front of the television and removed one of its cushions. At the base of the padded back of the sofa, he felt for the twelve-inch cut in the fabric that he had made with a small penknife the night he'd checked in. Sticking his hand into the slit, he found and removed the large envelope of cash given him by Wei. He pulled out twelve 100 dollar bills and threw the envelope in the dresser. He went back down to the street and paid the bondsman for the bail and his fee, thanked him, and went back to his room. After he closed the door, he flopped onto his back on the bed, facing up toward the ceiling, and covered his face. He couldn't believe what was happening to him. How could he have been so stupid the night before as to drive in search of a few beers? He could have just as easily walked.

Kurt looked at his cell phone. It was ten minutes past 1:00 p.m. The last ferry for Canada was scheduled to leave at 2:00 p.m. He had fifty minutes to board. Sheriff Thompson's comments had stunned him. Eric Savage was in China? Why? What did Eric have to gain by such a bold move? Next Kurt worried about Wei, who he knew couldn't be trusted. He accepted that he was in a serious mess and faced only bad choices—all because of misguided feelings of love towards Melissa, feelings that were never reciprocated. Had he really loved her, or had he simply craved the unobtainable? It really didn't matter now. He'd felt rapture the nights he was lucky enough to share her bed. Now it hardly seemed worth it.

Five minutes later, he jumped up from the bed and started packing his bag. He took documents with his legal name on them and stuffed them deep inside. Then he took his falsified driver's license and put it in the see-through window of his wallet. He looked around the room to make sure he hadn't forgotten anything. Confident that the room was cleared out, Kurt picked up his car keys, placed them on the top of the nightstand, and walked out the door.

Kurt walked hunched over, in the miserable rain, from Second Street down to Lincoln and then onto E. Railroad Avenue. Ahead, he saw the 341-foot long *MV Coho* tied to the dock. Cars were loading through large doors at the boat's stern. He picked up his pace until he arrived at the ticket office. Kurt felt his chest begin to tighten as he stood in line waiting to buy a ticket. A quick glance at the wall clock reassured him he still had twenty minutes before the ship sailed. When his turn at the window came, he paid the seventeen-dollar fare for walk-on passengers and received his ticket. The clerk looked at his identification and told him to have it ready for inspection in the departure lounge. He then walked out the rear door of the ticket office and followed the pedestrian pathway across the auto lot to the departure building.

As he walked across the lot, Kurt recalled the events of December 14th, 1999, when Al Qaeda terrorist Ahmed Ressam arrived in Port

Angeles at 6:00 p.m. after crossing into the U.S. from Canada on the last ferry of the day from Victoria. As Ressam received standard questioning in the auto arrivals area, an alert U.S. Customs inspector became suspicious of his behavior when he was non- cooperative. The inspector ordered a secondary examination of his car, and they discovered bomb-making materials in the trunk. Ressam had been planning to detonate a bomb at the Los Angeles Airport on New Year's Eve to mark the new millennium. He had been captured not more than forty feet from where Kurt was now walking, all because of suspicious behavior and a falsified driver's license from Canada.

Kurt's stomach tightened as he passed through the double doors leading into the departure building. The floors of the industrial-style building were fashioned of poured concrete. Steel beams and an exposed air duct crisscrossed the ceiling. He hung back near the entrance and pretended to admire the collection of historical photographs hanging from the building's interior walls. One photo recorded the keel of the *MV Coho* being laid in drydock in 1959. Others captured old steamships, plying the waters of Puget Sound. Kurt eyed the long line of passengers, waiting to board the ferry, kept in place by a red rope. At the head of the line, serious-looking U.S. Customs and Border Protection officers examined travel documents and occasionally looked inside bags. In a few minutes, while Kurt continued to look at photos and watch the rest of the room through his peripheral vision, he knew he'd soon have to get in line. He was now among a handful of passengers remaining to be screened, and the ship would sail in just ten more minutes.

Kurt counted only four passengers left in line. He considered his options. He was confident that his new identification would get him into Canada. But what would he do after that? How long could he survive on the money Wei had given him? Maybe a year? It all depended on how frugally he could live. And what about getting a new job? How hard would that be? And what if Sheriff Thompson was right, that he would ultimately be implicated in the burglary and theft? What about getting back into the United States? Kurt's apprehension increased as he watched the final few passengers clear security and pass out of sight through the back of the room and into a passageway that presumably led to the boarding ramp for the ship. A Customs agent waved him forward and said, "Son, if you're departing on this sailing, you'd better hurry."

Sweat broke out on Kurt's forehead, and his heart began to pound faster. Abruptly, Kurt turned around and went back out through the double doors and into the pelting rain. With his bag in hand, he quickly crossed the auto lot and headed back toward the ticket office. He was shaking from the anxiety he experienced at the security checkpoint. His stomach lurched into his chest. Almost staggering now, he passed through the glass door, out of the weather, and into the ticket office. He put his bag down and looked back toward the ship. The loading doors were closing. He almost felt a sense of relief at the sight. He picked up his bag and turned toward the street door of the building. He was shocked by what he saw next: Sheriff Thompson and a Clallam County Sheriff's Officer stood by the exit, watching him intently.

Scott walked up and put a hand on Kurt's shoulder. "You made the right decision, Mr. Hughes. Let's go talk."

The three men walked outside and climbed into a Clallam County patrol car parked on the street. It was only a four-block drive back to the county courthouse and jail complex. Scott requested use of the conference room and escorted Kurt inside.

"Mr. Hughes, I'm going to go back to the courthouse and find your attorney, Mr. Becker. He'll want to talk to you first and be present while I question you. I'm glad you decided not to get on the ferry. I had a hunch you might try to go to Canada, but I think you were smart to stay here and face up to what happened."

It took forty-five minutes before Scott and Mr. Becker returned to the conference room. In private, Mr. Becker advised Kurt to discuss only the burglary and theft, not the murder. He then invited Scott to join them.

"I know I'm in trouble for stealing Eric's wine, but I had nothing to do with Jeff Russell's murder," Kurt said.

Scott set up a voice recorder, switched it on, and took out his note-book and a pen. "Tell me what happened the night wine was removed from Eric Savage's winery."

Kurt explained how he broke into the winery that night, using a key he'd copied from Melissa without her knowledge. He entered her security code on the keypad, having memorized it while watching her enter the same code during trips together to the winery. He then described Wei's arrival in a car, followed immediately by a truck carrying a shipping container.

"When did you meet Mr. Huang?" Scott asked.

"Not until that night. We'd only spoken by phone before then," Kurt replied.

"Then what happened?"

"I pumped wine from many barrels into the shipping container. It took several hours."

"Did Mr. Huang pay you for your help?"

"Yes, he paid me fifty grand."

"Did he give you cash?" Scott began to have an idea.

"Yes, he gave me a large manila envelope with money inside. He told me not to talk about it with anyone and sort of threatened me."

"Threatened you, how? What did he say, as far as you can remember?" Scott asked.

"He said I had to leave the area and if I spoke with anyone, he'd find me."

Scott imagined that Wei was instrumental in convincing Kurt that he should flee to Canada. "What did you do next?"

"Wei had me worried, so I drove to a friend's house in Seattle and hung out there for a while. Then I drove up here where I've been for about a week. Man, this is a boring place." Kurt leaned back in his chair and frowned.

"So what did you do with the money?"

Kurt reached for the duffel bag he'd brought with him into the room. "It's in here," he said. He lifted the bag up onto the table top and opened it. He then removed a large manila envelope that Scott quickly noticed had been opened at the top with a knife, leaving the flap and its adhesive intact. Kurt dumped the bundles of tightly wrapped 100 dollar bills onto the conference room's table.

"Is all fifty thousand there?"

"No, I've spent about five thousand on bail, a forged driver's license, and expenses since leaving Walla Walla."

"I need to enter this money and the envelope into evidence," Scott said. "Please don't handle it again." Scott planned to bag it to avoid any additional contamination.

"Are you going to arrest me?" Kurt leaned back in his chair, with a look of resignation. His face had returned to a normal color and his features had softened.

"No, my main interest is in finding Mr. Huang and charging him with murder if I can prove his guilt. As my investigation concludes, I believe the prosecuting attorney will file charges against you in connection with the burglary. You have my word, however, that I will work with him and the court to make sure your cooperation is taken into consideration at sentencing. You know you also have to face the DUI charge."

"Yeah, I know." Kurt's face fell flat and he looked defeated. After staring at the desk, he glanced up at Scott and asked, "Why did Eric go to China?"

Scott remained silent. He found it interesting that Kurt had asked the question, and wondered if he was feeling some sense of regret.

"Tell Eric he needs to be careful," Kurt said.

"I'm sure he knows."

"Tell him I'm sorry. I was angry. It was a dumb mistake." Kurt started pulling at his hands again.

"Mr. Hughes, cooperating with me was a great decision. You can get through this and then start rebuilding your life."

Before releasing Kurt, Scott wrote down his contact information, instructing Kurt to inform him of any changes in his whereabouts and to check in weekly. Kurt said he planned to go back to Walla Walla to see if he could get his old job back. He knew it wouldn't be easy, but he was willing to give it a try.

Scott watched Kurt as he walked out of the conference room. While Scott had seen many criminals over the years, it always struck him as tragic when someone let their emotions cause them to make bad choices. Whatever had gone on between Kurt and Melissa, Kurt had to let it go. Scott was somewhat optimistic though, and he truly believed that with some hard work and a willingness to accept what he had done, Kurt could recover. However, from his past experience, he felt there was a fifty-fifty chance that Kurt would commit another crime.

After Kurt left, Scott arranged for the State Patrol's plane to fly him back to Seattle. He planned to take the evidentiary envelope of money to the State Patrol's lab located there and have any DNA samples analyzed and recorded into the Combined DNA Index System (CODIS). If Wei's DNA was found on the envelope containing the money and could be successfully profiled and matched to the foreign DNA found on Jeff Russell's body, Scott was confident the Walla Walla County Prosecuting Attorney would have enough probable cause to charge Wei with murder and seek an arrest warrant from the Superior Court. For Scott, it had been a successful day.

27

November 29th

Yinchuan

At 7:30 a.m., Eric's cell phone rang. He didn't recognize the interior of the unfamiliar hotel room. After locating and answering his phone, he smiled at hearing Ashley's voice.

"Hey, good morning," Eric said. "What time is it there?"

"Five thirty in the evening here in Houston. How are you?"

"I'm fine. Sorry I haven't called. We've been a little busy." Eric sat up in bed and ran his hand over his face. His long pajama pants and T-shirt were heavily wrinkled, and he thought they smelled stale. As was his habit when he woke up, he wished for a cup of coffee.

"How's the detective working out?" Ashley asked.

"Jiao Ming? He's been a great help, but he's a bit of a character. I'll tell you more another time. We followed the container for a few days to a winery here in Yinchuan. We arrived late yesterday afternoon. I'm heading over there this morning to take a tour and look around the winery. Hopefully I can find a way to get into the production area and taste my wine. I'm confident I'll recognize it, though I'm not sure how I'm going to get inside. I'm hoping the tour will give me some ideas."

"You need to be careful," Ashley said. She wished she were there with him. Not just to see him, but to protect him.

"We have been careful," Eric said. He knew Ashley didn't believe him. "I liked your friend Grace," he added. He was curious to see if Ashley knew of the evening at the Long Bar in Shanghai.

"I hear Champagne is expensive in Shanghai," Ashley quipped.

"Your surveillance is far-flung, Ashley," Eric laughed.

"Grace is a good friend who was watching my back. She approved of you 100 percent, but said I'd better keep an eye on you. She found you pretty tempting."

"Glad I passed the test," Eric said. "Now tell me why you called."

"I want to give you an update on a couple of things. Scott had a breakthrough in the burglary of your winery, and there's a way we can prove to the authorities the authenticity of your wine in that container. I've found a research institute in Perth, Australia, that can scientifically match a sample of your Eagle Cap blend to a sample from the shipping container. Melissa is sending a sample from your winery, and I need you to get a sample from the container. Ship it overnight, if possible, to the facility in Perth."

"I think getting the wine will be challenging," Eric said. "Huang Wei, the man Scott suspects of murdering Jeff Russell, was by the loading dock and signed for the container after it arrived. We were stopped by some private security guards at the winery as we looked around. They took photographs of our passports and then left us alone. If Wei finds out I'm here and accompanied by a private investigator, he won't be happy."

"I suggest you get a sample of the wine and get out of there as quickly as possible."

"I agree. What's up with Scott?"

Ashley gave Eric an abbreviated version of the circumstances surrounding Kurt's DUI arrest in Port Angeles. She highlighted the discovery of the shipping container's identification number in Kurt's wallet. "Eric," she said, "Kurt confessed to helping Wei with the burglary and theft of your wine. He was there that night."

"That's what we suspected. But why do you think he did it?"

"Scott believes it was because Kurt held a grudge against you over your relationship with Melissa."

"But I don't have a relationship with Melissa," Eric protested.

"That's not the way Kurt saw it. And honestly, Eric, I'm not sure that's the way Melissa sees it. Scott thinks Kurt was jealous of you. But that's not important now. He is cooperating, and Scott has evidence from Kurt that might contain some of Wei's DNA. It's now being analyzed at the Washington State Patrol Lab in Seattle. We should know more in a few days. If there is a match with the DNA sample from Jeff Russell's body, then Scott will ask the prosecuting attorney to file murder charges against Wei and obtain an arrest warrant in conjunction with the murder of Jeff Russell. That's another reason you need to get out of there. If Wei gets wind of the warrant, he might become even more dangerous."

Eric couldn't get his mind past the comment that Kurt was jealous of him. He thought back to the dinner at his house and remembered how Kurt had stormed out in anger. He wondered what transpired between Melissa and Kurt after they'd left his house together. Although he viewed his relationship with Melissa as platonic, perhaps others perceived it differently. He wondered if Ashley suspected a romantic relationship between them as Kurt had?

Remembering Ashley's request, Eric said, "I'll try to get a wine sample today and ship it to Australia. Please text me the address."

"I'll send it after we finish our call. Eric, be careful. Do you think this detective, Jiao Ming, knows what he's doing? Can he keep you out of trouble?" Ashley had heard only good things about Ming, but still, Eric wasn't trained in self-defense. If they ran into some tough guys, she knew Eric would be at a big disadvantage.

"We'll be fine as long as I can keep Ming sober," Eric said. "I think he has a slight drinking problem."

"What do you mean?" Ashley hadn't heard about this trait in the detective.

"I think he self-medicates for pain from some old injuries. He's fine. We'll be okay." Eric didn't feel as confident as he tried to sound.

"Let me know when you get a wine sample sent to Perth. I'll call you if I hear anything else from Scott regarding an arrest warrant. When it's issued, the FBI office in Beijing will assist the local authorities. I miss you, Eric."

"I miss you too, Ashley." Eric had frequently thought of Ashley during the quiet hours of the drive across China. He concluded that the only way their relationship could work would be if they lived closer to each other. He knew Ashley's children and his winery posed a challenge to a possible change in location. "We need to talk about us when I get back. I've been doing a lot of thinking."

"So have I, Eric. Houston and Walla Walla are too far apart. Yes, let's talk about it when you get back. I love you. Bye."

Eric hadn't missed that this was the first time Ashley had said she loved him. Eric's own feelings had strengthened while in China, and he wished he'd responded in kind before Ashley had ended the call. He sat on the bed for a minute, taking stock of his own feelings for Ashley. He did love her. Vowing to tell her the next time they spoke, he took a shower and got dressed.

Afterward, he went down to the lobby where he found Jiao Ming eating breakfast in the hotel's restaurant. Eric sat down and ordered some coffee. Ming appeared tired. He wore a rumpled suit, his eyes were bloodshot, and his face looked like it hadn't been shaved for a couple of days. Eric assumed he'd been drinking again. Eric got up and went to the buffet and prepared a plate of typical Chinese breakfast foods, including soup made with fried tofu and cellophane noodles; *congee,* a plain rice porridge; salted duck eggs; and, pickled vegetables on the side. He couldn't wait to get back to Walla Walla and his favorite breakfast of pancakes, scrambled eggs, and bacon.

"Ready for the winery tour?" Ming asked.

"Honestly, I'm ready to finish this adventure and go home." Eric's thoughts were elsewhere, focused on Ashley, Melissa, and Kurt. He had to forget them and concentrate on the day ahead.

"I imagine you are. Not many tourists explore this part of China. It must feel very foreign to you," Ming said.

"I'm enjoying seeing China, but I'm more concerned about Wei and the winery. I spoke with my FBI friend in Houston this morning, and she's requested that I get a sample of wine and send it to a laboratory in Perth, Australia. They should be able to prove the authenticity of the wine and that it came from my winery. But I'm not sure how I'm going to get a sample until I get inside and survey the building."

"We need to leave for the winery in ten minutes to arrive in time for the ten o'clock tour. Let's discuss it in the car on the way over," Ming said.

After paying the check, they returned to their rooms to grab their coats. They met outside by the car and Ming drove them back to the winery. "I assume security is tight inside the winery. You'll probably get to see public areas, but I'd be surprised if they let you onto the production floor."

Eric agreed. "By now they will be unloading the container. I hope I can see into the production area and determine what's going on. We may have to get in through the loading dock where we watched the container arrive last night. Given how quickly they came to ask us questions, they must have been monitoring the video cameras you saw on the fence."

"Just take the tour and size up the place. It lasts an hour. I'll drop you off and then return to pick you up in front. Do you have your phone?"

"Yes," Eric said.

Ming dropped Eric off at the circular driveway near the winery's front entrance and drove off. Eric walked inside where he filled out the requested information and paid for the tour, a refundable amount if he chose to purchase wine in the tasting room. As the other members of the tour milled around the foyer, Eric noticed that he appeared to be the only non-Asian. Because the tour's commentary wouldn't be translated, he was given a recorded narration in English to listen to as he walked around the various buildings.

Prior to starting the tour, the group was shown a short video presentation inside a small theater off the winery's entrance. English subtitles highlighted the success of the winery, which had shipped over forty-five thousand cases the previous year, and won many awards. With over ninety-five acres of vineyards under management, the vineyard produced Cabernet Sauvignon, Merlot, Cabernet Franc, and Chardonnay grapes. It was explained that red wine is a symbol of good luck in China. While a narrator discussed the winery's achievements, the video featured an aerial view of the remarkable French-style château, surrounded by verdant green vineyards and nestled against the nearby Helan Mountains. The video switched to an interview with Red Star Winery President and Head Winemaker, Lily Kwong. Eric remembered the story Ming had told him about her ascent to the head winemaking position. Some of the clips in the interview recorded her speaking perfect English, and the subtitles changed to Chinese characters. In her comments, Lily attributed her dedication to making Red Star Winery the best winery in China to lessons she had learned from her father, the Chairman of Shanghai Star Industrial Group. With over seventy wineries in the region, and more planned, Lily said she faced many challenges, but was confident of her success. From the video it was clear to Eric that Lily was very passionate about her work.

After the house lights went up, Eric and the rest of the tour members were escorted outside the theater to begin their tour. Their first stop was the château. A replica of traditional Renaissance architecture, its design integrated the styles of a number of châteaux in the Loire valley of France. The design included an abundance of masonry with four traditional bastion towers at its corners and multiple chimneys piercing the roofline. The interior of the building was mostly modern, except for a grand staircase designed in the shape of a double helix and built of marble, roped off and not accessible to the public. Eric's recording stated that Chinese architects borrowed heavily from the Leonardo da Vinci-designed staircase found in the sixteenth-century Château de Chambord at Chambord, Loir-et-Cher, France.

Eric surmised the upstairs area included guest rooms and offices. On the main floor were a number of richly appointed spaces, including a large dining room and an industrial-style kitchen, complete with French flat-top stoves and old fashioned ice boxes with large pull handles on the doors. A great room finished the floor.

After exiting the château, the group went into a building that housed a large private tasting room. It contained four tables in rows, each seating seven people. Each seating position featured built-in sinks with water taps for swirling, sipping, spitting, and rinsing. Next door to this room was a large wine library that likely housed thousands of bottles of wine, including all of the vintages ever produced at the winery. Eric hadn't yet seen the production area, but was already awestruck by the size of the investment that had gone into the facilities.

His anticipation grew as they passed through a tunnel to another building. Eric assumed they would finally get to see where the wine was made. After taking an elevator from the tunnel up a few floors, the group entered a hallway and passed a door with a security keypad on it. Several employees entered this door as the tour group passed by. He also noticed all the employees wore photo badges, and video cameras were stationed to provide visibility of the hallways and door. At the end of the hallway was a long viewing area with floor to ceiling windows. It looked down into the production area. Eric was amazed by what he saw below.

The two-story room was at least ten times as big as his winery. Along one wall were six stainless-steel tanks, almost reaching the top of the two-story building's ceiling. Ranging along another wall were additional stainless-steel tanks, sitting below a half-height platform, with grape destemmers on top. It was clear the winery had been designed to provide gravity feed processing, whereby grapes, as they arrive from the vineyards, are emptied onto sorting tables on the crush pad outside of the building. Leaves, loose stems, and bad clusters are removed by hand; the clean fruit falls onto a lift conveyor belt before being carried up to an access point on the side of the building. Once the grapes arrive inside, they fall into one of the many mechanical destemmers. After processing in the destemmer, grapes and juice flow by gravity into tanks on the floor inside the winery where they begin fermentation. No mechanical pumps are required, which is desirable as pumps could be rough on grapes.

Eric assumed there was probably another floor below the viewing area where juice could flow down into barrels for aging. He'd only read about leading edge winery designs such as this one. He looked around the building awhile longer, until he noticed some open shipping doors leading to the crush pad outside and the loading dock beyond. He saw that the container truck was parked outside. A four-inch hose ran from the back of the truck and along the floor until it connected to a mechanical pump, and from there continued down to one of the steel tanks along the lower wall. He had just pulled out his phone to take a photo when the tour guide turned to him and said,

"No photographs please." Eric returned the phone to his pocket and noted the exact location of the tank.

After the recording concluded, Eric removed his headset and walked with the rest of the group toward another exit. It, too, had a keypad, and the tour guide opened it with a code. They passed through the doorway into a different stairwell and followed the stairs down to another tunnel. After walking a short distance, they entered the public tasting room, where a bar with glasses awaited them.

Eric approached the young female tour guide, who spoke English quite well. "I'm a winemaker visiting from the United States. I'm wondering if it would be possible to meet with Miss Kwong. I'm very impressed by her work."

"No, that is not possible," the guide said. "She is not available."

"Well, I'm staying in town for a few days. Could I make an appointment?"

"Miss Kwong is out of town. She will not be back until Monday."

It was Friday, and by Monday, Eric hoped he would be far away from Yinchuan. But, he decided to set up a meeting anyway. "May I have a phone number for Miss Kwong's assistant, so I may call and make an appointment?"

"Yes, come with me and I will give you her business card."

Eric followed the woman to a reception desk, where she presented a card. "Her assistant should be there now if you'd like to call."

"Thank you," Eric said.

He exited the building and walked past the fountains and gardens on his way back toward the front entrance. He saw Ming's car waiting for him. He held up his hand to indicate that Ming should wait for him as he dialed the assistant's number on his cell phone. An older-sounding woman answered in Chinese, but quickly shifted to English as Eric said his name. Eric introduced himself and explained his interest in meeting with Miss Kwong. The assistant was happy to set up an appointment for 11:00 a.m. the following Monday morning.

Eric climbed inside Ming's car and they sped off.

28

November 29th

Yinchuan

Eric and Ming met in the parking lot of the hotel at 9:00 p.m. for the drive back to the winery. Their plan seemed simple enough. Ming would drive to the back of the winery, where he and Eric had seen the container arrive the previous day. After dropping Eric off at the gate, Ming would return in one hour. That was the easy part. The hard part would be for Eric to get inside the winery, obtain the samples, and get back out, all while remaining undetected.

Standing outside the car in the parking lot, Eric asked, "Ming, do you have a pry bar?"

"Let me look in my detective kit," Ming said, with a laugh. He opened the trunk and pulled out an old and frayed canvas bag, its rips sealed with duct tape.

"That's a detective kit?"

"You were expecting ballistic metal? You've been watching too many detective shows."

Ming unzipped the bag and rummaged around inside for a minute. Eric watched as he pulled out a flashlight, various tools, a roll of duct tape, and finally a small pry bar. "Here you go."

Eric took the bar and reached for the flashlight as well. "Are you really a detective, Ming?"

"Yes, Eric, I'm really a detective. Make sure you keep your cell phone close. If you have any trouble, call me. I won't be far away. I'll be back at the gate in one hour."

"Let's go." Eric placed the tools in a small bag and got into the passenger side of the car.

The drive back to the winery took about twenty minutes. Ming extinguished the car's lights as he drove around the masonry fence that marked the periphery of the property. As they approached the back gate, Eric zipped up his dark windbreaker and made sure to put its hood up over his head. Just past the gate, where the security guards had approached them, Ming barely came to a stop. Eric stepped out and then watched the car disappear into the night.

Eric made his way to a cast-iron gate, which broke the uniformity of the masonry wall. It was about eight feet tall and had gold-colored spears at the top. He peered through the darkness along the wall and saw a tree about twenty-five yards away. Having climbed many trees as a boy, he didn't think this one would be too hard. He made his way to the tree, placed his bag around his shoulder, and started climbing. He found a few fortunately placed handholds and was soon up on a branch, working his way further up the trunk. He calculated he would have to climb higher than the wall, then leap out in an arc from the tree and attempt to land on the top of the wall's two-feet-wide surface, or at least grab hold of it.

After he was up on the third branch, he felt he had enough height to make the leap. He made sure he had the bag strapped tight around his body, then jumped out toward the top of the wall. His aim was pretty good, but after he hit the top of the wall, his momentum carried him over to the other side. He ended up rolling off the wall and falling to the dirt eight feet below. Eric remembered from his football days to absorb the impact and roll, not to use his arms to break his fall. He landed on his hip, which hurt like hell. He lay on the ground for a minute and took a quick inventory of his body. Everything seemed intact as he slowly rose up onto his knees.

During the tour earlier that day when Eric had viewed the production room from the observation windows inside the winery, he had noticed small doors in the walls above the crush pad. The doors provided access for lift conveyors, which looked like baggage belts typically used to load luggage into cargo holds of airplanes, only longer and higher. These conveyors were used to move grapes from the sorting table outside the winery at ground level, up through the small door at the top of the production room. From there, they fell into the top chute of the destemming equipment located on the inside of the building. His plan was to gain entry into the winery through one of these access doors. After gathering himself and his bag, Eric got up and hobbled slowly across the gravel parking lot toward the winery building. Even though it was dark, a couple of lights on the side of the building gave him enough visibility to see where he was going. Approaching the cement crush pad, he saw that several of the conveyors were parked at the far end of the building, along with other equipment. They would likely stay there until the next harvest. As he neared the winery, he realized that the row of access doors was about ten feet off the ground. He chose one of the lift conveyors and tried to roll it over to the wall. It wouldn't budge. That's when he remembered the foot brakes on the conveyor's casters. He pulled out his flashlight so he could see and used his foot to release the brakes on each one.

The conveyor moved easily as Eric rolled it next to the building and positioned the high end at the access door. He locked the foot brakes on the casters again, then went to the end of the belt and crawled up to the top. Now he was at the same height as the access door to the inside of the winery. He used his flashlight to survey the door. As there was no latch on the outside, Eric assumed it was probably latched from within. Fortunately, there were two hinges on one side, so he took out his pry bar and started loosening them. The door appeared to be made out of plywood and the hinges were simply screwed in to the masonry wall. It wasn't hard to get the bar under the hinge plates with enough purchase to pry them off. Once that was done, he simply pried out the side of the door from the wall, to an angle of about forty-five degrees. He was then able to reach through, undo the latch, and remove the whole door. He laid it behind him on the conveyor belt.

Using his flashlight, Eric peered into the dark room. He could see it was an easy drop to the bare floor. He grabbed his bag and lowered himself down the wall until he was hanging on by his fingers at the base of the opening. He let go, and landed on his feet with a thud after a drop of only about four feet.

Remembering the layout of the winery from his observations during the tour, he set out for the lab area. He went through the doorway of the glass-enclosed lab and searched the cabinets inside for sample tubes. Also known as "test tubes," they were frequently used to send wine samples to labs for chemical analysis. Wineries needed a spectrum of tests performed, to make sure the wine had no chemical faults or spoilage bacteria, and also to confirm alcohol content. In the fourth cabinet, Eric found what he was looking for: a box of clean tubes and another box of rubber stoppers. After throwing a handful of each into his bag, he left the lab and went back into the winery.

Things were going well. *Too* well, perhaps. He looked at his watch and saw that he only had twenty minutes before Ming would return. He had to press on. His next stop was to find a wine glass. Grabbing a glass from a rack near the office, he found his way to the tank he'd seen earlier in the day: the one to which they were transferring wine from the shipping container. He'd memorized its location. When he arrived at the tank, he noted that the pump and hoses were gone. He was impressed with how neat and clean everything was throughout the winery. He put his glass under the sample valve, opened it, and watched as his wine poured out. He took his flashlight and shined it through the glass so he could see the liquid. As he hoped, it was deep ruby colored. He swirled the glass, smelled it, and then took a sip. After tasting, he spit it out, smiled, and took another sip, swallowing a mouthful. Yes, it was definitely his wine.

Eric put the glass down on the ground and took three sample tubes from his bag, filled them, and put rubber stoppers in each of them. He put them back in the bag and made his way back to the wall beneath the access door where he had entered. Looking around for a way to climb back to the door up above, he shined his flashlight around the winery but didn't see anything useful. Starting to panic, he looked behind the row of steel tanks and found just what he needed, a folding ladder. He picked it up and carried it over to the wall. It was high enough that he could stand on the top and crawl through the door. Just as he put his foot on the first step, he heard a door open.

Suddenly, the room was bathed in dim light as high-powered metal halide lights came on and began their slow warm-up. Eric looked toward the sound and saw a security guard at the door next to the observation windows. From that landing there was a double flight of metal stairs down to the production area. The guard looked around as if everything was normal. Then he saw Eric standing on the ladder. Pulling out his radio, he started yelling something into the microphone. Eric wasted no time in turning back around and climbing the ladder's steps. He had just squeezed through the door and onto the conveyor belt when he heard a second voice yelling something. He crawled down the belt, remembering to climb over the access door he'd left there. He jumped off the bottom and pulled out his cell phone to call Ming. He dialed the number and then started running across the gravel parking area back toward the wall. As he ran, he waited for Ming to answer. About halfway across the open space, he heard the large receiving doors of the winery groan as the guards rolled them open. The sound he heard next sent chills down his spine: growling and barking dogs. Suddenly, the area was bathed in bright light as outdoor floodlights were switched on. "Damn it, Ming," Eric yelled, "answer the phone."

"This is Jiao Ming, please leave a message." Eric couldn't believe it.

"Ming, they've found me. I'm running toward the wall by the gate, right by where you dropped me off. I'm going to toss the samples over. If they catch me, you've got to get them delivered to the lab in Perth. Hurry." Eric reached the wall and tossed the bag. He then ran toward the gate to lead the person chasing him away from the wall. Just as he reached it, a German Shepherd clenched its powerful jaws over his calf and began to shake his leg like it was attached to a child's doll. Overcome by pain, he fell to the ground. Just as suddenly, the dog released its grip and retreated after one of the guards issued commands in Mandarin. Eric sat up and grabbed his calf. He saw circles of blood soaking into the fabric of his pants. He remained seated on the ground and wrapped his hands around his calf to stop the bleeding. The pain made him feel nauseous. The guards lifted him to his feet and began dragging him back inside the winery, where he saw a medical technician descending the stairs with a bag. He approached Eric, opened the bag, withdrew some scissors, and started cutting away Eric's torn pants. After methodically cleaning and bandaging the open bite marks and cuts in Eric's leg, the technician retrieved a syringe from the bag and filled it from a small vile. As Eric struggled, the guards held him down. He could only watch as the needle entered his arm.

29

November 30th

Yinchuan

When Eric awoke, he was lying on a four-poster bed in an exquisitely appointed room. He presumed he was in the château. As
his eyes started to focus, he looked down at his leg and saw that it was
professionally wrapped in a clean bandage. Besides being a bit lightheaded, he felt some slight pain. He struggled to remember what had
happened the night before.

He sat up in the bed and noticed that he was wearing a nice set of
flannel pajamas. A white mat on the floor held a pair of bedroom slippers. He put the slippers on and shuffled over to the window. Outside,
dormant vineyards stretched into the distance, confirming his assumption that he was in the château. He tried to open the window, but the
latch was removed. There was a knock on the door, then it opened,
and a pleasant-looking woman walked in with a tray of food. She was
neatly dressed in a maid's uniform. "Good morning, Mr. Savage. I
bring you coffee or tea, whichever you prefer, and some pastries." She
put the tray on a table and turned to leave. "Mr. Huang Wei will be in
to see you shortly."

After she left, Eric tried the handle on the door and determined it
was locked. His comfortable bedroom now seemed more like a jail cell.
He returned to the table, poured himself a cup of coffee, then bit into
a croissant. He was hungry and still lightheaded from whatever drug
they had given him. The coffee tasted great.

There was another knock on the door. Eric looked up and when it
opened, he saw the same man he and Ming had seen accepting delivery

of the shipping container the day before. "Mr. Eric Savage, how nice of you to visit us," Wei said. "You should have let me know you were coming. I would have had time to prepare a more entertaining visit."

"I didn't know I was coming until a few days ago," Eric replied, sarcasm in his voice.

"Mr. Savage, I hear you've been touring around the property. Trespassing is a serious offense. Care to tell me why you broke into my winery last night?" Wei took a seat in a richly upholstered Bergère armchair located next to the window.

Eric, wearing only pajamas, felt intimated by the burly and impeccably dressed Wei. "Do you care to tell me why I'm in a room I can't leave?"

"May I call you Eric? Please call me Wei, and let's stop the pleasantries. Eric, you broke into my winery last night, and I want to know why."

"I think you know why. Someone stole fifty-four barrels of my wine from Walla Walla three weeks ago, and I think it's in a tank here at Red Star Winery. I want to understand why someone took my wine and is trying to put me out of business."

"Eric, I don't know what you are talking about. True, I did purchase some wine in Washington and had it shipped here on one of our company's container ships. The purchase was legitimate, and I can show you the bill of sale."

Eric quickly considered how much to let on at that point. He knew from speaking to Scott that the bill of sale was forged, but until he had irrefutable proof, something that could stand up to legal review, he was hesitant to overplay his hand. He certainly wanted to steer clear of any discussion about murder.

"Wei, I think we both know the wine is mine. I tasted it last night and I have no doubt. What I don't understand is what you plan to do with it. Why would you come all the way to Walla Walla and steal my wine?" Eric was angry and felt his face growing flushed.

"Eric," Wei said, "you are at a distinct disadvantage. I caught you breaking and entering my property; I could simply have you thrown in jail. It's not a very pleasant place and you'd find it very difficult to get out. Instead, I have a proposition for you."

"Go on," Eric said.

"I'd like you to help me today. I have a new shipment of wine that needs to be transferred into barrels for a few more months of aging before bottling."

"What! You want me to help you with my wine?"

"I didn't say it's your wine, but I'd like your help. You have a great reputation as a winemaker."

Wei's hubris was insulting, as was his unctuous manner. What bothered Eric even more was the cunning in Wei's idea, as though he anticipated Eric's wanting to be sure his wine was handled with care.

"Why should I agree to help you?"

"Because it's better than going to jail."

"What if I can prove to the authorities that it's my wine? Have you considered it might be you who goes to jail?"

"Eric, you have no proof, and the police in Yinchuan take direction from me. They would never believe you."

Eric considered his options and concluded that for now, he had no choice but to cooperate. He wondered what had happened to Jiao Ming. Had he gotten Eric's message? Did he find the samples? And where were Eric's phone and other personal belongings? Until he knew more, there wasn't much he could do, especially since it was becoming clear he had been kidnapped. "All right, I'll help," he said.

"Excellent. I'll have some clothes brought over. You can dress, and then I'll have you escorted over to the winery. Today is Saturday, so it will be very quiet around here. I have a couple of assistants who will help you."

"Where's my phone?"

"Eric, I have your phone, but I'd prefer you don't speak with anyone right now," Wei said. "Also, my personal nurse will stop by to check on your bandages. Sorry about the dog bite, but the medical technician told me you will be fine." Wei rose from his chair, and walked over to the door. He knocked on it lightly, and it opened from the outside. He walked into the hallway and the door closed behind him with a mechanical click.

After Eric removed the bandage and took a long hot shower, a nurse came in to examine his leg. It must have looked okay to her because she calmly applied some new gauze dressing and tape. She made a few comments in Mandarin, but Eric didn't understand any of them. A half-hour later, Eric was escorted to the production floor of the winery, dressed in blue jeans and a *Red Star Winery* hooded sweatshirt. When he arrived, two young-looking Chinese staff were standing by, quietly awaiting instructions.

Wei arrived shortly after Eric. "The wine is in two six-thousand liter tanks, numbered sixteen and seventeen, over by the back wall near the crush pad." With his own bit of sarcasm he added, "But I'm sure you already know that. I'd like you to work with my assistants." He pointed to the two men. "And transfer the wine from the tanks to barrels. Before you do, I suggest you measure the level of sulfur dioxide and make sure it's at the right level after our addition yesterday."

"Where are the barrels?" Eric asked.

"That's the interesting part," Wei said. "You're going to dump the wine currently stored in fifty-two barrels in the barrel room, rinse them, and then fill them with some wine that arrived yesterday and is now stored in the tanks. The barrels are all labeled with the number 88, a lucky number in China, and they contain a blend we call Celestial Red." Wei looked at Eric and waited for the response he knew was coming.

Eric thought for a second. It didn't make a lot of sense to throw away good wine only to replace it with his. Maybe their wine had some faults they were trying to hide. Perhaps it contained high levels of acetaldehyde, acetic acid, or brettanomyces, with its accompanying barnyard smell. "What's wrong with the Celestial Red?" Eric asked.

"Nothing; it's perfectly fine," Wei replied. "But it won't win any awards. I believe this new wine will."

Eric was stunned as Wei's comment sank in. He realized Wei was turning the idea of wine counterfeiting on its head. Instead of using cheap wine and selling it with counterfeit labels as an expensive knock-off at a huge profit, Wei was stealing his wine and trying to turn Red Star's brand into a prestige wine. Eric felt like laughing at Wei, but didn't. "Why are you doing this? It can't be for money. You have plenty here at Red Star Winery." Eric didn't expect a straight answer.

"Enough questions, Eric. It's time to get to work. I have told the assistants about the work for today. The security guard watching you from the corner over there speaks English and can translate if necessary. It's now ten o'clock. I think you should be able to finish your work by the end of the day. Lunch will be delivered." Wei turned and left the winery.

Eric looked around. With lights on and daylight streaming in through rows of windows along the upper walls near the ceiling, he was able to appreciate the building's size and design. He remembered his drop to the floor from the access window, which he could see had already been repaired. The floor was spotless and finished in a hard glaze, which made cleaning simpler and more effective. Floor drains ran the length of the winery and were ideally placed for cleaning equipment. All of the tanks, pumps, tools, and fittings were top-notch and shiny new. The building was plumbed throughout with hot water for cleaning and cold water for cooling jackets on fermentation tanks. He walked over to the lab. With more light than his flashlight had provided the night before, he saw that it was equally as clean, and well provisioned with the latest equipment.

Eric left the lab and returned to the winery floor. When he beckoned toward the guard with his hand, the guard nodded and walked over. The two assistants joined him. Eric said to the guard, "Ask them to get the barrel washstand ready and start sanitizing the pump and hoses. When that's completed, have them bring the barrels of Celestial Red from the barrel room and stack them on the floor here." He pointed to a large open area next to the drains. "I'm going to test the wine in the tanks for sulfur dioxide."

The guard spoke to the assistants and pointed in different directions. As soon as they understood what Eric wanted them to do, they almost ran to get started. Within a few minutes, he heard the forklift start moving in what he guessed was the barrel room below them, and one of the assistants came into view pushing the wine pump. After putting the wine pump near the tanks, the assistant gathered all the cleaning supplies. He began cleaning the clamps and attaching the hoses and racking wand to the pump. Eric was impressed by the competency of the two men. It was clear they knew exactly what to do.

While the assistants worked quietly and efficiently, Eric went to the lab and found two clean beakers. He returned to the wine tanks that contained his wine and took a two hundred milliliter sample from each. He brought the samples back to the lab and was happy to see a piece of Australian equipment sitting on the counter, known as a Wine Analyser for Free and Total SO_2. He'd read about this measuring device that he knew was prohibitively expensive for a small winemaker. Eric found the instruction booklet, which was thankfully written in English, and reviewed the operation of the device. Within thirty minutes, he had the measurements he needed and determined that the current levels of sulfur dioxide were within the optimal limits for continued aging in barrels. He was impressed that Wei's assistants had accurately measured the wine the previous day and added the right amount of SO_2. The wine had survived its time in the shipping container quite well.

When Eric returned to the winery floor, he saw that the equipment was set up, and twelve barrels had already been retrieved from the barrel room and stacked on the floor. He loathed what he was about to do. He took the racking wand and connected it to the pump. Next, he picked up the pump's hand control, walked over to a rack of two full barrels, and removed their silicone stoppers, referred to as bungs. He placed the racking wand deep inside the barrel and started the pump. The wine began to flow into the pump, then out through a two-inch hose on the pump's output side, and finally onto the winery floor near the drain. Believing winemaking was as much art as science, Eric hated to see someone's hard work and creativity literally go down the drain.

The process of emptying the barrels of wine went on for nearly four hours. After each pair of barrels was emptied, one of the assistants drove the barrels over to the washstand where the other gave them a quick one-minute cold rinse with a high-pressure spray wand and water. The barrels were then stacked with their bung holes pointing down, and any remaining water gurgled out onto the floor. Lunch arrived while they were working. When they finished around 2:00 p.m., they sat down at an old wooden picnic table and began to devour the assortment of local cuisine like hungry dogs, filling the winery with the sounds of their energetic slurping and chewing.

The next step in the process was to refill the barrels with Eric's wine and insert clean bungs. Eric had noticed that one of the assistants had been cleaning and sanitizing the bungs taken out of the previously full barrels. He was beginning to enjoy having such well-trained staff to help him.

The rest of the afternoon went smoothly. After another five hours, all of the barrels were refilled with Eric's wine, rinsed off, and returned to the barrel room. Each barrel still displayed the lucky number 88, and while the actual taste and aroma profile of the wine would be different, no one other than the assistants would be aware of the switch. Even though he ruminated over it most of the afternoon, Eric still couldn't understand why Wei had gone to so much trouble, including a suspected homicide, just to swap Red Star's wine with his.

The assistants finished cleaning all of the dirtied equipment and tanks while Eric watched and occasionally gave them direction. By about 7:00 p.m., his leg really ached from the dog bite and from standing all day. He wanted to lie down. He also wanted to get his phone back, something he suspected was unlikely. Eric fretted over what Wei had in store for him now that he was done racking the wine. A clicking sound at the doorway announced someone's arrival. Eric looked up and saw Wei descend the steps down to the winery floor.

"It looks like you have finished your work for the day," Wei said. "Well done. I will have you escorted back to your room."

"I'd like to have my phone back," Eric said.

"No, I don't want you making any calls right now. I need to decide what I'm going to do with you. Your unexpected appearance here has created a bit of a problem."

"You can't just hold me here against my will," Eric protested.

"Eric, have you forgotten that you were illegally on my property and that you broke into my winery? Trust me, you will be much more comfortable here than in the Yinchuan detention center with Jiao Ming."

"Jiao Ming is in jail?"

"Yes, we finally located him about noon at the hotel where you were both staying. We searched your credit card records through our government's security agency, similar to your NSA, and found you had used a credit card to check into a hotel in town two nights ago. I assumed that Jiao Ming was likely staying at the same hotel. He was with you on the day my wine arrived, when you were questioned. After we caught you trying to escape last night, I placed one of my security men at the hotel to watch for Mr. Jiao. He did not return until noon. When he did, we called the police and had him arrested." Wei seemed very bored by the events.

"Arrested, for what?"

"For aiding and abetting the trespass onto my private property," Wei calmly replied.

"But you don't have any proof."

"He's being held while the local police complete their investigation." Wei turned toward the stairs and said, "Come, I want to return you to your room. I'll have some dinner served shortly. I'm sure you are tired and very hungry."

Eric realized his situation was dire. He had assumed all along that Wei was dangerous, but now he began to think he might also be mentally unstable and possibly violent.

As they arrived at Eric's room in the château, Wei said, "Enjoy your dinner. You do have television available; you might like some of our local programming. I suggest we meet after lunch tomorrow. I will give you a tour of the grounds and vineyard. Then, we will have dinner together and discuss your future here in Yinchuan."

"How can I refuse?" Eric said. *I have to find a way out of here.*

30

November 30th

Houston

Ashley woke up at 6:00 a.m. that Saturday. She did the calculation in her head and determined that it was 8:00 p.m. in Yinchuan. It had been over thirty-six hours since she'd spoken to Eric about the wine sample. If she didn't hear anything soon, she'd call her friend Grace.

She checked her email and found a confirmation that Melissa had shipped a sample of wine from Walla Walla to Professor Fletcher. It was scheduled to arrive on Monday, in two days' time. That was encouraging news.

She also read an email from Sheriff Thompson, who had briefed the prosecuting attorney in Walla Walla County on the facts of the case against Huang Wei, a foreign national of China, in the murder of Jeff Russell and the burglary of Eric Savage's winery. Scott confirmed that the prosecuting attorney would proceed to file charges if the lab analysis matched Wei's DNA on the envelope to the foreign DNA found on Jeff Russell's corpse. The results should be ready on Monday. That was all: there was no news about Eric.

Ashley was frustrated that there was nothing else she could do. She felt helpless and worried about Eric. It looked like she would have to wait twelve hours to call her friend Grace at the FBI's office in the U.S. Embassy in Beijing.

Yinchuan

Eric sat at the small table in his room and surveyed the surroundings. He saw a keyboard with the television. He discovered that he had limited Internet access, so he decided to see if he could access his email account. As he expected, it was blocked. The Internet was closely controlled in China. Reportedly more than two million monitors worked for the government and commercial companies as Internet opinion analysts who continually reviewed and censored web page content. He tried several other sites that he thought might give him access to an email application, but they were either blocked or unavailable. He wasn't surprised.

Researching the history of the Yinchuan region, he found that about a third of the population is considered Hui, a predominantly Muslim ethnic group in China. Hui people are found throughout the country, though they were concentrated mainly in the Northwestern provinces and the Central Plain. The research suggested that most are Chinese-speaking practitioners of Islam, influenced by their proximity to the Silk Road between China and the Mediterranean Sea. As he reflected on their history, he remembered seeing a number of mosques as he and Jiao Ming had driven around the city looking for a place to stay.

With nothing else to do, he decided to eat the dinner that had been delivered to his room. The first thing he wanted to do was try a glass of wine. He picked up the bottle of *Celestial Red* and removed the foil capsule. Using a corkscrew from the serving tray, he opened the bottle and poured himself a small glass. His first impressions were that it was acceptable. It was the same wine he'd tried at the wine shop in Shanghai, but this vintage was a few years older and its red hue had changed from ruby to brick. The nose was muted. On the palate, the wine was balanced and full of dark fruit, which unfortunately tasted slightly vegetal, a common trait imparted by grapes not fully ripened or faulty vineyard technique. However, the tannins were supple and the finish was long. While the winemaking technique probably allowed some exposure to oxygen, the main problem was with the fruit. Once their vineyards were more established and producing higher quality grapes, Eric believed their wine could steadily improve.

He ate his dinner while watching some local television shows, trying to understand what was going on. The dishes he was served with his dinner were of typical Muslim cuisine. They included steamed lamb, pita bread soaked in lamb soup, crispy chicken, and rice. Accompanying the meal was a pot of Gaiwancha, a tea which, according to a search on the Internet, had been traced back to the Tang dynasty in the years of 618–907 A.D. Its flavor was called five-savory and was made from tea leaf, crystal sugar, longan, raisin, and dried apricot. Eric found it quite refreshing.

After finishing his dinner, Eric pushed the call button near his door. Several minutes later the door opened, and a young woman came in and retrieved his tray. As she left, he noticed a cardkey on a long lanyard around her neck. Through the door opening, he observed a security guard posted in the hallway outside. Alone again, he put on the pajamas and walked around the room once more. All the windows were locked, and the hand cranks had been removed. Even if he could get out through a window, it appeared to be at least a thirty-foot drop straight down to the ground below. The only exit was the door.

Houston

Around 6:00 p.m., Ashley started preparing dinner for herself and her boys. Elliot and William loved her fajitas, and it was an easy meal to prepare. She was just putting the dish into the oven to stay warm when her phone rang.

"Ashley, this is Grace."

"Grace, I was just about to call you. It's eight in the morning there, right?"

"Yes. The reason I'm calling is I just received a troubling phone call from Jiao Ming, the private detective who's working with your friend Eric. He's in the Yinchuan detention center."

"Is Eric with him?"

"No," Grace said. "He thinks Eric is being held against his will by Wei. He called me because he fears Eric needs help, and Ming's not sure when he'll be released from detention."

"Did he say why he's being held?"

"He didn't want to talk about it because his guards were listening to him."

Ashley tried to sound calm. "Grace, is there some way you can help him?"

"I've requested permission from my supervisor to travel to Yinchuan, but he needs some justification. You mentioned in our last call that murder charges might be filed against Wei and an arrest warrant issued. When might that happen?"

"The prosecuting attorney is waiting for lab results of some DNA testing. They should be available on Monday. By Tuesday morning, your time, he should have something," Ashley said. She wondered if there was a way she could help move things along. "Tell your boss I'll have the prosecuting attorney send him a summary. That should give him confidence that you're on to something serious."

"I'm convinced the Ministry of Foreign Affairs for the People's Republic of China will want to see a formal request from the U.S. State Department before they even consider taking any action regarding Wei. In the interim, I hope I can throw some weight around in Yinchuan and try to get Ming released. Since he's a Chinese national, it may be difficult. When I arrive in Yinchuan, I'll make contact with a local attorney and see what I can do."

"What about Eric?" Ashley asked.

Grace hesitated. "Ashley, I don't think there's anything either of us can do until I arrive in Yinchuan. I hope to be on a flight later today and arrive early enough to make contact with Ming this afternoon. It's only a two-hour flight from Beijing. Until then, sit tight and let me know as soon as you have any information about an arrest warrant."

"Okay. Thanks, Grace." After hanging up, Ashley went to the refrigerator and retrieved a bottle of beer. Prying off the cap, she sat down at the kitchen table and reflected on the call. She hated feeling so helpless. She had to trust that her friend Grace would learn something from Jiao Ming. Until then, she'd just have to wait, though she much preferred being in the game to just sitting on the bench. She took a couple of sips of the beer and went off in search of her boys to let them know dinner was ready.

31

December 1st

On Sunday afternoon at two, Wei came to Eric's room for the planned tour of Red Star Winery's property. Eric was growing increasingly frustrated by his predicament. He felt as if he had been taken hostage, and with the tight, almost military-like security of the facility, he didn't see how he could escape.

The two men left the château through the rear entrance and walked toward the vineyards. Eric was glad he had been given a warm overcoat, hat, and gloves because he estimated the temperature was in the high thirties and a steady wind made it feel colder. The gray sky and the dried leaves on the hardened canes of the vines imparted a feeling of loneliness to Eric's psyche. He missed the companionship of Jiao Ming, even though he had probably been drunk most of the time they were together. What was happening to him in the detention facility? He hadn't heard good things about Chinese prisons and knew confinement would be hard on Ming.

Eric and Wei walked together across the dense earth while Wei enthusiastically described the plans of the Chinese government to develop the wine industry in the Ningxia region. "By 2020, our plan is to have a grape corridor of up to 170,000 acres of vineyards, a wine center, three grape culture cities, and over one hundred châteaux," he boasted.

"Do you have enough labor to farm so much land?" Eric asked.

"Yes. The government has a program to resettle the indigenous population, often Muslim, from the harsh mountains in the south, closer to settlements around Yinchuan in the north. As you can see, the vines are buried during the winter, and it takes a lot of labor to farm our grapes."

Wei went on to describe the grape varieties grown on their ninety-five acre property leased from the government. "In the vineyards around our winery, we predominantly grow Cabernet Sauvignon and Merlot, but also some Cabernet Gernischt, known as Chinese Cabernet, Chardonnay, and smaller portions of Chenin Blanc, Shiraz, and Aglianico. We tried Pinot Noir several years ago, but it was so bad we ripped out the vines. We intend to replant this spring with new cuttings imported from France. It took three years for the government to approve them."

Eric observed the trellis systems used to manage grape canopies and sun exposure and thought they looked a bit haphazard. Rows were not very uniform and it would be hard to add any mechanization for harvesting or winter pruning. Of course, labor was cheap and plentiful, and it would be many years before mechanical harvesting would be an economic requirement.

Eric was curious about the plants which had been used for cover crops between vine rows. Most vineyards used some sort of cover crop to add nutrients when tilled, minimize wind erosion, balance water supply in the soil, and improve soil structure. But he didn't recognize the remaining roots and dead growth of the plants he saw there. "What are these cover crops?" he asked.

"Those are onions and radishes. Not only do we think they make good cover, the workers pick them, and we use the vegetables for cooking in the house. Pumpkins are grown in some areas as well."

Eric and Wei walked over to the central barn to look at the farm tools used by the workers. Eric was surprised to see mostly hand tools. There were a number of tractors for pulling flat farm trailers, a couple of riding lawn mowers, and what looked like an old tilling attachment. But most of the tools were hand trowels, shovels, clippers for pruning vines, bins for hauling fruit, and some hand spreaders for fertilizer. He felt like he'd stepped into a history museum and was looking at a diorama of early nineteenth-century farming methods.

Eric picked up one of the shovels and turned it over in his hands, as if examining its blade. He noticed that Wei had turned a quarter turn to his right and stepped in the direction of the barn's exit. Impulsively, Eric raised the shovel with both hands and swung it as hard as he could at Wei's head. Wei must have anticipated the move because as the blade accelerated toward him, he stepped back, turned to face Eric, and grabbed the handle near the blade with only one hand, stopping it cold. Then using both hands, Wei snatched the shovel out of Eric's hands and holding it like a spear, punched Eric in the solar plexus with the round end of the handle. Eric hit the ground hard, gasping for breath.

"That was stupid," Wei said. "Did you really think you could surprise me?"

It was Eric who was surprised by Wei's reflexes. The man's strength was obvious, but his quickness came as a shock. "You didn't leave me much choice. You can't hold me here."

"Yes, I can. And now that you have transferred the wine for me, your usefulness is over."

"No, it's not," Eric said.

"What do you mean?"

"If you want my wine to taste its best, I need to make some adjustments." Eric was bluffing, but he needed to buy time.

"What kind of adjustments?"

"Adding tartaric acid. You don't want the wine to taste flabby do you? No awards for that. But I have to wait until the sulfur dioxide we added has reached equilibrium."

"How long do you have to wait?"

"At least three days," Eric replied.

"You are really beginning to annoy me, Eric. But since I'm stuck with you for now, let's go back to the winery. I believe you saw our library of wines and our special events tasting room, but didn't get to go in as part of the tour. I'll give you a bit of history of our wines, and you can taste the progress we've made. We can talk about these 'adjustments' later."

As they walked together along the road from the barn toward the château, Eric noticed security guards loitering nearby. They had been within eyesight since the walk began. Eric considered whether he could make a run for the fence, but thought it would be a mistake. He still hadn't regained his breath from the punch with the shovel. Wei's offer was peculiar, Eric concluded, but he was happy for a chance to regain his composure.

Across town, at the Yinchuan Hedong International Airport, Grace stepped off a Shenzhen Airlines flight from Beijing at 3:30 p.m. and made her way to the rental car desk. She wore a navy blue pants suit with a light blue blouse. Her long, dark hair was clipped back with an enameled floral-designed barrette, and flowed down to a point midway on her back. She had successfully convinced her boss, the Legal Attaché in charge of the FBI's office in the United States Embassy, that charges would soon be filed in Washington State against Huang Wei in the murder of Jeff Russell. Furthermore, she told him she suspected that a U.S. citizen was being held against his will by Huang Wei and was now in imminent danger. The Legal Attaché counseled Grace that without a formal request for extradition from the State Department, and an accompanying request for a provisional arrest warrant, she didn't have any authority in the matter. Until charges were filed against Huang Wei, Grace was only authorized to attempt an interview with Jiao Ming at the Yinchuan detention center with the cooperation of the local authorities.

Before departing Beijing, Grace had contacted a Yinchuan criminal defense attorney, who agreed to meet her at the detention center. After securing a rental car and letting her phone's mapping software lead her across town, she pulled into the large parking area at the entrance to the facility's main building. She switched off her car and waited. Detention facilities in rural China always appeared foreboding to Grace. Public investment logically went toward facilities and infrastructure to help grow the economy; there was no reason to make jails look more attractive. The single level building was made of stark gray painted cement that was fading and severely peeling. High chain-link fencing, with concertina wire on top, encircled the grounds. Additional buildings, resembling old army barracks, were located toward the rear.

Within minutes, another car entered the lot and pulled up next to hers. An older Chinese man in a dark suit and white dress shirt stepped out and introduced himself as attorney Zhū Jie. They conferred outside for a minute before walking into the building's entrance. At the front desk, the officer on duty asked to help them. Fortunately, Grace had learned Mandarin from her parents while growing up in San Francisco and was conversant in the language.

Zhū Jie handed his business card, along with his government license to practice law in the region, to the officer on duty. "I am an attorney and want to visit a detainee named Jiao Ming. I understand he is being held here."

The officer examined the documents and wrote down some notes. Looking at Grace, the officer said, "What is your name and the purpose of your visit?"

Grace produced her FBI badge and China Ministry of Justice identification and handed them over. "I am interested in Jiao Ming as well. I understand he has been here in Yinchuan with a U.S. citizen we are trying to locate, Eric Savage."

As she spoke, the officer's eyebrows rose and his eyes shifted their gaze toward the documents. He then turned his attention to his computer screen and started typing. Grace assumed he was looking for information on Jiao Ming. After a moment, he wrote additional notes. "Yes, Mr. Jiao Ming is here, but you cannot see him. Visiting hours are over for today."

"Can you tell me why he is being held here? What are the charges against him?" asked Mr. Zhū.

"He is suspected of aiding an individual with breaking and entering into private property."

"I am here representing the United States," Grace said. "We believe that one of our citizens is here in Yinchuan and may be in danger, perhaps even kidnapped. It is important that we speak with Mr. Jiao. I'm happy to call your bosses in Beijing if you won't help us." Grace leaned over the counter and spoke in a stern voice to convey as much gravitas as possible.

"Ms. Chin, you have no authority here in China. I am under no obligation to cooperate with you. However, I will make an exception and allow the attorney to speak with Mr. Jiao for ten minutes. You will remain here in the lobby." He picked up the phone and requested that prisoner Jiao Ming be brought to interrogation room C2. He stood and directed Mr. Zhū to meet him over at the door on the left.

Mr. Zhū walked to the door and waited. A buzzer and click sounded, and the door swung open allowing him to walk inside. Grace walked over to some hard wooden chairs and sat down in one to wait.

Fifteen minutes later, Mr. Zhū returned. They both walked over to the desk to retrieve their credentials. As the officer handed them over, Grace looked at Mr. Zhū expectantly. "Is he all right?"

"Outside," Mr. Zhū said.

After exiting the building, they sat in Grace's car to get out of the wind.

"He's not in good shape. It appears that they beat him severely. He has a few abrasions to his cheek and jaw, and his eyes are extremely swollen and bruised. I doubt he has received much sleep. They keep the lights on twenty-four hours per day in there."

"What did he say?" Grace asked.

"He said they wanted him to confess to the crime of trespassing, but he refused. That's probably why they beat him."

"What about Mr. Savage?"

"He said he thinks Mr. Savage is in trouble and probably being held by someone named Huang Wei in the Red Star Winery. He specifically said to tell you that he sent the shipment on Saturday morning, before he was arrested in his hotel. Do you know what shipment he's talking about?" Mr. Zhū asked.

"Yes, but it's not important now. What else?"

"He pleaded for us to get him out of there."

"When is his trial?" Grace guessed the answer was probably unknowable.

"The officer wouldn't say. As you know, the legal system is very different here in China than in your country. The police are currently in the investigative stage in which they take statements, collect evidence, and interview witnesses. During this phase, lawyers' roles are very limited. I was surprised they allowed me to speak with Mr. Jiao. I assume it was because you are here. I doubt the FBI shows up at a local Public Security Bureau very often. But until they move on to the prosecution phase, I will be allowed little contact. And they can take as much time to investigate as they want." Mr. Zhū was sure he was only reinforcing what Grace already understood of their legal customs.

"We need to get him out of there and get some help investigating whether Huang Wei has Mr. Savage in the winery."

"I don't think you're going to have much luck here," said Mr. Zhū. "I think you'll need the Ministry of Public Security, which is the principal police authority in China, to intervene at this local bureau. And for that to happen, I expect your State Department will need to bring pressure on the Ministry of Justice here in China. They are responsible for extraterritorial legal relationships. And there's one more issue."

"What's that?" asked Grace.

"You said that the citizen you are concerned with, Eric Savage, is at the Red Star Winery?"

"Yes."

"They are owned by Shanghai Star Industrial Group, one of the larger and more powerful corporations here in China. I suspect they are well-connected within the People's Republic of China and will likely have significant influence." Mr. Zhū frowned as he extended his hand. "I'm sorry."

Grace shook it and said, "Thank you, Mr. Zhū. Please do whatever you can for Jiao Ming. I will be in touch."

Mr. Zhū got into his car and drove away from the detention center. Grace sat quietly for a moment then pulled out her cell phone and called her supervisor.

Wei and Eric walked back inside the château and into the library room. In the center was a large round table for sixteen, set up with four wine glasses at each seat, white paper placemats for examining color, and silver spit buckets engraved with the Red Star Winery logo: a single five-pointed red star.

Wei led Eric into the climate-controlled walk-in cellar, where Eric admired row upon row of wines. Wei pointed toward several *vertical* collections, wines of the same style produced over many contiguous years. He also proudly claimed that the library housed one of the more notable collections of Bordeaux wines in China. After selecting four bottles, Wei returned to the tasting table. He handled each of the bottles with aplomb, cutting away the capsules and removing the corks with a stylishness that suggested a professional's touch. "Please sit," Wei said.

He poured the first wine, a white, and motioned to Eric to try it. Eric sniffed the glass and then tasted the wine before spitting it into the bucket. Eric couldn't translate the Chinese label. "What is this?" he asked.

"It's our second vintage of Chenin Blanc." Eric thought the wine had a fragrance of honeysuckle and flavors of melon. It was very crisp, indicating high acidity. "This is quite good," Eric said. "This is a hard wine to make, and you made it here?"

"Yes." Wei said. "We grew the vines for several years before getting what we thought was acceptable fruit. Our first vintage wasn't very good, so we disposed of it. However, this particular vintage has been well received by critics."

One of the guards who had been positioned outside the door to the wine library opened it and stepped inside. He walked over to Wei and whispered into his ear.

"Eric, I must take a phone call. It will only be a minute." Wei left the room and the security guard positioned himself at the door. He watched Eric warily. Eric sipped some more of the Chenin Blanc while waiting for Wei's return.

After about five minutes, Wei came through the door and returned to his seat. Eric could feel the intensity of Wei's glare. "I don't know what to do with you, Eric."

"Just let me go."

"You know I can't do that. I just received a call from a friend at the Yinchuan detention facility. He reported that a man and a woman were there earlier today inquiring about your friend Jiao Ming. He didn't know who they were or what was discussed, but he thought I should know."

Eric found the admission encouraging. He might have reason for hope yet.

"We might as well have dinner," Wei said. "We can discuss your predicament over a decent meal."

They left the library and walked across the hall to the dining room. It was paneled in dark wood and had an elegant table set with expensive china, crystal, and linens. Wei took a chair across from Eric and clapped his hands. A young Chinese girl wearing a French maid's uniform walked in and poured water into each of their glasses and placed napkins in their laps. Wei started speaking in Mandarin, then paused and looked at Eric. "Is locally grown rack of lamb satisfactory?"

"Sure," was Eric's tepid response. He was suspicious of Wei's hospitality and wondered about his mental condition. *Psychosis perhaps?*

After the young woman departed, Wei said, "What am I going to do with you here at Yinchuan? I've tried to show you our Chinese hospitality and make you feel comfortable."

"You need to release me," Eric said. "Based on the phone call you received, I think the FBI is looking for me, and they won't approve of your kidnapping a U.S. citizen."

"Eric, you forget that you are in China. Your FBI has no authority here, and I make sure the police look after me."

"You can't legally keep me here," Eric said. He was more worried about another option of course, the possibility that Wei might murder him, just as he had Jeff Russell back in Walla Walla.

"Right now, you have no choice. I expect you to make the adjustments you mentioned in three days' time. Until then, try to enjoy your time here. I will continue to make you as comfortable as possible. But don't try to escape again. I think I might have underestimated you, Eric. You're more resourceful than I thought."

The young woman returned with their first course of salad, and brought out a bottle of Chablis. She poured a glass for Wei who nodded his approval after tasting it. After filling both glasses, the young woman departed. Eric and Wei ate the rest of their meal mostly in silence. Eric asked questions about the winery operation and other seemingly benign subjects.

They ate their lamb, accompanied by a bottle of 1982 Château Latour from Pauillac in the Haut-Médoc region of Bordeaux. It was likely the most expensive wine Eric had ever tasted. He guessed that it would have been priced around $3,000 per bottle and recalled it had received a 100-point score from Robert Parker, the respected U.S. wine critic. It was dark crimson in color, expressed great minerality, and was surprisingly youthful for its age. Eric was thrilled to taste it, despite the unpleasant circumstances.

Over dessert and tea, Eric mustered the courage to say, "Wei, I scheduled a meeting with Lily Kwong tomorrow at eleven in her office. I'd like to meet with her to discuss her philosophy toward winemaking. It would help me better understand how I should make adjustments to my wine." Eric really didn't need to talk with her; it was another bluff.

"When did you make the appointment?" Wei demanded.

"I called her assistant, Ling, after taking the tour on Friday." If Wei allowed the meeting to go ahead, Eric expected that he wouldn't be alone.

"She knows nothing about the work you did in the winery yesterday. She's been out of town. I expect you to keep silent about it. I'll attend the meeting with you to make sure you don't mention it."

"I understand." Eric was relieved that Wei had agreed. Perhaps Lily could help.

After the dinner was over, Wei escorted Eric, with the ever-present guards nearby, up the grand marble stairway to his room in the château. Once Eric was locked inside, he had to admit his only hope was for someone to rescue him.

32

December 1st

Walla Walla

It was the middle of the night when Sheriff Thompson answered his ringing phone and heard Ashley say, "Good morning."

Scott sat up in bed and switched on the lamp on his nightstand. He could barely make out his clock in the sudden bright light. "Ashley, it's four in the morning."

"I know, but I really need to speak with you," Ashley pleaded.

"Can you give me ten minutes to put some coffee on, and I'll call you back?" Scott was still wiping sleep from his eyes as he watched his wife roll away from him in bed.

"Sure, call me back on my cell phone. Be ready to take some notes." Ashley ended the call.

Fifteen minutes later, Scott was in his study with a hot cup of coffee and a legal notepad. He dialed Ashley's number.

"Thanks for calling me back, Scott," Ashley said. "I need to give you an update on Eric and some conversations I've had within the FBI."

"I'm ready."

"I received a call from the Special Agent in Charge of the Beijing LEGAT a little while ago."

"LEGAT, what's that?" Scott asked.

"A LEGAT is an FBI operational office in a foreign country. The office in Beijing has a staff of four. They're located in a controlled access area within the diplomatically protected premises of the U.S. embassy. An old friend of mine, a Special Agent named Grace Chin, works there as an Assistant Legal Attaché. I just got off the phone with her supervisor, the Legal Attaché, who is in charge of the LEGAT." Ashley wanted to get straight to the issue but knew she had to bring Scott up to speed first.

"What did he want?" Scott asked, picking up his pen to take notes.

"He told me that he had authorized Grace to go to the city of Yinchuan, where we think Eric might have been kidnapped. Eric had been working with a private investigator named Jiao Ming. Ming was helping Eric follow the wine and attempt to obtain a sample. He was arrested in Yinchuan sometime Saturday afternoon. He's accused of helping Eric get inside the Red Star Winery. He hasn't been charged yet, but is being held pending an investigation."

"Did Grace get to meet with him?" Scott asked.

"No. The local police wouldn't allow it, but they did allow a local attorney to speak with him briefly. Ming said that he thought Eric was being held captive at the winery and that he had been able to send the shipment on Saturday. I'm hoping that means Ming was able to ship a wine sample to Perth."

"That's the research facility where they're going to attempt to prove that the wine in China is Eric's?" Remembering an earlier conversation with Ashley about wine fingerprinting, he began a separate sheet of notes for a call he expected he'd soon have with the prosecuting attorney. He was accustomed to multitasking.

"Yes, if I'm right, the lab should receive the shipment tomorrow. I'll check with Professor Fletcher after we finish our call. It's evening there, and I hope I won't be getting him out of bed like I did with you."

"What about Eric?"

"The LEGAT in Beijing won't be able to officially help us until the Walla Walla judge issues an arrest warrant. You told me that this means the prosecuting attorney needs the DNA evidence to be conclusive before he can file murder charges, correct?"

"Yes. The State Patrol CODIS lab in Seattle promised the results tomorrow morning. I hope to hear from them first thing." Scott continued writing his notes.

"Scott, a concern we have is that China does not have an extradition treaty with the United States. The FBI's primary function there is to establish, maintain, and enhance liaison with foreign law enforcement agencies. LEGAT personnel have no direct law enforcement authority in foreign countries. They have no arrest powers and are not allowed to carry guns. However, they can request cooperation from the Chinese legal authorities once your prosecuting attorney charges Huang Wei with murder and the judge issues the warrant." Ashley paused while Scott considered the information.

"Did the Legal Attaché you spoke with in Beijing say what's required to request formal assistance from the Chinese authorities?"

"He recommended the following procedures and submission of the necessary affidavits. First, you'll want to request that the prosecuting attorney file charges in Superior Court, and the court issue an arrest warrant. Next, the prosecuting attorney should file a request for a provisional arrest warrant, have it executed by the judge, and then submit it to the Department of Justice's Office of International Affairs. They will review these affidavits and supporting documents and, if they find everything satisfactory, will forward the request through the State Department to the Ministry of Foreign Affairs of the People's Republic of China. Scott, in the last hour I've studied the procedures in the Office of International Affairs manual. I found out that very specific information must be presented. I think you need to get started today. You should assume the DNA evidence will come back positive on Monday and get the prosecuting attorney started now."

"Ashley, it's five in the morning on Sunday. I'll see what I can do, but it's a small department over here."

"Scott, I truly believe Eric's life is in danger." Ashley gripped the phone and waited.

"I'll call the prosecuting attorney after breakfast and let him know it's urgent. We're on good terms." Scott leaned back in his chair and rubbed his head. He hated to ask, "Anything else?"

"Yes, you also need to request an INTERPOL Red Notice. This is the closest instrument to an international arrest warrant we have available to us. The provisional arrest warrant, combined with the INTERPOL Red Notice, should get the cooperation of the Ministry of

Public Security, which controls the police. That organization should be able to locate Eric and arrest Wei in Yinchuan."

"Okay," Scott said, "please send me the information you've been reviewing, and I'll start working with the prosecuting attorney as soon as possible on the required affidavits. What about the evidence proving the wine is Eric's?"

"I'll follow up on that. I'll make sure the lab submits any evidence to the FBI's LEGAT office in Beijing and to your office in Walla Walla. Scott, I know I'm asking for a lot of work here, but we need to get Eric out of there. I'm worried about him. I'll be in touch." Ashley ended the call.

Scott examined his notes. It was going to be a long day. He knew getting the prosecuting attorney to work on a Sunday would take some convincing. But, with any luck, they would be ready for the judge on Monday if the DNA results came back positive.

33

December 1st

Walla Walla

It was dinner time when Sheriff Scott Thompson walked through the front door of his house. His wife was expecting him and was in the kitchen making dinner when he arrived. "I need a beer," Scott said, announcing his return.

"There's some in the refrigerator," she replied. "Pour a glass of wine for me as well, will you? How did your work with the attorney go?"

Scott grabbed a bottle of beer and the bottle of local Chardonnay from the refrigerator. He poured a glass of the wine then opened the beer. "I'll be back in a minute. I need to make a quick phone call. Smells great in here, by the way." After handing the glass of wine to his wife, Scott walked into his study with his beer and sat down to call Ashley.

"How'd it go?" Ashley asked.

"Great. I caught the prosecuting attorney at home before he left for church. Then I went over to my office and started working on the required affidavits. He joined me later. We have drafts completed of the murder charges, a request for a warrant of arrest from the Superior Court judge, a request that a provisional arrest warrant be issued by the U.S. Department of Justice, and a request for issuance of an INTERPOL Red Notice."

"Wow, you worked hard. Thank you."

"Submissions are contingent on positive confirmation of the DNA," Scott emphasized. "If there is a match, we'll take the report from the State Patrol and attach it to the documents. Once we get the necessary signatures from the judge, we can send them off. This could all happen pretty quickly. What I don't know is how long it takes for these to receive approval by the U.S. Office of International Affairs and then be forwarded to the embassy in Beijing. Have you spoken to the Legal Attaché?"

"Yes, he knows what we are working on and promised to expedite the necessary communications with the Chinese Ministry of Public Security as soon as he has the documents."

"Ashley, I think there's some risk in this strategy," Scott cautioned.

"What is it?" Ashley asked.

"I don't know how secure the embassy is, but in my experience, you have to worry about back-channel communications. Word of this activity could leak out to the Chinese authorities before all the i's are dotted and t's are crossed. Someone might get wind of this before it's official."

"That's what we are hoping for, Scott. It's what the Legal Attaché is counting on."

Yinchuan

At exactly 11:00 a.m. Monday, Wei arrived at Eric's room to escort him to the executive offices in the château. They walked together up a flight of stairs and toward the far end of the building. Before arriving at the massive hand-carved wooden double doors, Wei reminded Eric to be careful with what he said. Lily's assistant Ling asked them to be seated while their arrival was announced. After a short wait, they were escorted into the office of Red Star Winery's President and Head Winemaker, Lily Kwong.

Lily rose from behind her large desk and said, "Good morning, Mr. Savage. How nice to meet you. I hear you are staying in one of our guest rooms. I hope your accommodations have been satisfactory."

"Thank you, Miss Kwong," Eric said. "Please call me Eric. Yes, Wei has made sure I'm quite comfortable. You have an impressive facility here."

"We continually strive to make the winery better," Lily said. "I remember my father once taught me a saying of Confucius: *He that would perfect his work must first sharpen his tools.* Wei makes sure we have the best tools. I strive to learn the best methods."

"That reminds me of a quote attributed to Winston Churchill," Eric said. *"Success consists of going from failure to failure without loss of enthusiasm."*

"Both are true. Now how may I help you, Eric?" Lily sat in a large red leather chair and wore a simple floral blouse printed in muted tones, and a loose pair of dark tailored slacks. Eric thought she looked like a combination of a young college professor and an inquisitive attorney. Her eyes behind her glasses were intense yet at the same time welcoming.

Wei spoke and said, "I was thinking of asking Eric if he might like to consult with us. He's an experienced winemaker from Washington and took one of our tours on Friday. From some conversations we've had, I think he might be able to help us."

Eric looked toward Wei, trying to read his expression. He wondered if Wei was attempting to create a plausible scenario for as to why Eric might be working on the barrels of *Celestial Red* later in the week.

"What's your philosophy for making wine, Eric?" Lily asked.

"I believe in using the best fruit and the least intervention possible. The winemaker should merely help the grapes express themselves, and not make mistakes along the way. I currently use commercial yeasts, but eventually I'd like to use indigenous yeasts instead. I know that the benefits of improved aroma profile and mouthfeel supposedly outweigh the risks of using wild yeasts, such as stuck fermentations, but as a small winemaker, I still want to sleep at night knowing that everything is going well in the winery. As the winery grows larger, I may start some trials of fermentations using indigenous yeasts."

"I've studied this subject at length," Lily responded. "I know of Ridge Vineyards and their winemaker Paul Draper who espouses this style. He always uses native yeasts for his fermentations. He claims to have one of the most sophisticated analytical laboratories of any winery his size. Any problems are detected early on, which allows him to correct them. I think his style is correct." Lily smiled, indicating to Eric she approved of his philosophy.

"Yes," Eric said, "Draper calls it pre-industrial style. I believe some of Ridge's vineyards are over fifty years old. His wines are very expressive of the region's *terroir*, and reflect its unique climate, geography, and topography. I hope the day comes when I am crafting wines as consistently excellent as his."

"So, why don't you help us? I'm always looking for fresh ideas and enthusiasm. I can see you have both." Lily's expression didn't give away whether she was serious, or just supportive of Wei.

"I appreciate your interest," Eric replied, "but I have my winery back home to consider."

"I have an idea," Lily said, "why don't you go down to our production area and look around. Taste our wines. Look at our equipment. Examine our lab. I think you will be impressed. I could afford to provide you with any tools you need if you were working here. And feel free to use a *wine thief* and taste some of the wines." Eric knew that Lily was referring to a glass tube with a handle which winemakers use to remove samples of wine from barrels.

"Thank you, Lily. I would enjoy that. Maybe we could have lunch together after I'm finished." Eric took a side glance and detected a slight expression of anger as Wei's jaw tightened.

"Excellent idea. Let's meet in the dining room at one o'clock. Wei, I don't think you need to join us." Lily stood, signifying the meeting was over.

Wei and Eric left the office and stepped into the hallway. "You better be careful, Eric. I'll take you down to the winery. Guards will continue to monitor you, so don't try anything. I'm losing my patience with you." They continued down the hallway.

Alone in her office, Lily was turning her attention to her work when her assistant came in. "Miss Kwong, your father just called and asked that you call him right away. He said it's a matter of some urgency." Lily found it odd that her father would want to speak with her so soon after their week together in Hong Kong.

Eric spent several hours examining the production area of the Red Star Winery. As Wei had promised, a guard followed him the whole time. The more he explored, the more impressed he became. Everything was of the best possible quality. All equipment was modern and well maintained, the floors spotless, the equipment stored or hung with precision, and the space airy and inviting with lots of natural light. He was easily able to imagine working there. Having unlimited assistant labor and money were a definite advantage. However, he knew money alone would not produce great fruit, and he had been spoiled in Washington by having an abundance of top-quality grapes available.

Would Yinchuan's geographic location ever enable grapevines to produce consistently outstanding fruit? With global warming, anything was possible. Maybe the vines wouldn't always need to be buried during the winters. The nearby Yellow River provided plenty of irrigation. The altitude was beneficial, and the latitude provided ample amounts of sunlight during the summers. It could be done, he thought, especially if the Chinese government made a national commitment to be the best in winemaking, as they had in so many other fields, like electronics, communications, and weaponry. No, he couldn't rule out success here as well.

Among some of the equipment, Eric came across a prototype of a combined fermentation tank and press which allowed for less movement of wine from one vessel to another. He'd read about such designs in the U.S., but was surprised to see one here. They were serious about their efforts.

As Lily had suggested, he worked his way through the barrel room with a wine thief and a tasting glass to sample wines from a number of barrels. After pulling small samples of wine from the barrel and filling his glass, he stuck his nose near the bung hole and inhaled the aromas to see if he could detect any faults. When he was done with the samples, he poured the remaining liquid from his glass down one of the nearby floor drains. His overall impression was that some wines were better than others, but generally they were all solid efforts.

His time exploring the winery went by quickly. He looked at his watch and wanted to get cleaned up before lunch. He motioned to his guard that he was ready to leave. The guard understood and walked him back to the château and his room. Back in the room, Eric washed up and changed into a clean shirt, which he noticed had been added to his closet. They were taking good care of him.

As the guard escorted him back down to the dining room, Eric considered what he would say to Lily. *What if she and Wei were working together? Did she know about the theft of his wine and the murder?* He doubted that was possible since Wei had given explicit instructions not to say anything to her. Yet Wei himself had mentioned the idea of having Eric help them. He decided to be cautious with his words and talk with Lily over lunch to better understand her perspective.

The guard escorted him into the dining room, and then left him alone. Eric admired the exquisitely appointed room that looked as it had the night of his dinner with Wei, with the table set for two. In a few more minutes, Lily appeared from a private doorway toward the rear of the room near the kitchen. She strode over to where Eric was standing at the table.

Lily spoke in a low voice. "Eric, please sit down."

Eric took a seat at the table, and Lily sat in a chair at its head.

"Eric, what do you really know about Wei?" Lily asked.

Eric just stared at her, frozen in thought. *How honest should I be?* He didn't know her, but based on their brief conversation and the history of her exemplary education and career, Eric felt he could trust her. She seemed very sincere. He also realized he really had no other choice.

"I think he's dangerous, perhaps even mentally unstable," Eric said.

Now it was Lily's turn to go quiet. Lily stared past Eric toward the guard standing outside the dining room. Shifting her eyes back toward Eric, she said, "I think we must leave now. Please come with me." She took his hand and they both stood. She led him back toward the door near the kitchen from which she had entered.

"Why, where are we going?"

"I spoke with my father a few minutes ago. He's the Chairman of Shanghai Star Industrial Group, and he thinks you may be in some danger. He wants me to bring you to Shanghai. He will meet you at our local offices there." Lily led Eric through the kitchen and to a stairway toward the back. They descended to the main level of the château.

"What did your father say?"

"He received a call from a comrade in the Ministry of Foreign Affairs. He told my father that your government is preparing documents charging Huang Wei for murder. He said they are awaiting the results of some lab work. If the evidence is conclusive, they will also seek an INTERPOL Red Notice."

"Where is Wei now?" Eric asked.

"He's on the property somewhere. I requested that one of our cars meet us in back of the winery. I hope we don't confront him; he has quite a temper. Eric, has Wei been keeping you here against your will?"

"Yes, since Saturday night. I knew that Wei was suspected of murder, but I didn't know the authorities were close to issuing a warrant."

Lily and Eric walked briskly across the grounds leading from the château to the winery. "Eric, what brought you to China? You didn't really come to tour wineries in our country, did you?"

"I came here to find Wei, because the man he is suspected of murdering back home was a friend of mine. Wei also took something very important to me."

"What?"

"I'd rather not say." Eric wasn't yet ready to admit his role in the wine transfer.

Once they had passed through the public entrance to the winery, Lily used her keycard to get them into the production area. They walked quickly across the winery floor and out to the loading dock toward the back of the building. A new black Mercedes SUV was parked at the bottom of the stairs on the gravel lot. Eric thought back to the early morning hours on Saturday when the area had looked like an illuminated prison yard, and he had tried to flee the guards and the German Shepherd. They both heard Wei bellow in his loud voice. "Wait!"

Wei was moving toward them across the floor of the winery. Lily told Eric to get into the SUV and shouted some orders in Mandarin to the driver. "Where am I going?" Eric asked.

"To the airport. My father's plane will take you to Shanghai."

"And you—will you be safe?" Eric asked.

"Yes, the guards know who pays their salary. They'll follow my orders. I will see you there."

Lily closed the door to the SUV and the driver accelerated out of the lot, sending gravel flying from under the tires. Eric looked out the rear window and saw Wei, just as he arrived at Lily's side. Two security guards ran out of the winery and joined them. Wei was yelling wildly at Lily, flailing his arms. She simply stepped back and watched as the two guards grabbed Wei's wrists and secured him.

34

December 2nd

Walla Walla

It was around 8:00 a.m. when Sheriff Thompson received a call from the CODIS lab. They informed him that DNA testing showed a positive match between the foreign DNA material taken from Jeff Russell's body and the DNA taken from licked adhesive on the envelope of money Wei had given to Kurt. The conclusion was that the DNA was from the same person with a reliability of 99.99 percent. Furthermore, and importantly for the prosecuting attorney, the samples contained sufficient amounts of DNA, were of significant quality, and were unique, meaning that they were from only one DNA source and had not been mixed. The CODIS lab had recently been certified for its quality control and assurance, so the test results would likely sustain challenge. They were conclusive.

Scott instructed the lab to send him a copy of the results by email and also to send a copy to the Walla Walla Prosecuting Attorney. After he finished speaking with the lab, Scott called the prosecuting attorney and told him of the results. The prosecutor confirmed that he had been in contact with a Superior Court Judge, who would be available to review and sign documents once murder charges had been filed against Wei. The prosecuting attorney fully expected to see the requests for a provisional arrest warrant and INTERPOL Red Notice signed and forwarded to the Department of Justice's Office of International Affairs by the end of the day. Scott thanked him and hung up.

Scott looked at his watch and calculated that the current time in Yinchuan was around midnight on Monday. Hopefully, by Tuesday morning their time, the embassy would receive notice from the State Department of the legal action that was proceeding against Wei. What Scott couldn't have known, because Ashley didn't tell him, was that the FBI was already one step ahead of him.

Houston

About the same time the prosecuting attorney delivered the necessary legal documents in the case against Huang Wei to the Walla Walla County Courthouse for filing by a judge, Ashley was calling Professor Fletcher in Perth. He confirmed that the lab had indeed received the wine samples from China the day before and that the analysis was almost complete. He promised to distribute them by email late in the afternoon. Ashley confirmed he had the email addresses for Scott, the prosecuting attorney, and the legal attaché in Beijing.

Shanghai

Eric was overcome with feelings of relief on the Shanghai Star Industrial Group's private jet during his flight from Yinchuan to Shanghai. But it was hard not to worry about what awaited him there. *Is my trust in Lily misplaced?* He'd soon find out. He also felt growing guilt that he was now free while Ming was probably being abused in a Chinese jail. He could only hope that the FBI would be able to free him.

Upon arrival in Shanghai, Eric was taken by private car to the Jin Mao Tower and given a room at the Grand Hyatt Hotel. The view looking out the floor-to-ceiling windows was fantastic, even though the night sky was hazy with pollution. He didn't care about the view; he was just glad to be safely out of the château in Yinchuan. As he turned back toward the center of the room, he saw a bottle of wine and two glasses sitting on the coffee table. He immediately recognized the Red Star Winery label on the bottle. An accompanying note card read *Mr. Savage, Welcome to the Shanghai Grand Hyatt,* and bore the signature of the hotel manager. There was another note card which said, *The Chairman of the Shanghai Star Industrial Group requests your presence in his office on the forty-first floor at 9:00 a.m. tomorrow.* Eric wasted no time in opening the bottle of wine and pouring himself a large glass.

After taking a long hot shower, Eric called Ashley. Since he didn't have his confiscated cell phone, he used the room phone. He wondered if the line was secure, but knew he lacked better options.

"Hi Ashley."

"Eric, is it really you? Where are you? I didn't recognize your phone number."

"I just arrived in Shanghai. It's been a weird couple of days. Wei has my cell phone. It's a long story."

"How did you get there? Are you okay?" Eric appreciated the concern in Ashley's voice, confirming the emotion she felt for him and matching the love he now admitted he felt for her.

Eric relayed the events at the winery leading up to his release and flight to Shanghai, as well as his meeting with the Chairman the next morning. "Ashley, do you know who arranged my release?"

"Eric, it's a bit complicated. The short story is that the staff of the FBI's LEGAT office in Beijing suspected that the Chairman of Shanghai Star Industrial Group was highly placed within the People's Republic of China. We believe he has communications access to most of the ministries in China and possibly into some less secure channels of the U.S. Embassy. We intentionally leaked word that Wei was being investigated for the murder of a U.S. citizen. Our thinking was that our communications might motivate the Chairman to take action. The fact that you were released confirms these communication channels exist. What we are unsure of is what the Chairman plans next."

"What about Jiao Ming? I haven't seen him since Friday night, over four days ago."

"Eric, he was arrested. My friend Grace—I'm sure you remember Grace, don't you?"

"Champagne Grace?" Eric smiled on his end of the call.

"Yes, that Grace. She and an attorney in Yinchuan went to the detention center. The attorney was allowed to meet with Ming. That's when we confirmed that you were being held at the winery and that Ming had shipped the wine sample to Perth."

"He got it!" Eric exclaimed. "That's great news."

"We don't have results from the wine fingerprinting analysis yet, but I hope to receive them later today. I'll forward them to you as soon as they arrive. You might need them when you meet with the Chairman tomorrow morning.

"Eric, I'm afraid they were pretty rough on Ming while he was in the detention center. It sounds like they beat him badly while trying to gain a confession."

"Is he going to be okay? Is there anything I can do?"

"I just heard a few minutes ago that he was released and is now being treated at a local hospital for some severe cuts and abrasions. Thankfully, the attorney told Grace he should be fine."

"That's such a relief. I was really worried about Ming. By the way, where is Grace?" Eric asked.

"She's on a commercial flight back to Beijing," Ashley said.

Eric was silent for a few moments as he digested Ashley's news. He took a drink from his glass of wine. "Wow, I can't tell you how relieved I am to be here. I think Wei is delusional. The last time I saw him, he was being restrained by security guards at the winery. By the way, I was pretty impressed by Lily. She's the president of the winery and the Chairman's daughter. I don't think she knows much about what's happened."

"Really, you think Wei was acting by himself?"

"I do. I suppose Lily could have known what Wei was up to, but once her father told her of the pending murder charges against Wei, she decided to let me go. However, Wei was adamant that I not speak with Lily, so I think she was in the dark."

"Eric, I'll ask the FBI to leave you a new cell phone at the front desk along with a credit card you can use while in China. The local police in Shanghai promised the FBI that they'd keep an eye on you. They have a pretty good relationship. You should go ahead and meet with the Chairman tomorrow as requested and see what happens. Everything we know about him suggests he's very honorable and not dangerous. I'm sure he'd like to see this whole problem go away. The last thing he will want is negative publicity. Hopefully, you can come home soon.

Grace will probably need to debrief you before you leave. Why don't you do it over lunch this time?" Eric loved Ashley's sense of humor and her trust in him.

"No more bars in Shanghai, I promise," Eric laughed. "Good night. I love you, Ashley."

"Good night, Eric. I love you, too, and can't wait for you to get home. You have some unfinished business from Hawaii to take care of."

Before going to bed, Eric sent his clothes with a valet to be cleaned and returned in the morning. After the best night of sleep he'd had in days, Eric woke up around 7:00 a.m. He ordered breakfast from room service, and then called the concierge to enquire about a package. Just as Ashley had promised, one was waiting for him. He asked for it to be delivered to his room. The package, his clothes, and breakfast all arrived within thirty minutes of each other.

Eric used the new phone to check email and found that he had over three hundred messages. He sorted the new messages by sender, and concentrated on those from Ashley. He quickly found what he had hoped for: a forwarded copy of the test results from Perth. He opened the message and read the attachment. The summary contained the usual disclaimers about sample error, imperfect data from the source vineyards, sensitivity of the test equipment, and the limitations of the test protocol. Then he read the important part:

> **Conclusion:** *Based on spectrographic analysis of over 46 elements contained in the wine samples submitted to the lab and the soil elements measured in the source vineyards, these tests show a 95% confidence that both samples are the same wine from the vineyards in Washington State. While there is a 5% chance that the wines are from different locations, we find it highly unlikely that the wine sample purported to be from China was actually produced in China, as the soils there would not support the unique concentration of elements present in the sample from that location.*

Eric was pleased. He knew from his own tasting at the winery in Yinchuan that it was indeed his wine, but these results would help him to make the point if required during the meeting.

Eric left his room and headed to the one elevator that could take him from his level down to the forty-first floor. After descending to the correct level, Eric stepped out of the elevator and into a professional office with a reception desk on the right. A very attractive and stylishly dressed young woman said, "I am Zhao Xiaojie. May I help you?"

"Yes, I am here to see the Chairman," Eric replied.

"You must be Mr. Savage. I've been expecting you. Please come with me." Zhao Xiaojie stepped out from behind the desk and motioned Eric to follow her. Eric couldn't help but admire the shapely legs and high-heeled black pumps of the young receptionist as she led him down a hallway toward the corner of the building. After walking about fifty yards, they entered another reception area with a desk and sofa arrangement. Eric was surprised to see Lily Kwong sitting by herself on one of the white sofas. She nodded at Eric, as the receptionist of that area took charge. The new receptionist thanked and dismissed Zhao Xiaojie before turning her attention to Eric. Bowing slightly, she said, "Good morning, Mr. Savage. I'll take you in to see Chairman Kwong now. He's waiting for you."

She walked him to a large oak door and opened it inward, allowing Eric to enter Chairman Kwong's office. She closed the door behind him after he passed through. Eric advanced a few steps toward a massive mahogany desk, as a distinguished and very fit looking man of sixty years rose and walked around the desk to meet him. They shook hands in the middle of the room.

In perfect English, the Chairman said, "Welcome, Mr. Savage. I'm glad you could join us."

It was then that Eric looked toward the side of the office and saw Wei and another man standing next to some armchairs.

"I believe you know Huang Wei, Facilities Manager of the Yinchuan Division, but I don't believe you've met Huang Cheng, Wei's father and President of our Real Estate Division. I've asked them to join us today."

"Thank you, Mr. Kwong. It is a pleasure to meet you. Yes, I've met Wei. And I'm pleased to meet you, Mr. Huang." The names of both men matched the business cards that Luc DuPont had given Eric.

"I also believe you've met my daughter, who is sitting outside. I plan to ask her to join us later. Now Mr. Savage, please have a seat. The reason I've asked you here is so you may share with me the events that brought you to China. I have heard from Wei, Cheng, and Lily, now I'm curious to hear your version."

Eric sat transfixed for a moment. The situation was surreal; he wasn't sure what to say. Sensing his discomfort, Mr. Kwong asked, "Would you like a glass of water?"

"Yes, please."

Eric took the glass the Chairman offered him and sipped. It gave him a moment to collect his thoughts. He decided now was not the time for finesse or subterfuge. He hoped the truth would serve him well. That's what he'd always been taught. He began a thoughtful retelling of the events of the past several months, starting with the request from Jeff Russell for a wine tasting with a Chinese client, looking to buy some wine similar to Bordeaux in style. He described the discovery of Russell's lifeless body, the disappearance of Eric's fifty-four barrels of wine, investigative work to trace a shipping container believed to contain his wine to a containership bound for Shanghai, his decision to travel to China, the employment of a private investigator, and the most recent events at the Red Star Winery in Yinchuan. After twenty minutes, Eric concluded his comments and said, "I assume I have you to thank, Mr. Kwong, for releasing me from my captivity in Yinchuan and bringing me here to Shanghai. If so, then you have my most heartfelt appreciation."

"Yes, you do. Thank you for your thorough review, Mr. Savage. I have an additional question. How do you know the wine in our winery is actually yours? Do you have any proof?"

"Yes, I do. Did you know that there are scientific tests that can confirm the authenticity of a wine? This process is called *fingerprinting*, and there's a lab in Perth that is able to conduct these tests. The FBI contacted this lab last week. We sent them wine samples from my winery in Washington and samples I took Friday night from your winery in Yinchuan, which was when Wei kidnapped me. The results of their tests came back yesterday and prove that the wines are the same. It is my wine in Yinchuan."

"May I see the results, Mr. Savage?"

Eric handed over his cell phone. The Chairman scrolled through the same message Eric had read in the hotel room earlier.

The Chairman glared at Wei and Cheng while handing the phone back to Eric. "Do you have family, Mr. Savage?"

"Yes, I have a daughter," Eric replied.

"As you know, I, too have a daughter, my only child. Family in China is very important, Mr. Savage. The work unit comes next. In my corporation, I treat my executives the same as family. Their families are, by extension, part of my family too. This brings me to the dilemma I face here today. Wei is the son of Cheng. Cheng has been a faithful and loyal employee of mine for over twenty-five years. He is a good man, a trustworthy man. Not only is Wei a son to Cheng, he is like a son to me as well.

"After listening to all of the statements this morning, I believe what you have told me is true, Mr. Savage. The facts align closely, but you have provided an additional level of detail. Now I think we need to understand why this happened. Wei, please tell us why you embarked on such a dishonorable plan."

Eric looked toward Wei whose appearance suggested he was going into a state of psychological shock. All color was gone from his face and his brow appeared shiny from a slight sweat. When he tried to speak, he was barely audible.

Finally, his father spoke for him. "It was for love," Huang Cheng said.

"Love! How could this possibly be about love?" the Chairman demanded, while lightly pounding his fist on his desk.

Wei said, in a whisper and without emotion, "I wanted her to love me."

"Who?" the Chairman asked.

"Lily. I wanted Lily to love me," Wei said.

Cheng spoke again. "Wei thought that if he could substitute excellent wine for the wine Lily had made, the Celestial Red, she would win awards and become famous. This would bring her great honor in your eyes, Mr. Chairman. At some point in the future, Wei would explain to Lily how he had helped her achieve this success, and she would love him for it. Wei has been infatuated with Lily since they were in high school. Unfortunately, she has never shared his feelings."

The Chairman sat back in silence and stared at Wei. "Not only have you made a fool of yourself, you have potentially brought great shame to this company. If one of my senior employees is accused of murder, and Red Star Winery is charged with counterfeiting wine, you will have destroyed everything I have ever worked for. My reputation is unassailable in China. I plan to keep it that way. Does Lily know anything about this?"

"No," was all Wei could say.

"Well, she knows about the murder investigation and pending charges coming from the United States because I told her myself. What about the wine? Does she know that Mr. Savage's wine is in Red Star Winery?"

"No, Mr. Chairman." Wei's voice was barely audible.

"Cheng, did you know about this?"

"I accompanied Wei to Washington. We planned to purchase wine and ship it back on one of our container ships. I was not aware of the murder and theft until after I returned."

"But you knew and yet you didn't tell me?"

"No, Mr. Chairman." Cheng's eyes were cast downward, looking toward the floor in shame.

The Chairman leaned back in his chair. He surveyed the room and then stared out the massive windows of his office for a few moments while thinking. Turning his attention back to the men, he said, "Mr. Savage, if I compensate you for the loss of your wine, make reparations to the family of Jeff Russell, and ensure that Wei is given a sufficient level of punishment for his crimes, do you think you could convince the prosecuting attorney to drop the provisional arrest warrant and the INTERPOL Red Notice before they are transmitted by your State Department?"

"I can't speak for them directly, but since China and the U.S. have not signed an extradition treaty, I'm aware prosecutorial options are limited. I think the authorities might share your interest in finding a negotiated solution that could be kept confidential." Eric was quick to appreciate that the Chairman would want to make everything go away and avoid what would be embarrassing publicity for himself, his daughter, and Red Star Winery.

"Thank you, Mr. Savage," the Chairman said. "I'd like to finish my conversation with Wei and Cheng privately. Join my daughter outside, and I will ask you to return in a few minutes. Please, do not discuss any of this with her."

"Yes, Mr. Kwong," Eric said. He got up and left the room.

Eric sat across from Lily and waited quietly, wondering about the conversation then occurring in the chairman's office. After only five minutes, two security guards appeared at the entrance to the waiting area. The receptionist motioned them into the inner office. It wasn't long before the guards, escorting Wei and Cheng, came out from the chairman's doorway, passed through the waiting area, and then walked down the hallway and out of sight. The Chairman reappeared and said, "Lily, Mr. Savage, please join me."

Eric and Lily walked into the empty office and sat down. The Chairman returned to the leather seat behind his desk.

"Mr. Savage," Mr. Kwong began, "I'm sorry and embarrassed by the actions which have brought you here to China. You have my word that Huang Wei will never commit such crimes again. And for the hardships you've experienced in coming to China, I offer you one million dollars as recompense. Would that be satisfactory?"

"You are most kind," Eric said. "I'm just thankful we located Jeff Russell's murderer."

"I also plan to offer Mr. Russell's family a payment in the amount of five million dollars," the Chairman continued. "I know that nothing can replace the loss of a son, but I would like to help make their lives more comfortable."

"I can't speak for Mr. Russell's widow and family, of course, but I think it's a generous offer."

"Mr. Savage, I'd also like to offer you a job working with my daughter as Assistant Winemaker and Vice President of Red Star Winery. Lily tells me that your philosophy is very compatible with her winemaking style, and she believes you can bring tremendous skill to her efforts." The Chairman paused. "Would you be interested?"

Eric was stunned by what he had just heard. "Mr. Kwong, I'm not sure what to say. As I'm sure you are aware, I already have a full-time job managing my own winery in Washington."

"I appreciate that, Mr. Savage. But think about the opportunity here in China. This will be the world's biggest market someday. China will become one of the great global wine producers because there are not enough vineyards in the world to supply the growing demand from our domestic market. As you must have seen at our winery, no expense will be spared. We will continue to invest and make Red Star Winery one of the elite facilities in the country. Wouldn't you like to be a part of that effort?"

"Sir, I appreciate everything about Lily and her efforts. And yes, I would surely enjoy the challenge of building a great winery here. I think your success will ultimately depend on establishing great vineyards, and you are making impressive strides. The recent wines I have tasted are very good. But I have my winery to think of and my own family."

"Mr. Savage, what if I bought wine from you under an annual contract? Then, confident you have a guaranteed market for some of your production, you could come visit us on a regular basis. Become a flying winemaker as they're called. We'll give you your own room at the château—one you can leave." The Chairman showed a slight smile as he said it, the first one Eric had seen from him all morning.

Neither the Chairman, nor his daughter Lily, said anything about his wine now sitting in barrels inside Red Star Winery. Eric understood why the Chairman would not want to tell his daughter. Honor is everything in China, and shame a painful corollary. The deception nagged at Eric, but he also knew there was nothing to be gained from mentioning it.

"Mr. Kwong, I am honored by your most generous offer. May I think about it? I would like to discuss it with my family."

"Of course," the Chairman said. "Why don't you think it over and then send me a proposal for an annual purchase agreement. In the meantime, I expect you will be leaving China soon?"

"Yes," Eric said. "I plan to take a flight tomorrow after I debrief with the FBI in Beijing. I will present your request for the Justice Department to quash any criminal proceedings and warrants against Huang Wei, in exchange for victim compensation and equivalent punishment delivered here in China. I'm curious though. How will we know the details of Wei's punishment once it has been imposed?"

While he spoke, out of the far corner of his eye, Eric's vision was distracted by a shadow that passed outside the window farthest away, located at the end of the chairman's office. By the time he turned to look, whatever was there had disappeared. It was almost as if a large bird had flown past the window in a downward direction.

"You'll know," the Chairman replied.

Beijing

Eric took the high-speed bullet train from Shanghai to Beijing immediately after his meeting with the Chairman. The five-hour leisurely ride was a perfect anecdote to the stress he'd felt over the past few days. Covering a distance of over eight hundred miles, the train would travel up to 230 miles per hour. Eric was impressed that China had already installed over six thousand miles of high-speed rail, double the length of the Japanese and European high-speed rail systems combined. As he gazed out the window, watching small farms and villages speed by, Eric appreciated having seen first-hand the economic miracle that is China. However, he didn't appreciate the human density and sickening smog present in most major cities.

After a quiet night walking around the city of Beijing, followed by an early dinner in his hotel room, Eric awoke the next morning and prepared to meet Grace over at the U.S. Embassy. She wanted to discuss the details of his time in Yinchuan and his meeting with the Chairman. Afterwards, he planned to depart Beijing on the nonstop flight to Seattle that afternoon. As he sat down to eat breakfast in his room, he opened a copy of that morning's edition of *China Daily*, the most widely circulated English language newspaper in China. After glancing at a few national headlines, his attention was immediately drawn to the following story:

Facilities Manager Falls to Death in Apparent Suicide

Shanghai – A thirty-three-year-old resident of Yinchuan was found dead Monday morning after an apparent suicide leap off of the eighty-eight story Jin Mao Tower. Fortunately, no passersby on the ground below were injured. The man, Huang Wei, was employed as Facilities Manager at Red Star Winery, an up-and-coming winery located in the Ningxia Hui Autonomous Region of China.

No explanation was given for the apparent suicide. However, according to a spokesperson, Huang Wei reportedly had been recently despondent over some romantic troubles. He is survived by his father, Huang Cheng, a former President of the Real Estate Division of Shanghai Star Industrial Group, Ltd., who recently retired.

Eric was astounded. Was the shadow he'd seen passing by the window yesterday in the chairman's office actually the body of Wei plummeting from the top of the building? The Chairman had said that Wei would never bring harm to anyone again; is that what he meant? In a bit of irony, he realized that the need for an arrest warrant had just gone away.

35

December 3rd

Seattle

By crossing the international dateline on his return, Eric stepped off the plane in Seattle at 11:00 a.m. the same day he'd departed Beijing at 4:30 p.m. The nearly eleven-hour flight was uneventful, and Eric slept half the time. He couldn't remember ever being so happy to return home. The process of passing through Immigration and Customs took about forty-five minutes, ending with the standard comforting words from the officer: "Welcome home, Mr. Savage."

As Eric arrived at the top of the escalator and stepped into the publicly accessible area, he was surprised to see Ashley standing nearby, dressed in blue jeans and a cashmere sweater. "What are you doing here?"

"Grace called me after your meeting yesterday. She told me you were coming home and I arranged some time off. I wanted to surprise you. My flight from Houston just arrived a few minutes ago."

Eric kissed her on the lips and was met with an equally passionate response. After a lingering embrace, Eric said, "I'm so happy to see you." It was hard to believe less than four weeks earlier he'd left her back in Maui. After the way things had turned out, he was glad he'd made the decision to go to China. He also recognized his life had been immeasurably changed because of it.

"I was beginning to wonder if I'd ever see you again," Ashley said. "Anything could have happened over there, Eric."

"I know. I was probably being foolish, but I'm glad I went. I have lots to tell you about." Eric looked at Ashley, almost as if he were admiring her for the first time. He slowly drank in her beauty.

"What are you staring at?" Ashley said, looking embarrassed, her face feeling warm.

"Just the most beautiful crime fighter in the world. Come on, let's go rent a car. We can be back in Walla Walla before dark."

During the four-hour drive to Eric's house in Walla Walla, Eric and Ashley recounted the events of the past four weeks and, at times, simply held hands and watched the scenery go by. Their conversation was a process of becoming reacquainted. They covered a number of topics, such as how Ashley's sons William, who Ashley informed him wanted to be called Will, and Elliot were doing in school and sports; how Eric felt about missing Thanksgiving with his daughter; a cursory overview of the drive from Shanghai to Yinchuan with Jiao Ming, and Eric's impressions of China; and, the cases Ashley had been working on at the FBI since returning from Hawaii. The deeper stuff would come later. They both had the luxury of a few days without distraction.

They took turns driving, which gave Eric a chance to text Melissa and his daughter to let both of them know he was back. He asked Melissa to take the dogs to his house that night and to meet him at the winery the following morning to catch up. He also sent an email to Sheriff Thompson inviting him and his wife to join Ashley and him for dinner at his house the following evening. He was going to enjoy being home and spending time with Ashley.

By the time they arrived at Eric's restored bungalow near the Whitman College campus, the sky had turned almost completely dark. The air was cold, with a north wind blowing briskly. Eric pulled the rental car up the drive and switched off the ignition. The lights of his house were on. He and Ashley walked to the porch and unlocked the front door. As soon as they walked in, they heard the sounds of Max and Ginger, nails clicking on the hardwood floor, as they came running down the hallway. The golden retrievers leapt up onto Eric's chest where they rested their front paws and wagged their tails like metronomes. Eric loved these greetings.

They all made their way back to the kitchen where Eric found a note:

Welcome home, Eric. I missed you. The dogs have been fed and I look forward to catching up in the morning. Everything is fine at the winery. —XOXO, Melissa.

"Do you mind if I order some pizza?" Eric asked. "After the strange foods I've been eating in China, pizza sounds unbelievably good."

"Sure," Ashley said. "Anything with you will be great. I could use a glass of wine, however."

Eric called in a pizza order for home delivery and then found a bottle of Chianti and some glasses. The dogs continued to follow him around the kitchen as he located an opener and uncorked the wine. He joined Ashley at the kitchen table and poured them each a glass.

"I have fond memories of this house, Eric. It's where we enjoyed our first passionate night together after our time in London. Remember?"

"How could I forget? I took some wine up to my bedroom and left it for you as you took a bath. I remember seeing your service weapon and badge lying on the bed and photos of William—I mean Will—and Elliot in a travel frame on my nightstand. It was seeing the two most important things in your life side by side, your job and your family, that gave me deeper insight into you. I think that was the moment my love for you was complete."

"And then I had to leave," added Ashley, a touch of regret in her voice.

"Yes, which brings me to a subject I've wanted to discuss with you since stepping off the plane in Seattle. We need to talk about us." Eric knew it was time to disclose the offers from the Chairman to compensate him for the theft and to buy some of his production.

"May I go first?" Ashley asked.

"Sure."

"You mentioned the two most important things in my life are my career and my family. I want to think of you as part of my family. The boys like you, and I'm beginning to have a hard time imagining my life without you in it. And I don't see how we can continue to build a relationship with me in Houston and you in Walla Walla." Eric wasn't sure what Ashley was getting at. But in his past experience, this kind of talk usually led to comments like "we should slow things down," "this isn't fair to you," or the more brutally honest "it's over."

"So what are you saying?" Eric asked, trying his best to read Ashley's facial response for any clues.

"I'm thinking of transferring to the FBI office in Seattle."

Eric hadn't expected that. "You'd do that?"

"I think it's the best answer. I want to stay with the FBI and I want to be nearer to you. I don't see you leaving Walla Walla anytime soon. I've already spoken with my supervisor, and he mentioned they are looking for someone to head the Puget Sound Joint Terrorism Task Force. It's a big job and I'd have to compete for it, but he thinks I'd have a good chance."

"What about Will and Elliot?" Eric asked.

"That's been the hardest thing to wrap my mind around. I'm thinking of asking their father to keep them during the school year and let me have them over holidays and during the summer. We'd try our best to keep it an equal split."

"The three of you are so close; wouldn't that be hard on them?" As soon as he said it, Eric knew he'd probably been too direct.

Ashley's eyes started to glisten, and she reached for her wine glass. "I'm not saying it would be easy, but I don't know any other way to make this work for us."

"Ashley, I know it's difficult to consider such big gaps in time with your boys. You know, they'll soon be going off to college. I'm not saying your job is done, but they are so independent already, thanks to the great job you've done raising them."

Ashley's tears were flowing freely by then, and Eric scooted his chair over toward her to wrap his arms around her shoulders and offer comfort. "I'm sorry, that was insensitive."

They were silent for a few moments until Ashley spoke up. "So now that I've spilled the beans, what did you want to say, Eric?"

Just then the doorbell rang. Eric went to get the pizza and returned with the pie and two plates. They both dug in.

"I received an interesting offer while I was in China." Eric took his first bite of pizza. It tasted heavenly. He was happy to be eating one of his favorite foods again.

"I think I may have heard some of this from Grace," Ashley volunteered, before taking another bite.

"The Chairman of Shanghai Star Industrial Group offered me a job working as a consultant with his daughter at their winery in Yinchuan. It's a pretty tempting idea." Eric laid out in detail the whole story behind his captivity in the winery, his assessment of the facility and its equipment, and the meeting in Shanghai when the Chairman presented the idea of signing a consulting agreement with him.

"Would you want to spend a lot of time over there?" Ashley asked, sounding incredulous.

"I'm thinking about it. He also offered me a guaranteed annual contract to purchase my wine. With the guaranteed revenue, I'd feel much more comfortable hiring some additional help here and then traveling to China on a regular basis. The opportunity to help them is exciting. With their financial resources, I know we could create a world-renowned winery. It will take time, but it's the beginning of a new era over there."

"Don't you think you could continue to do that right here in Walla Walla?" Ashley countered. She was already thinking ahead, contemplating how a schedule might work in this scenario. "What about Melissa?"

"What do you mean?"

"How's your relationship with her? My intuition tells me you might have an issue." Ashley put down her pizza and picked up her glass of wine. Her eyes remained focused on Eric.

"What makes you think so?" Eric struggled not to become defensive.

"Well, when Scott told me of the comments Kurt made during questioning in Port Angeles, about how he was jealous of the relationship between you and Melissa, I began to suspect she might have a crush on you."

Eric decided to put all his cards on the table. "She's a great employee. A couple of times she mentioned wanting a romantic relationship with me. I thought I made it completely clear that it's out of the question. In retrospect, I think I may have given her some mixed signals during harvest. Spending time with her outside of work might not have been the best idea. Heck, she's attractive, energetic, and fun to be around. I enjoy her company. After many hours thinking about this in China, I think I should make a change."

"You mean terminate her employment?"

"Yes. I appreciate the commitment you are making to our relationship by moving to Seattle. I don't want Melissa to become an issue."

Ashley was pleased by Eric's newfound self-awareness, which she found unusual in a man. "Could you manage the winery without her?"

"It would be difficult, especially if I'm making regular trips to China. She held things together while I was away. She manages all of the sales and marketing efforts and is beginning to understand how I make wine. It would be a major setback at a time when I need to recover from the theft."

"Eric, I think you need to fully understand the influence you have with Melissa as her employer and mentor. If you accept that responsibility, then give her clear direction, keep her focused on the job, and don't give into temptation. I trust you."

"Anything else?" Eric was again impressed by Ashley's insight and maturity.

"You need to make sure that she understands her relationship with you is that of a student and employee. Put her job description and responsibilities in writing. Then if she slips up, you can terminate her employment with cause."

"Did you previously work in human resources?"

"I did. And Eric, when you unzip those cute jeans of yours, make sure it's with me." Ashley smiled as she delivered the last part, wanting it to sound not as a threat, but an acknowledgment of the situation.

Eric took Ashley's hand and squeezed it. He rose out of his chair and leaned over toward her. They kissed longingly for a moment before continuing the conversation.

"There's another part of the situation in China that's bothering me," Eric said.

"What is it?" Ashley guessed it might be the challenge of living in China while working there. That would bother her.

"It's a moral dilemma. My wine is now sitting in barrels at Red Star Winery. They plan to bottle it later this spring and sell it as their wine. It doesn't feel right." Eric had struggled with the situation on the flight home.

"So what's the issue? Is it that you won't get recognition?" Ashley knew this would be hard for him to swallow.

"Maybe. It's illegal in China to sell wine labeled as domestically produced when the wine is imported from outside the country. Realistically, however, smuggling is widespread."

"Right. So what are your options?" Ashley hoped to lead Eric's thought process to a logical conclusion.

"I could go to the press with the wine fingerprinting evidence you obtained from Professor Fletcher, but that would humiliate the Chairman and his daughter Lily. I'd never be able to set foot in China again."

"What else?"

"I could tell Lily about it and ask that she destroy the wine." Eric sounded unconvinced that this was a viable option.

"So then you'd have two vintages of wine poured down the drain. And for what? So you can feel morally consistent?" Ashley hoped Eric would take the final logical step.

"I see what you mean. Why not at least let people enjoy the wine and let Lily enjoy success."

"And if you choose to consult with her, then you'll have another opportunity to create your own success." There was a ghost of a smile on Ashley's lips as she looked expectantly at Eric.

"You make a lot of sense," Eric replied.

"Don't ever forget it." Ashley poked Eric in the shoulder.

"Aren't you concerned about the law enforcement aspects of this?" Eric asked.

"It does concern me, and if this were happening in the United States, I'd feel differently. Pragmatically, I have to accept that this is a law enforcement issue internal to China. It's not in our jurisdiction. Red Star Winery is paying you for the wine, so it can't be considered stolen. The only issue in my mind is labeling the wine as domestically produced when it was actually imported. After your involvement with murder, kidnapping, and theft, I think you should let it go. Remember the other two individuals who know the details of the deception. One of them is dead and the other is retired. What are you going to do?"

"I need to think it over," Eric said. "I have a week before I agreed to send the Chairman a proposal."

"If we are done with dinner, I'd like to go take a bath. Don't forget, you have some unfinished business to attend to. How about you clean up this mess and come join me later?"

"Yes, ma'am," Eric replied, returning her mirth. He refilled Ashley's wine glass before she headed for the stairway and to his bedroom.

"Don't be long, handsome," Ashley said, from the top of the stairs.

Eric cleaned the kitchen and opened another bottle of wine. He let the dogs outside and watched them through the window in the back door. After a few minutes, both dogs scampered back to the door and waited for him to let them in. Instead, Eric stepped outside to join them, even though it was cold, and he wasn't wearing a coat. He gazed toward the clear sky and noted the constellation Ursa Minor and Polaris, the North Star, shining brightly above.

When Eric was a boy, his grandfather, the one who had served in the U.S. Navy in China, told Eric many stories of celestial navigation and how he had been required to learn the use of a sextant. His grandfather had always said, "Like early ocean navigators, everyone needs a North Star to show them the way forward." Eric looked at the sky and smiled. It was apparent that Ashley was becoming his North Star.

After Eric and the dogs went back inside the house, he turned down the kitchen lights, picked up his glass and the open bottle of wine, and walked toward the stairway. After ascending the stairs to the darkened landing at the top, he saw his bedroom door was open a crack. Soft candlelight streamed through, illuminating the way forward.

He opened the door and stepped inside. His eyes filled with the sight of Ashley. She sat on his bed with her legs crossed. She wore one of his dress shirts, buttoned halfway, and nothing else. A wine glass was in her hand and her long blond hair was still wet from washing. "Do you remember Hawaii?" she asked, as Eric sat on the bed next to her.

"I think I remember everything," Eric said.

Ashley set her wine glass on the night stand and with both hands started unfastening the belt on Eric's trousers. "Don't worry," she said, giving it a tug, "if you get lost, I'll show you the way."

Epilogue

Sometime the following spring

Walla Walla

In the end, and after much consideration and discussion with Ashley, Eric signed a purchase agreement for his wine and a consulting agreement with Red Star Winery. The agreement specified that Red Star would purchase 25 percent of the production of Eric's winery on an annual basis at a transfer price of retail less 40 percent, and Red Star would pay all shipping costs. These purchases would help Lily with her plans to start a second brand based on imported wines and enable her to grow the winery's volume more quickly as she methodically increased fruit production from their domestic vineyards.

Eric agreed to make six trips annually to Yinchuan. He knew the worst time to leave would be during harvest when he should be home working in his own winery. Hiring additional help became an immediate priority. He would be given a room in the château. A room that, as the Chairman had joked, he would be free to enter and exit as he pleased. His first trip was coming up in two weeks, which would give him a chance to spend time in the vineyards during the spring growing season and provision the winery for the upcoming harvest. He would be paid a handsome consulting fee for these trips.

Ashley received a promotion to head the Puget Sound Joint Terrorism Task Force in Seattle. She and her ex-husband had negotiated an agreeable parenting plan for the boys for the following year, and planned to renegotiate it annually. She had already begun looking for a condominium to rent in downtown Seattle as she wanted to have it ready for the boys when their summer vacation commenced in June.

Eric spoke with Melissa at the winery the morning after his return. He told her of the consulting agreement and plans to export part of his production to China. The implication, he explained, was that he was going to need her more than ever. He emphasized it was critical they accept their roles as employer and employee—and nothing more. He revisited the discussion he had with Melissa before his trip to China when she had suggested he find someone else because she was going to leave. She had changed her mind, she said. She asked to stay on, adding that her comments were made in haste after feeling hurt by Eric's rejection. She promised to respect his relationship with Ashley and agreed that she would keep their working relationship professional. Eric promised to do the same.

Other than his trips to China, Eric and Ashley expected to see each other every weekend, alternating trips between Seattle and Walla Walla. Eric sensed Ashley's trepidation about sending the boys back to Houston when school started up again in the fall, but she had all summer to grow comfortable with the transition.

Kurt Hughes pleaded guilty to burglary and was given a suspended sentence on the condition that he serve four months in the Walla Walla county jail. For his cooperation in the investigation of the murder of Jeff Russell, the theft charge was dismissed and the lighter sentence imposed. After pleading guilty to the DUI and paying a $1,000 fine, the Clallam County prosecutor suspended the sentence. In addition, Wei's remaining $45,000 payment to Kurt would be forfeited to pay restitution and court costs.

Jeff Russell's widow and immediate family agreed to the generous payment of five million dollars from the Chairman. To a family that had always lived in rented apartments or double-wide trailers, such a sum seemed surreal.

Only a few weeks after signing documents to sell his wine and establish a consulting schedule with Lily, Eric received the following email. He read it with interest.

From: Lily Kwong <lily.kwong@redstarwinery.cn>
To: Eric Savage <eric.savage@bluemtcellars.com>
Subject: Wine Review

Dear Eric,

I look forward to your visit in two weeks. I am happy you have agreed to consult with Red Star Winery and I am confident that together we will build the most sustainable and esteemed winery in greater China. I assure you that this trip will be more enjoyable than your most recent visit last December. Please let me know if there is anything I can do to help prepare for your arrival.

After you departed Yinchuan, I spent a lot of time reviewing records, trying to better understand the activities of Huang Wei in the days before his death. I found receipts of wine delivered here during the week I was away, visiting my father in Hong Kong. That was the same week you were here in Yinchuan. I questioned some of my cellar workers, and they were unwilling to speak of any work in the winery at that time. It wasn't until I tasted the Celestial Red blend in barrel that I understood. Your comment that Wei "had taken something valuable from you" finally gave me the answer.

I appreciate that this must be difficult for you. But I also sense you understand the nature of honor and disgrace here in China. Thank you for not making this an issue with my father. As we work together in the future, I promise you that you will receive all the recognition you so obviously deserve.

I've included a copy of a newsletter from a well-known wine merchant in Seattle who visited me recently. I think you will enjoy what he has to say. He mentioned he knows you.

Best wishes,

Lily

Honorable Wine Merchants
May Newsletter

Dear Friends of the Vine,

The wines I am sharing with you this month come, surprisingly, from China. My tireless efforts to secure only the best wines for you recently led me to the Ningxia region. I just returned from my annual sojourn to measure the

Middle Kingdom's progress toward making outstanding wines. Loyal readers will recall that after my trip last year, I was encouraged by the maturity of specific vineyards and winemaking style in a select number of producers. At that time, I tasted what I concluded were twelve acceptable vintages.

Yesterday I had the pleasure of meeting Red Star Winery's President and Head Winemaker, Lily Kwong, in her beautiful château in Ningxia. Lily was kind enough to offer me a barrel sample of her top of the line Bordeaux blend, the 2012 Celestial Red. This wine did not disappoint. My past criticism of Chinese wines has involved green notes and the presence of early oxidation. Not a hint of vegetable could be found in this wine, and no early oxidation was observed. Lily demurred when I asked her what changes had occurred in the vineyard or the winery to make such a marked improvement in her wine.

The wine is deeper, richer, and more polished than the vintage I first tasted in 2011. The complex nose explodes with caramel, espresso bean, blackberries, and earth. Intense, polished, lush, and deep, the wine finishes with a beautiful sensation of purity and silk. Had I closed my eyes, I would have thought I was swirling a glass of this beauty at the recent *en primeur*. Scheduled for bottling later this spring, I expect this wine will only improve with six months of bottle aging.

Imagine riding a camel across the high and arid Tengger Desert before arriving at the scenic base of the Helan Mountains. You enjoy wolfberries and local cuisine of lamb braised in soy sauce. Perhaps you survived the arrival of Genghis Khan who conquered Yinchuan in the early 13th century. You, my friends, will taste the history of this great land in the wine I am making available to you. I have secured only fifty cases of the 2012 Celestial Blend, which will be considered one of the finest wines ever produced in China when it is released. Act now to secure your order before this unique offer expires in two weeks.

Your humble wine merchant,
Luc DuPont

Eric laughed as he read the newsletter. His refusal to work with Luc DuPont had come full circle. Now Honorable Wine Merchants was selling his wine in Seattle after an epic round trip to China. His involvement would remain a mystery. At least his name would soon be on his bottles of wine sold by Red Star. Though he hadn't received the praise and high scores he'd imagined for his Eagle Cap blend, this journey had been just as satisfying.

The End

About the Author

Steve Wells lives in Medina, Washington. His formal education includes a Bachelor of Science degree from the University of Colorado and an MBA from Seattle University. After a long career in the high-tech industry, Steve decided to study nonfiction writing at the University of Washington and winemaking at South Seattle Community College, where he received a degree in wine production.

Steve has published several magazine articles, a short book titled *Ginger's Story: A Golden Retriever Reflects Upon Her Life With Humans*, and the first book in the Winemaker Series, *Killer Cuvée*. He has also worked in a number of local wineries in the Seattle area.

While not writing, drinking wine, or walking his dogs, Steve is involved with a number of nonprofit organizations in the Seattle area, serving as board chair, volunteer, or consultant. He also likes to hike, bike, and swim.

Author's Note

For me, learning to make wine was a bit like a return to childhood. Connecting hoses, running pumps, performing lab tests, and ending the day wet and sticky from wine—all brought back memories of playing with Legos, building model rockets, and using my first chemistry set, found under a Christmas tree. In short, it was a lot of fun. After two years of school and three years working in some great wineries, I decided I wanted to write about my experiences.

The idea for Harvest Homicide came to me during a Friday afternoon visit to a local Seattle wine distributor. The owner was excited about the imminent shipment of a container full of packaged wine bound for Beijing. In business for many years, this would be his first shipment to China. Understanding the required rules and regulations took extended coordination with his customers in China and local freight forwarders and legal entities in Washington State. Unfortunately, earlier in the week, they'd hit a snag. They were informed that Chinese Customs officials required a Chinese language sticker of authenticity be placed on the back of each bottle shipped. After a mild panic getting the stickers printed in Chinese, the day after my visit, on a Saturday, the distributor, his employees and their spouses, would spend all day unpacking the already stacked pallets of wine, opening each of the several hundred cases, removing each bottle, gluing on a label, resealing, and then restacking them. The shipment would go out on Monday as scheduled.

For the owner, it would be memorable folklore on the way to opening up significant business opportunities in China. It's hard to pick up any wine-related trade press and not read about growth in China's consumption, efforts toward improving and increasing domestic production, proliferation of counterfeit wines, capital investment in China by famous wine houses from around the world, and the massive amount of Chinese investment in French and United States vineyards and châteaux. Wine and Spirits Education Trust courses are immensely popular in Hong Kong and Shanghai. Chinese students represent the biggest national group outside of the UK who are taking these popular courses. One large Chinese wine importer has no less than fourteen WSET educators on its staff and holds Wine Residences in Shanghai and Beijing.

For my story, I chose the port city of Shanghai as the location for several scenes. Not only is Shanghai among the largest ports in the world, it is considered by some to be one of the most dynamic cities as well. My father, who served there as a young seaman in the U.S. Navy, had described Shanghai to me. After several tours on the USS Sacramento, the famous "Galloping Ghost of the China Coast," he also completed several Pacific tours on the USS Arizona before it was torpedoed and sunk in Pearl Harbor.

A lot of people enjoy wine, and most know how it's made. But not everyone has the opportunity to look inside a winery and experience the hard work and daily routine that delivers a bottle of wine to their dinner tables. However, a story solely about winemaking is better served by technical journals and research papers than by a fictional novel. So, I decided to tell a tale that weaves the life of a winemaker into a more interesting story of murder, romance, and personal discovery, set in the real town of Walla Walla, Washington. Throughout the book, scenes of winemaking should ring true, thanks to my own experience and the helpful eye of reviewers of my writing.

The rest of the story is purely imagined and hopefully provides the reader with an engaging and thoughtful experience. This book is the second in The Winemaker Series. Updates, background information, and new releases can be found at www.thewinemakerseries.com.

Acknowledgments

This project would not have been possible without the contribution of so many. Their insight and efforts are felt throughout the book. Bill Kinzel, well-known and widely respected attorney in Seattle, gave me invaluable insight into criminal legal procedures from his years working in the King County Prosecuting Attorney's office, and perhaps more importantly, immeasurable personal inspiration. Editor Christine Go, whose deft touch with all things wine and relationship related, steadily edited this book from the very beginning. Mike MacMorran, head Winemaker at Mark Ryan Winery in Woodinville, Washington, offered his keen-eyed review to keep me honest in the winemaking scenes. Jeff Havlin, who owns and manages a successful vineyard in Oregon, and recently lived in Shanghai, helped me understand the nuances of Chinese culture. And Mary Becker, whose graphics design expertise helped create the book's cover.

The communications staffs of the FBI and the Justice Department were very helpful locally and from their headquarters in educating me on procedural issues related to extradition, provisional arrest, and INTERPOL. Thanks to the Port of Tacoma for helping me understand how shipping containers actually travel through the port system.

Lastly, and most importantly, thanks to Leslie, my partner, for living with me through another year and a half of writing a book. She offered me blunt criticism and patiently watched as I went from road blocks, to dead-ends, to flawed characters, and all points in-between, on the way to writing *The End*.

Also by Steven M Wells

Ginger's Story: A Golden Retriever Reflects Upon Her Life With Humans

A young girl of divorced parents finds love in the eyes of a golden retriever. As their relationship grows, the girl and her puppy find they share something in common—a broken heart. Their time together pays tribute to the richness dogs bring to our lives and the lessons they teach us about love.

Killer Cuvée

In the first novel in The Winemaker Series, Eric Savage follows his passion for winemaking and moves to Walla Walla, Washington, to start a new winery. Small town living agrees with Eric until his ex-wife is found dead. Suspected of the crime, Eric travels to London to track down the real killer. As he follows the clues, Eric meets FBI Special Agent Ashley Hunter. Romance blossoms as together they try to solve the crime.

Made in the USA
San Bernardino, CA
18 March 2015